Graham Sutherland

The Unwanted Inheritance

novum ⬢ pro

This book is also
available as
e-book.

www.novum-publishing.co.uk

Author's Note

In 1999, Michael Packham a twenty-six-year-old doctor working in his local hospital's Accident and Emergency Department receives a letter from a distinguished London law firm, who are seeking to identify the beneficiary of the Last Will and Testament of a former German Panzer tank radio operator who fought against the Allied Forces in the Battle of Normandy in 1944.

Otto Wagner, who's will it is, has left a huge house and farm estate in Southern Bavaria to a British Army Surgeon who saved his life during the Battle of Falaise. The question is, how did a private soldier in the German army obtain such wealth?

Why is an organisation of ex Nazis so keen to obtain this estate for themselves and will do everything they can in order for this to happen?

This is a work of fiction based around well-known German historical figures before World War Two. My characters are all purely imaginary.

Chapter 1

The time was 7.50 a.m. I was due to finish my shift as a doctor in A&E in just ten minutes at eight. It had been a routine Thursday night Friday morning in casualty. The first four or five to present themselves were all feeling unwell. One had stomach pains, another earache and another who was being very abusive towards everyone and to be fair was in much pain, was enduring a terrible boil in the lower middle of his back. Once lanced, his demeanour changed immediately from being aggressive to being apologetic and grateful.

After midnight patients attending A&E quite often change from those with natural causes of illness or unfortunate accidents to those of the more preventable type. The first of these to arrive was a man who had got into an argument over a girl in one of the town pubs. The argument had escalated, resulting in the man having a beer glass smashed into his face requiring stitches. He was lucky not to have lost the sight in his left eye!

Then there were two young women who quite clearly had had too many drinks and were puking up all over themselves shortly followed by a man in his late teens who was suffering from drug abuse. You might say a typical shift in A&E.

I was just finishing writing up the notes of one of the casualties before preparing to leave for home, when the doors swung open, revealing two paramedics pushing a man on a stretcher whose head was covered in blood. The paramedics advised me that he had crashed his Mercedes into a telegraph pole at speed. They speculated that the initial cause might have been, that he had fallen asleep at the wheel and had woken up when he realised that the car was leaving the road, because of the skid marks caused by severe braking which was too late to avoid the impact.

He was still very much alive but unconscious. Without the safety feature of air bags, I could well have been looking at a corpse. My next two hours were spent cleaning him up and determining what injuries had been sustained to his body. After the various x-rays and scans it was apparent that he had damaged his spinal cord. During this time, he regained consciousness although he had no recollection as to what had happened. One of my colleagues, then took over and I wearily left the hospital to make my way home.

Home for me was a two bedroomed flat in the middle of town that I shared with my partner Louise. I had first met Louise after moving into the area to start my job at the local hospital. She was working at the estate agents when I was looking to buy. I immediately found her attractive. She was witty, smart, confident, and vivacious. I deliberately prolonged my search for a suitable place, with her showing me several properties over the course of several weeks before I plucked up the courage to ask her out.

As a teenager, I had had truly little confidence with girls. I never quite knew what words to find to strike up a conversation. It was always the fear of being turned down and the feeling that followed of utter rejection and humiliation. It appeared to me that most of my male friends at that time did not share these inhibitions as they went from one girlfriend to another, sometimes dating two girls at the same time.

We had been dating for a couple of months before she showed me the two bedroomed flat in the middle of town. She was so enthused with it, it ticked all the boxes according to her, that she liked. Although now twenty-four years old, she was still living with her parents and had never left the area where she had been born.

I then agreed with her that I also loved it, and that I would love it even more if she moved in with me. It was marvellous, there was no hesitation whatsoever. She threw her arms around my neck and kissed me with such passion and laughed excitedly and said, 'Yes, yes, yes.' That all happened two years ago. Louise and I get on very well, mainly because of our sporting interest. We both enjoy playing tennis and golf when we can. She is a better golfer than I am playing off a handicap of 14 whereas I am 18. Our other love is to go off into the hills on our mountain bikes. It is so exhilarating.

I arrived home a little after eleven in the morning. Usually if I am on the night shift, I am just arriving home as Louise is leaving for work. We generally have a quick five-minute discussion. Me telling her what I have dealt with in A&E, her advising me of the latest developments in the TV series 'Sex and the City'. A fleeting kiss 'goodbye' and she is gone. I normally make my way into the kitchen and make coffee and toast. I then scan the newspaper, after which I go upstairs to sleep.

I have found that the quality of sleep is never as good during the daytime as it is during the normal expected hours of nighttime. Because I was late home this morning, Louise had long departed for work at the estate agents and would not return home until two in the afternoon. Feeling unusually tired, I skipped coffee, toast and the newspaper and instead crawled into bed.

After what seemed a noticeably short period of sleep, Louise woke me gently stroking the side of my face. I enquired as to the time and was advised that it was five forty in the afternoon. I was encouraged to get up out of bed by the promise of a cup of freshly ground coffee accompanied by two poached eggs on toast. First, I took a long, luxuriant shower and slowly shaved with the shower water pleasantly cascading over my head and shoulders and running down my body. The therapeutic benefits of a shower can never be understated.

After applying the aftershave that Louise most liked on me, I slipped into a nice crisp white short-sleeve shirt and summer slacks and made my way downstairs. The steaming mug of coffee was already sitting on the breakfast bar and Louise was just slipping the two poached eggs onto the toast. Louise was incredibly pleased with herself as she announced that she had sold two properties that day and together with the other sales that she had made during the previous couple of weeks, was now looking forward to a healthy end of the month bonus.

After consuming my poached eggs and toast, I noticed four or five letters from the morning's postal delivery that Louise had picked up on her way in and had placed at the end of the breakfast bar. The first three were the usual household bills. The fourth was an invitation to attend an interview at a neighbouring hospital. I had applied for a more senior position which offered greater prospects and a substantial increase in salary. The last envelope that I inspected was of remarkably high quality. On the back was the embossed name of a City of London Law Firm, Hildreth and Watkins, established in 1906.

My heart immediately sunk. In this litigious age, so many health authorities are being taken to court for failures in medical care. Many are unjustified but are settled out of court because defending such claims usually is more costly than settling. A colleague of mine who had just returned from working in a hospital in California had been successfully sued for apparently misdiagnosing the condition of an 87-year-old lady who died a year later. I was wracking my brains to think if there had been any patient that I had diagnosed and treated that had made a complaint afterwards. I could think of none.

I opened the envelope and retrieved the letter inside which was typed also on an incredibly heavy bond paper with the watermark of 'Hildreth and Watkins' running through the middle from bottom to top. I then proceeded to read the contents.

Dear Mr Packham – We have been instructed by an overseas law firm to trace and establish the so far missing beneficiary of a large estate in Southern Germany of their deceased client. We have spent almost two years in researching military archives as well as engaging a firm of genealogists. With all the information that has been collated and drawn together, there is a distinct possibility that we may have concluded our search and that you are that beneficiary.

To establish if this is the case or not, we would be most grateful if you could arrange an appointment and travel to London and we will then explain all. If you and your partner Louise, I believe that that is her name, would require an overnight stay, then all your expenses will be taken care of.
Respectfully Yours,
Daniel Watkins

I sat there for a moment or two with what must have been a puzzled look before hearing Louise say, 'Anything of interest?'

'I'm not sure. This could be genuine, or it could be a scam. What do you think?'

Louise took the letter from me whilst at the same time dunking her plain digestive biscuit in her coffee and proceeding to eat the soggy biscuit at the same time.

'Hmm,' she muttered. 'Could be interesting. There is no harm in giving them a phone call. An evening spent in a London hotel with my favourite man with all expenses paid, I find quite appealing.'

Before I had chance to reply, my mobile phone went off. I immediately recognised the number as the hospitals. It was Irene, one of our senior administrators. She explained that there had been a serious accident on the nearby motorway involving a coach full of German tourists that had rolled down the motorway embankment resulting in many serious casualties. All hands to the pump were required.

I looked at Louise, I knew that she would be disappointed as it was unlikely that I would be back home for several hours. We had booked a meal for two at our favourite Italian Restaurant and had tickets to the Theatre afterwards to see 'The Buddy Holly Story'. We both loved the music of the late 50s and 60s.

'I am so sorry my sweet,' I said. 'There has been a major incident involving a coach full of tourists. An emergency has been declared at the hospital, they are requesting as many doctors, medics and nurses as possible to help out.'

Ever since we moved in together, Louise has always been a pragmatist. We both share a deep love and understanding for one another and fully respect each other's decisions. Louise concealed her disappointment, in the knowledge that I had to do what I had to do.

'Well, you had better do what your duty and training demands. After all we would expect the same if it were us who were passengers on that coach.'

'Thank you for your understanding, I will call you when I am able to. May I suggest that you don't cancel this evening and instead invite your young sister? She has after all just broken up with her boyfriend and I am sure would enjoy an evening out with her older, wiser sibling.'

'Yes. That is a good idea. I may just do that. Take care. Love you.'

'I love you too.' With that, a quick hug and a kiss that was all too short, I found myself exiting the front door and running towards my cars parking space.

I arrived at the hospital some ten minutes after the first casualties had arrived. Generally, they were the less serious cases. I was advised that the fire brigade was at that very moment cutting passengers out of the coach who were still trapped in their seats. Sadly, several passengers had been thrown through the side windows and had died at the scene despite the valiant efforts of the paramedics to save them.

A fleet of ambulances had been sent to the scene. One by one, they began to return, now carrying the more seriously injured patients. When such an emergency occurs, which fortunately is rare, whereby several casualties arrive at the same time. The scene can resemble that of a busy kitchen in a top London hotel. Everyone seems to be shouting instructions at once. It is the nearest that I know to organised chaos. But there is an order to it.

The first casualty that I am taking responsibility for is a young woman who I would judge to be in her late thirties. She has a serious head wound and her left arm appears to be badly broken. As we are wheeling her into the first available A&E bay, the senior paramedic is giving me a prognosis and advising me of the care that they have administered, including injections to relieve the pain.

As the attending physician it is my duty to carry out the investigations and procedures necessary to establish a diagnosis and then give advice and provide treatment where necessary and if necessary, calling the appropriate consultant should an urgent operation be deemed to be required. There were so many urgent things that needed to be done, and just for a fleeting moment I thought of my grandfather David McKay who was an army surgeon taking part in the Normandy Landings and the utter chaos and lack of facilities afforded to him to saving lives. It must have been as close to being in Hell as one could imagine.

In comparison, my situation was a good deal better. Lighting, medicines, nurses were all available. In these situations, it is always a question of limited time. The most pressing thing in this case was to discover if there was damage to the brain caused by the impact to her head. After cleaning and stitching the gaping head wound, I then authorised an MRI scan.

The scan revealed a burst cerebral aneurysm which was causing a haemorrhage. I realised immediately the implications for this and called for our neurosurgeon, who like me had responded to the appeal and returned to give help. After studying the scans together, he advised me that a craniotomy was urgently required. This I realised would mean removing part of the skull to access the brain.

I am always amazed how surgeons can issue instructions with authority, speed, and calmness. There never seems to be any panic. Everything is under control. We were lucky to have Mike Dean our neurosurgeon at our hospital. He rapidly instructed the operating theatre to be readied and commanded me to assist with the operation as well as requesting that the senior anaesthetist on duty be present. We then went through the scrubbing routine where our hands and forearms are decontaminated before donning our sterile surgical gown and gloves.

When in an operating theatre, time seems to stand still. This was the first time I had assisted in such an operation. It is not until it is over, and you remove your gloves and gowns and wash again, that you feel physically and mentally exhausted.

I returned to A&E. It was now a quarter past two, Saturday morning. I was advised that all the casualties from the coach accident had now been dealt with. The latest count read for solemn reading. Out of thirty-four occupants on the coach, seven had died, including the driver and his female tour guide who was leading the trip. Nine others were in intensive care, including the patient of mine, whilst the rest had escaped with just minor injuries.

I walked into the A&E waiting area to see if there was anyone that I could help. I discovered a middle-aged gentleman who was complaining loudly that he had arrived at A&E two and a half hours before the coach accident and yet no one had come to examine his ingrowing toenail that was keeping him awake. There are times, especially like now, when you are extremely tired, when you would like to shout loudly at someone for being so stupid and for wasting the hospital's time. But you know you cannot do this. So, I invited him through, apologised for the delay, and explained the unusual emergency of the coach crash.

I examined the big toe on his right foot. I then got him a bowl of warm water for him to soak his foot and gave him some ibuprofen to ease the pain. I then advised him to wear some comfortable shoes or sandals. Mike Dean the neurosurgeon then popped his head around the curtain.

'Just like to thank you Doctor Packham for your assistance in theatre this evening. I have every confidence that our patient will make a full recovery. I believe that you were working last night, is that correct?'

'Yes, that is correct.'

'Well then, I suggest that you go home now and get some rest. When are you next due to work?'

'I am on days for the next two weeks, starting at eight on Monday morning.'

'Well, that doesn't give you much of a weekend to recover. Be sure before you leave at the end of your shift on Monday to look in on Tanya Wolfgang, the young German lady who we operated on just now. Take care.'

And with that, he was gone. At the same time one of the nurses appeared and advised me that she would take over and look after our ingrowing toenail casualty. I didn't argue.

On the way out to the car park, I grabbed a quick coffee from the vending machine in the hope of a caffeine boost. I wearily opened the door to the car and climbed in, sinking into the driver's seat for the fifteen-minute drive home.

I unlocked my front door, glancing at my wristwatch as I did so. It was just before four. I entered the kitchen and poured myself a glass of water, drinking it as I slowly crept up the stairs. I opened the bedroom door as quietly as I could, so as not to disturb Louise who I could sense was fast asleep. I undressed in the dark and slowly got inside and under the bedcovers.

I felt absolutely exhausted. However, I was amazed how snuggling up to the naked body of the woman that I loved could have such an immediate effect of arousal. Louise murmured and then slowly turned over to face me. In no time at all our two bodies were joined together as one. To my mind there is no greater pleasure in life.

The post reaction to our love making could not have been more in contrast between us. I was now totally zonked out and was fully asleep in just a couple of minutes. Louise on the other hand was now fully awake and unable to go back to sleep. I guess, that now feeling grumpy, she got up out of bed, went downstairs and made herself a coffee, before going into the office to catch up on some agency work.

I awoke at around eleven. Upon going downstairs, there was a note on the breakfast bar from Louise advising me that she had gone shopping and expected to be back at around noon. I then went and showered, got changed and made myself some coffee and toast. I was reading the daily paper when Louise returned.

We had a lovely weekend. On the Saturday afternoon we went and played tennis and, on the Sunday joined another couple for a competitive game of golf. It was during Sunday evening that Louise mentioned to me the letter from Hildreth and Watkins. As I was expecting a hectic workload on the Monday, Louise said that she would telephone Daniel Watkins and ascertain if it was genuine and if so, arrange for us to visit the following Friday when she knew we were both off work.

Louise was quite animated when I returned home on the Monday evening. She had spoken with Daniel Watkins himself. Although no additional information was gleaned to what was written in the letter, she said that he sounded very genuine.

'He asked me if we would like to have overnight accommodation, I jokingly said, Yes, we would like to stay at the Savoy,' to which he replied, 'I will get Carol my P.A. to arrange it and she will be in touch.'

'How about that? We could dine in the hotel and go to the theatre afterwards perhaps buy some tickets to see *Blood Brothers*. I know that it is a show that we have seen twice before, but we both love it don't we? Mr Watkins assured me that all expenses would be taken care of.'

Chapter 2

We arrived at the offices of Hildreth and Watkins shortly before two. They were part of the Gray's Inn complex. We pressed the door buzzer and after advising who we were via the intercom, the door automatically released, and we were allowed in. To say that we were impressed by what we saw is an understatement. All the walls were of dark oak panelling. The furniture was regency style. It was all beautiful and lent an air of warm charm which seemed very comforting.

'Hello, I'm Carol, Mr Watkins P.A. All the arrangements have been made for your stay at the Savoy. Can I offer you a tea or coffee?'

'No to coffee or tea but thank you for arranging our stay,' I replied.

'That is a pleasure, would you please follow me?'

We followed Carol up one flight of very ornate looking stairs. At the top of the stairs immediately to the front of us was an impressive looking door with the name of Daniel Watkins painted in gold italic lettering. Carol lightly tapped on the door twice and without waiting for a reply opened the door and stood to one side to allow us to enter.

An elderly distinguished and one would have to say, a fine-looking man for his age, with a full head of silver-grey hair greeted us warmly.

'Come in, come in, it is good of you to travel up and see me.' Giving us both a firm handshake. 'Please take a seat. Allow me to introduce myself. My name is Daniel Watkins, and I am the Senior Partner of this firm. Now you must be Louise Johnson and you sir, I believe to be Michael G. Packham, is that correct?'

'You are indeed correct,' I said. 'But how is it that you know so much about us, particularly about Louise?'

'My dear boy over two years has been spent endeavouring to trace the beneficiary of the Will in question. There were two or three occasions when we thought that we had found that person only to discover that we had not got the right man. And so, we continued investigating every avenue until we came to you. Once found we had to conduct as many background checks as possible to eliminate the possibility that you were not the right man that we were seeking. It was therefore straightforward to establish that this lovely lady, Louise has been your partner for just over two years now. Is that correct?'

'You are spot on,' I replied.

'Now, I need to ask you a series of questions to confirm what we already believe to be the case. Would you please tell me what your mother's maiden name was? Her date of birth? Where, and when did she and your father marry?

'My mother's maiden name was Anne-Marie McKay. She was born on 3rd September 1939. A date that I and others will always remember as being the date when Neville Chamberlain declared at eleven fifteen a.m. that Britain was at War with Germany. They married in a small town called Frome in Somerset and this was in 1969.'

'Do you know how they met?'

'Yes, they were both keen runners and met as members of the local running club.'

'What did your parents do to earn their living?'

'They opened up a children's book shop, called "Inquiring Minds" in the nearby town of Warminster.'

'Do they still run that bookshop?'

'No. Very sadly both of my parents were killed in a head on car collision just outside Ilminster on the A303. They were pronounced dead at the scene. This was in 1996. They were on their way to spend a week's holiday in Cornwall. The car that hit them suffered a blow out and consequently skewed across the road. Not only were my parents killed but also a young couple in the other car. Their one-year-old son survived the accident and is now I believe being cared for by grandparents. It was a difficult time for both families.'

'That must have been tough. My apologies for enquiring about them. It must still be very painful. Let us move on. Please tell me about yourself. Where you lived, where you were educated and your occupation?'

'Well, I was born in Frome Hospital, I believe in Victoria Road, I am not sure if that is the correct road, I do know though that the hospital there is no more and has been replaced with a new one not far from the sports centre. My birthday was on 3rd August 1970. I attended Frome College from 1981 until 1987 before studying at University College London where I obtained my Degree in Medicine. I then worked as a Junior Doctor at Guys Hospital in London for a while until I qualified and took up my present position almost two and half years ago.'

'Do you remember your grandparents from your mother's side of the family?'

'Yes, I do. Both of my grandparents died in the same year. Grandad passing away in July 1987 followed by grandma, two months later. I was not surprised that they died so shortly apart. They were devoted to one another. They are both buried together in the same plot in the Cemetery in Frome.'

'What characteristics do you remember?'

'Hmm. They were both incredibly, kind, thoughtful and encouraging. And loving. It was my grandad's experience as an army surgeon, which convinced me to follow him into the field of medicine. It was shortly before he died. I remember him asking me had I given any thought to what sort of career I might like to have.

'I was a twelve-year-old who was mad keen on football, I was an avid fan of Queens Park Rangers. That season they almost won the Old First Division, which has now morphed into today's Premier League, unfortunately they were just pipped to the title by Liverpool. I was enthralled with the cavalier play of Stan Bowles, but my true inspiration was Gerry Francis. I wanted to be Gerry Francis. So, I announced to grandad, that I wish to be a professional footballer.

'I remember, he didn't respond immediately. He sat there for a long minute or two just gazing at the flames in the open log fire. He then took a sip of his whisky before returning and looking at me.'

'It is certainly true Michael, that you are showing great promise as a footballer. I have been impressed whenever I and your grandmother have watched you play. You also though are playing a good game of tennis and I am pleased that your dad has recently introduced you to playing golf. Two excellent games.

'There is nothing wrong with anyone having dreams of ambition. With all of us, reality is what ultimately decides who we are and what we become.

'It is a fact that many really good footballers, just fall short of making the big time. And then there is a whole catalogue of players whose ambitions were cut short by career ending injuries many by horrendous tackles, with little thought of the consequence by the perpetrator. Most professional footballers leave school at sixteen or like you at seventeen. They are signed by professional clubs. Between sixteen and twenty-one can be, not always of course, so important in the gaining of qualifications that will set you up for life.

'My advice to you Michael, you are our only cherished grandson, do something which is worthwhile and can make a difference to the lives of others. I became a general practitioner before the war and returned to my practice after I was demobbed in 1947. I carried on there until 1968 when I retired.

'Serving my community and looking after their health was wonderful. In the end you know many people and they know you. When you go to the local supermarket, you are continually being greeted by patients and friends who respect you. It was not just medical advice I was dispensing; my patients would come to me with their tax return forms or if they had a problem with paying their rent to the Council or a myriad of problems. I felt like I was more than a doctor, I was their friend and someone in whom they could confide.

'Of course, I realise that things are changing now and that the pace of living has increased and the demand for instant results and having less time with people seems to be becoming the norm. In many ways I am pleased that I belonged to a by-gone era.'

'My grandad never spoke voluntarily about his wartime experiences. I knew from my own dad that grandad had been some sort of medic during the D-Day landings. When I asked him what it was like, he would just reply that it was not nice. The scenes that he had to witness would be etched on his mind until he died.

'I remember my mum saying to me that she thought that grandad had felt a condition I believe they now call 'survivors' guilt'. He was unable to help, assist and save as many as he would have like to have done, because of the appalling conditions that he found himself in. I guess, trying to attend a wounded comrade, when you yourself are under fire in the heat of battle, can never be easy?

'I was successful with my school examines. My grades were high enough for me to enter university and to embark on a career which enabled me to follow in my grandad's footsteps into medicine. Besides, deep down, I knew that I was not good enough to play professional football at a high level. Grandad was right, dreams do have to give way eventually to reality.'

There was a gentle knock on the door and Carol entered carrying a silver tray upon which was a china tea pot and three bone china teacups and saucers. Also, a plate of assorted biscuits.

'Thank you, Carol,' Daniel Watkins said. 'I usually have tea at this time in the afternoon. Also, as you may have observed from my waistline, I enjoy indulging in my love for chocolate biscuits. Louise, would you like to be mum and do the pouring please?'

Louise gave a startled giggle, picked up the pot, and poured whilst Daniel Watkins offered me the plate of biscuits. I took two whilst he also took two. After Louise had poured the tea, and taken her own two biscuits, Daniel Watkins stood up taking his tea and biscuits and walked to the window and looked out upon the world below. Slowly sipping his tea and then disposing of one of his biscuits he stood there for some time appearing to be in deep thought. Louise and I shot questioning glances to each other, but not daring for some reason to speak.

After a minute or two when the only sound heard in the room was the loud ticking of the grandfather clock, which we had not previously noticed, Daniel Watkins returned whilst finishing off his second chocolate biscuit. He then took his seat again and with one of the napkins provided he wiped the crumbs from his lips and then coughed slightly to clear his throat.

'Well Louise, Michael, I thank you again for taking the time to come along to see me. I suspect, as indeed I would have, after receiving such a letter out of the blue, to wonder if the contents of that invitation were genuine or merely some sort of scam. Unfortunately, we seem to be entering an age of sophisticated scams. No longer does a man enter a bank with a gun and a mask and demand money from the till, now he can sit at a desk in his home and hack bank accounts from his computer. It is a fascinating, intriguing world that we are now living in. Indeed, a changing world, with an entirely new set of standards.

'I digress please forgive me. You have not travelled all this way to hear the musing of an old fool. From what you have told me Michael, I do believe that we have finally discovered the identity of the person that we are seeking. I now reveal to you the circumstances, albeit briefly as to why you are here.

'As you no doubt already know, the D-Day landings in France took place on 6th June 1944. A force exceeding 156,000 military personnel consisting of American, British, and Canadian troops were tasked with breaching and then securing a 50 mile stretch of heavily fortified coastline in Normandy. The British 50th Infantry Division had been allocated a section of coastline codenamed Gold Beach. Their objective was to capture the town of Bayeux famous for its Cathedral and Tapestry and proceed to capture the Caen–Bayeux Road and to link up with the Americans at Omaha.

'As is often the case with any battle, things didn't go according to schedule. Dislodging the German defenders took far longer than had been anticipated. Your grandfather, David McKay was a Major in the Royal Army Medical Corps. He was a surgeon. He arrived by sea six days later when the beach head had been firmly secured and the 50th Infantry Division had made significant inroads.

'Our story really begins on 20th August in what was to be the decisive battle for Normandy. The Western Allies had encircled the German Army Group B, consisting amongst others of the Seventh Army and the Fifth Panzer Army around the town of Falaise. Your grandad was desperately working at a field hospital a few miles from the front line. There was a long stream of casualties constantly being ferried back by any means of transport available. Most had terrible wounds. Many had limbs missing or the injuries were so severe that amputation was the only answer.'

Clearing his throat, Daniel Watkins went on. 'I received this letter just over two years ago from a very well established and indeed highly respected law firm from Munich. Their name is Muller and Schneider. In fact, they are remarkably similar to our own practice. Dieter Muller and Ernst Schneider are both sons of the founding fathers of their firm as I and my recently deceased partner of many years James Hildreth are and were.

'You will understand, before responding and agreeing to this request from an overseas law firm, I did a little research of my own to establish the credentials of Messrs Muller and Schneider. It may be that they chose our firm because they also had done their relevant research. I believe that they had discovered that James my former partner had departed to another place and therefore addressed their letter to me. Here is what it said.

'Dear Mr Watkins – We have been engaged to carry out the instructions in a Will and Last Testament of our client, one Otto Wagner. Herr Wagner leaves quite a substantial estate near Berchtesgaden which although in Germany is in fact just a few kilometres south of Salzburg in Austria. Our client sadly passed away in 1952 at the age of 63.

'It is natural for you to ask, why it has taken this long for me to contact you? In December 1949, Mr Wagner engaged a young lady housekeeper cum cook and a male gardener. The house is large, and the grounds are extensive. The terms of the agreement were that they would both live in. Shortly before Mr Wagner died and drew up his last Will and Testament a clause was inserted that these two employees could remain living there rent free until their deaths. Only then after their deaths would his final wishes with regard as to who inherited his estate be carried out. Tanya van der Leyen, his housekeeper died in 1995 aged 71 and his gardener Frank Meyer died last year 1997 at the age of 74.

'Our client, Otto Wagner was an Austrian national and was born in 1889 in the town of Eisenstadt which is south of Vienna, indeed not far from the border with Hungary. Eisenstadt is quite well known for its castle but in musical circles the main church is the resting place for the composer, Haydn. Otto married Hildegard Krause in 1921 and they had one son, Helmut who was born a year later in 1922. Tragically they endured the fate of many families during war time with the news that their son had been killed in 1943. He was a Luftwaffe pilot, and his Junker Ju87 Stuka dive bomber was shot down whilst on a mission during the failed assault on Stalingrad.

'The news of losing her only son was too much to bear for his mother, who then sadly took her own life. We believe at this time that Otto was working for the Air Ministry in Berlin. He decided, we are not sure when, to resign and instead enlist and train as a tank radio operator. In August 1944 he was part of Field Marshal Walter Model's army that was encircled by the Western Allies. It became known as the Battle of the Falaise Pocket.

'Otto was part of the crew in a Panther tank which received a direct hit from a shell fired by a British Cromwell tank. He and his crew managed to evacuate their vehicle which by now was burning fiercely. They came under rifle fire in which two of his comrades were killed.

'Apparently, Otto stumbled over the body of a dead British rifleman and had the presence of mind to discard his own headgear and tunic and put on the dead man's greatcoat. He was hoping somehow to survive the immediate fire fight and pass-through British lines. Unfortunately for Otto, he was shot in the left shoulder which totally felled him.

'He lay there in the mud aware of all of the noise and chaos that surrounded him. Then miraculously two British Army stretcher bearers appeared. They must have noticed his movement because they immediately ran over and attended to him. Fortunately for Otto, he spoke fluent English, which probably saved his life. They then lifted him onto a stretcher and carried him back about half a kilometre where he was then transferred onto the back of an army lorry with three other stretcher cases and driven to a field hospital further back from the fighting.

'He was then taken to a tent which was being used as a makeshift operating theatre. It was here when the great coat was removed in order to inspect his injuries that it was discovered that he was not a British soldier, but instead the enemy. Apparently, a ruckus erupted involving the stretcher bearers who were shall we say, less than pleased that instead of saving one of their own, they had brought an enemy into the camp. Otto felt his life to be in danger and it would have been had it not been for the calm and authoritative intervention of the surgeon who would go on to remove the bullet from his shoulder.

'The Surgeon immediately thanked and dismissed the two stretcher bearers advising them as they left that it was the duty of all to save lives wherever possible of both friends and foes. The surgeon successfully removed the bullet.

'Otto remembers the kindness of this man and thought how could we be enemies? The surgeon during the procedure had spoken words of comfort and was very reassuring during the operation which was very painful. He seemed to be impressed that Otto spoke such good English.

'Immediately after the operation and before Otto was transferred to another medic who would apply the field dressings, Otto thanked the surgeon and asked his name. The man was clearly in a hurry as another bloodied body had just been brought in with a badly shattered leg. All Otto remembers is the man calling out something that sounded like McKee. Otto never set eyes on this man ever again.

'Otto Wagner, one week later was shipped across the English Chanel to Portland in Dorset before being transferred to Devizes in Wiltshire to be processed and the decision taken as to where to send him. After a week or so Otto was then transported to Yorkshire in the North of England and to a POW camp, Camp No. 83 better known as Eden Camp, Malton. Here he recuperated until he was well enough to be sent out to work on a farm. He was then repatriated back to Germany in 1948 and made his way back home to his estate in Southern Germany.

'Now I come to the main part of the will. Regrettably like so many other German families who had survived the War, Otto had no living relatives.

He then concluded that the one person who had given him the chance to live was the surgeon who he believed was called McKee. He was aware that the surgeon appeared to be a similar age to himself and might not still be alive. Therefore, Otto has stipulated in his will that he is leaving his entire estate to the surgeon or to the living descendants of the surgeon.

'We trust that you will accept this commission and locate the descendants of the surgeon who we believe is called something like McKee. Assuring you that we have a substantial budget to ensure that this task is successfully concluded.

Yours faithfully,
Dieter Muller

'Part of the reason why it has taken so long to trace you is because we had the wrong surname. We were checking up on over twenty McKees that were involved during the liberation of France. Not one of them it transpired was an army surgeon. We then pondered if Otto had misheard the name called back to him and started looking at alternatives. We then gained access to the names of all military personnel that had taken part in the D-Day landings. Still nothing, so we expanded our search to include those who were subsequent reinforcements and had arrived after D-Day. This is when we stumbled across four McKay's.

'Looking at army records we then established that only one, a Major David McKay was an army surgeon and that he had been in charge of the field hospital south of Falaise during August and September 1944. We then engaged a firm of genealogists who traced the Family Tree that has led us to you. From what you have told me today, it matches all of the known facts that we have about your grandad and therefore I am certain that our quest to find the beneficiary of Otto Wagner is now complete.'

Louise and I sat there in stunned silence for several moments trying to comprehend the significance of what we had just heard. Something to me, didn't seem quite right. Finally, I found my voice to ask the question that was bothering me.

Looking back across the desk at Daniel Watkins, I asked, 'Tell me Mr Watkins, how is it that a private soldier serving as a radio operator in a German Panzer tank unit could have amassed such a fortune in order to buy the estate that you have indicated is significant in size? And in which so much time, money and effort have been spent to pursue and establish the rightful beneficiary in order to satisfy the wishes of this Otto Wagner?'

'They are very good questions, and ones that I also have asked myself. But no doubt you will appreciate that my role in all of this was just to find the right person and not to go beyond that. This is a question that you might like to ask of Dieter Muller when no doubt he contacts you. Now I believe that Carol has arranged for you to stay at the Savoy Hotel. All expenses have been taken care of. Please when you return home contact Carol with details of your travel and miscellaneous expenses, these will be reimbursed.'

With that Daniel Watkins stood up, came around the desk and ushered us to the door. Shaking our hands and remarking that it had been his pleasure he opened the door and lo and behold there was Carol already waiting to guide us down the stairs and out of the offices and once more onto the pavement of a busy London street.

I am not sure that Louise and I had fully grasped just what had happened. We went for a coffee where we tried to make sense of it all before checking into the Savoy Hotel. We concluded after much discussion just to let things run and to see what transpires. In the meantime, we were determined to enjoy an expenses paid weekend in London. Which we duly did.

Chapter 3

Louise and I returned to our respective jobs the following Monday after making the most of a very enjoyable weekend spent in London. We soon both became absorbed once more with work related issues that we completely forgot about being potential benefactors. It was four weeks to the day of our meeting with Daniel Watkins that a letter arrived with the stamp mark showing that it had been posted in Munich, Germany. Louise could hardly contain her excitement which was borne out of curiosity and intrigue.

Before slitting open the envelope, I suggested that we opened a bottle of our favourite red wine and read the letter together, which is what we did. It read as follows.

Dear Mr Packham – I was delighted to have received a letter of confirmation that you are the person we are seeking in order to execute the wishes of a deceased client of ours with respect to his final Will and Testament. Daniel Watkins of Hildreth and Watkins in London, sent through all the supporting documentary evidence which we thoroughly checked. This clearly establishes that you are the beneficiary. I would like to congratulate you. Your grandfather must have been a remarkable man?

It has taken over two years of exhaustive research to establish the facts that have now been arrived at. We on our part would like to conclude this matter as quickly as possible. I would be grateful if you are able to visit us in Munich at your earliest convenience. All expenses will be paid. We are happy for those expenses to include your partner Miss Louise Johnson. I await your instructions.

Yours faithfully,

Dieter Muller

'How about we make it a bit of a holiday?' I said to Louise. 'We both have holiday owing to us. I could take a week off in around four weeks' time, how about you?'

'It is true, I do have some holiday owing. I will check with the boss. Giving four weeks' notice shouldn't be a problem I don't expect.'

After Louise and I had obtained the permissions of our respective employers for our week's leave, I telephoned the offices of Muller and Schneider to confirm our intended date of arrival. As with our trip to London for our meeting with Daniel Watkins, we were advised that all the arrangements would be taken care of. These would include return flights to Munich, travel, and hotel accommodation.

We were both amazed when the arrangements for our trip to Germany came through. A chauffeured limousine had been booked to pick us up from our home and to drop us off at Gatwick Airport. Upon our arrival at Munich's Franz Josef Strauss International Airport, we would once again be collected by a chauffeured limousine and taken to the Mandarin Oriental Hotel in Neuturmistrasse, which is in the City Centre.

Louise and I were so excited. During our time of living together we had only taken two one-week holidays. The first was a golfing trip to Scotland where we played five different courses on consecutive days. The second, six days trekking in the Brecon Beacons in Wales. Both holidays, most enjoyable. However, this would be our first time abroad together.

On the day of our departure, we were duly picked up at eight a.m. sharp by our chauffeured limousine and driven to Gatwick Airport. As promised as soon as we had cleared customs and entered the arrivals hall at Munich Airport, there to greet us with a big, printed sign with our names on was our chauffeur.

'Hello and Welcome,' he said. 'My name is Johann, and I will be your driver/guide during your stay with us in Germany. Please allow me to take your cases and follow me.'

We followed Johann to the short stay car park, and he led us to what appeared to be a spanking new BMW 3 series car. He remotely opened the doors and as I got into the front passenger seat and Louise got into the back Johann put our cases into the boot of the car.

'Right,' he said. 'Let's go to the hotel. Have you been to Munich before?'

'No,' I replied. 'It is the first time in Germany for both of us.'

'Ah, then that is good,' Johann responded. 'Bavaria is the most beautiful area in the whole of Germany.'

It took us around 40 minutes' drive before we reached the Mandarin Oriental. Johann handed our cases over to the greeting doorman and then advised us that he would pick us up sharp at ten the following morning. He would then take us on a tour of Munich and after we would meet Dieter Muller over lunch.

After checking in we were then shown to our room, and what a room? It must have been the hotel's best. It overlooked the city. Briefly glancing at the hotel's information brochure, we discovered that there was a rooftop terrace with a pool and café. We were so happy that it was only a minute or two later before we found our two naked bodies on top of the bed making passionate love. It was wonderful. Afterwards, both feeling exhausted through our physical exertions we crawled under the covers and took a well-earned nap.

Upon waking, Louise then decided to run a bath. 'Are you going to join me?' she enquired.

'I most certainly am,' I replied. 'How about a glass of Moet? I asked noticing the for the first time, the ice bucket with the bottle of Moet protruding.

We decided not to venture out as we would see Munich the following day. Instead, we would enjoy the facilities and the cuisine of the hotel. We concluded that they were top-notch.

Johann entered the hotel lobby at precisely ten a.m. the following morning.

'Good morning Michael, Louise, was everything to your satisfaction?'

'It most certainly was, and more,' Louise replied whilst straining not to giggle at the same time.

'That's good to hear, let us explore Munich.'

It was a three-hour drive taking in most of the sights including the impressive football stadium home to FC Bayern Munich, then the BMW factory as well as the Olympic Park. At one p.m. we arrived outside a restaurant in the district of Maxvorstadt.

We must have been expected because we were greeted by the Maître-D at the door and escorted to the far end of the restaurant to a table clearly chosen with discretion in mind. Waiting for us was a distinguished looking man not unlike Daniel Watkins both in age and demeanour.

'Louise, Michael, how lovely it is for me to meet you after all this time. I thought it would be good to have an informal lunch before going back to my office which is only a short walk from here to discuss what has brought us together.'

The lunch was an unhurried affair, lasting for just over two hours. The food was exquisite and was accompanied by an excellent bottle of Riesling followed by another. Dieter proved to be a charming host, gently prompting us into revealing more or less our life stories. One thing that I did notice, was that he revealed very little about himself.

When it was time to leave, we just got up and walked out with the Maître-D expressing the hope that we had enjoyed our meal and opening the door himself as we left. There was no presentation of a bill or any attempt to pay. I thought 'How ideal is this?'

Dieter's office was no more than a five-minute walk from the restaurant. Unlike the offices of Daniel Watkins, these were ultra-modern with the walls being adorned by equally modern art. The entire office seemed to be hi-tech. There were six employees that we could see. Four ladies and two men. Both men looked to be tall and were both fair haired and the ladies also were blue eyed blondes. I couldn't help thinking that this was the perfect Aryan race that was so desired by Hitler. Amazing to think that Hitler looked nothing like what he was seeking for his nation. Dieter's staff all looked like peas out of the same pod.

'Please be seated both of you.' Dieter's demeanour changed from that of being a convivial host to now one of a serious professional with work to do. 'Let us cut to the chase as you English speakers like to say.

'I believe that we have beyond all reasonable doubt established that you Michel Packham are the surviving descendant. Major David McKay was your grandfather. He married Estella Wright in 1926. They had one child, a daughter Anne-Marie who was born in 1939. She then marries John Packham in 1969 and you are their only child, born in 1970. Your parents were killed in a car accident in 1996. This has left you as the sole surviving member of David McKay's family. Is this accurate as I have told it?'

'Yes, totally,' I replied.

'Good. So far so good. Otto Wagner's Estate is quite unusual in that it is not only just a substantial property, but there is also a 2,000-acre mixed arable farm. Now I understand that you are a doctor at present working in A&E and that Louise works as an estate agent. Therefore, I would suspect that the prospect of living and working in Germany and especially managing a farm is not one that you would consider as being desirable or indeed feasible?

'There is a consortium of businessmen who were very surprised by the wishes that Otto Wagner made in his Will. Knowing that he had no family survivors they had fully expected that their organisation and one in which Otto served with great loyalty and distinction would have been the beneficiaries. It has been extremely frustrating for this organisation to have waited for so many years. Firstly, by the clause that the housekeeper and gardener could stay until their deaths and then the delay in tracing you.

'There is a solution to the problem, one which I believe that you will welcome. I have been instructed by this group to make you an offer of seven million euros to sell your newly acquired assets to them. Afterall, it is an unexpected windfall for you. This will set you and Louise up for the rest of your lives. No need to work any longer. You could travel the world. Stay in the best hotels and have an absolutely wonderful time. What are your thoughts regarding this unexpected outcome?'

One of the qualities that impressed me about Louise was how quickly she could assess a situation. While I was still pondering, she crossed her legs with the skirt now riding halfway up her exposed thigh, which I noticed drew an admiring glance from Dieter, causing him momentarily to lose focus and for Louise to speak out.

'You are right Herr Muller; it is a totally unexpected windfall and one that could if we accepted the offer that you have outlined on behalf of this organisation totally change our lives. Having travelled to Germany, our curiosity would not be satisfied if we did not at least visit the property. What do you think Michael?'

'I am as intrigued as Louise is,' I said. 'In fact if you could give us the address and the keys, then we will hire out a car and travel down there tomorrow and view it if that is okay with you?'

'I was rather hoping that that would not be necessary and that you would accept the generous offer that has been made to you. But as you are in effect, the rightful owners of the property, then of course you may travel down and view for yourself. I will arrange for Johann to pick you up tomorrow and drive you there. It is an easy drive of less than two hours. I know you said that this is your first visit to Germany, I would assume also that you have not been to Austria, would that be so?'

Louise shook her head and I confirmed that that was indeed the case.

'Salzburg is a beautiful city; it is only a few kilometres away from your property. I will arrange for you to stay the night at the NH Salzburg City Hotel, this is where my wife and I always stay when we visit this fine city.'

'That's very kind of you,' I said. 'Are you sure it is no trouble? Now that we are potential millionaires, I think it only right that we pay for this ourselves.'

'Nonsense Michael, all expenses are being taken care of. Now if you would kindly excuse me, I have an important meeting scheduled for four thirty. Johann will take you back to your hotel and will pick you up in the morning. It was a pleasure meeting you both.'

There must have been some sort of 'silent bell' beneath Dieter's desk which could only be heard by his personal assistant sitting at the desk outside his office. For no sooner had he finished speaking, then there was a slight tap at the door and standing there was his P.A. smiling pleasantly as she then proceeded to usher us into the main office complex where Johann was waiting.

I was surprised when Johann said that he would drive us back to our hotel and that he would pick us up at 10 the following morning and take us to the property in question. It made me suspect that our meeting with Herr Dieter was being monitored in real time. I believe that Louise must have sensed the same. Neither of us spoke until we got dropped off at the hotel.

Upon entering our room, I looked around, everything appeared to be normal. For some reason, I just felt suspicious.

I said to Louise, 'Well what an interesting meeting, it looks as though you and I have become millionaires. What say you that we go for a swim before celebrating our good fortune? It is not every day that you get to swim in a rooftop pool. And then this evening, we can really celebrate.'

'That sounds like a good plan to me,' she said.

The temperature in the pool was a comfortable 68 degrees. We both swam for around ten minutes before exiting the pool, towelling ourselves off and donning our white fluffy dressing gowns. We then ordered two cappuccino coffees and stretched out on the sun loungers.

We looked at one another before I spoke. 'Don't think that I am becoming paranoid Louise but despite the good news, I felt uncomfortable in Dieter's office this afternoon. Something isn't quite right. What are your thoughts?'

Louise didn't respond immediately. She just gazed at the water in the pool and then she said. 'Did you notice how Dieter's demeanour immediately changed when it was put to him that we would like to visit the property?'

'Yes, very much so.'

'It was as if he had fully expected us to accept his offer, sign there and then and then to bugger off, never to be seen again. Seven million euros is a huge sum to offer. The nagging question that we need an answer to which is intriguing me, is how did Otto end up as such a wealthy individual?'

'You have mirrored my own concern Louise. I am not sure if you know too much about the Second World War, but it is interesting to note Berchtesgaden is where Martin Bormann, who was one of Hitler's henchmen was responsible for the construction of The Eagles Nest, ostensibly to curry favour with Hitler and as a gift to celebrate the Fuhrer's fiftieth birthday on 20th April 1939.'

'How do you know so much about this?' Louise asked.

'Because of my grandfather's involvement in the war, I then became very interested as a teenager and read several books, the best being "*The Rise and Fall of the Third Reich*" by William Shirer. This in turn lead me to other books. The Eagles Nest is a tea house placed right on top of a mountain. It was a great feat of engineering when you consider that much of it was cut out by hand. From what I read, Hitler suffered from vertigo and only visited it on a dozen or so occasions. He was also paranoid that the lift taking him to the tea house, which was constructed inside the mountain, that the lift mechanism could be struck by lightning, which it had been on two occasions. But the views of the area known as the Obersalzberg are stunning.'

'No doubt I will see how stunning tomorrow is,' responded Louise. 'In the meantime I have to say that I am excited and curious to see just what my man has inherited. Shall we have another dip? And then perhaps have a walk around the city centre this evening?'

'Absolutely but let us see who is the quickest over twenty lengths in the pool.' We both immediately jumped up and dived in, me in the knowledge that I stood no chance of beating Louise in the pool.

Johann as we expected arrived promptly at ten. As always, he was very cheerful and polite. When we walked outside and reached the car, he opened the rear door for Louise and was surprised as indeed I was when she said, 'I would like to ride in the front if that's okay?'

Johann glanced at me to which I said, 'Sure, I don't have a problem with that.'

Louise was wearing a tight-fitting white jumper and a bottle green skirt which came a couple of inches above the knee and wore high heels. I thought then, how great she looked. Her legs were fantastic, she had always been mindful of keeping fit and active. It is not until other men, such as Johann take an exaggerated interest in how she looked that I realised how lucky I was that she should be my partner. I also quickly concluded that this was a status that I needed to upgrade from partner to fiancé and then to wife very quickly.

We headed out of Munich and soon found ourselves travelling along the A8 autobahn in the direction of Salzburg. I was surprised at how chatty Louise was with Johann. She was asking him about his family, where he came from, had he travelled much and had he always been a chauffeur?

It turned out that Johann was 33 years old and had spent ten years in the military in their equivalent of our SAS, the German Special forces. He was an expert in unarmed combat and was a highly accomplished marksman as well as being an expert in explosives. He also spoke fluent English, French and Spanish. He was married to Dieter's Personal Assistant, Maria.

'Tell me Johann,' Louise asked, 'about the property that you are taking us to?'

'The first thing I would say is that when you see it, you will realise that it is not suitable for you. It is far too large. It comprises eight bedrooms four of which are en-suite, two family bathrooms, three receptions rooms, a large kitchen, a library and a snooker/billiards room. Otto was a very accomplished snooker player, did you know that? He was also a fine artist and many of his paintings adorn the walls.'

Not wishing to be completely ignored as I could see that Johann was so engrossed with Louise that he had quite forgotten my presence in the rear of the car. I said, 'No, I didn't realise that. What did he do for a living?'

'He is or was a farmer. As you may know, there is a 2,000-acre mixed/arable farm included in the estate.'

We left the A8 a few miles to the west of Salzburg and drove south just for a few kilometres before turning off the main road and along a country lane. We then pulled into a driveway with a very impressive set of closed wrought iron gates. There was a speaker phone to the side with a security camera looking down. Johann pressed the buzzer and without any words being spoken, as though we were expected, the gates slowly swung open, and we then continued to proceed along a driveway.

The driveway was an avenue with tall trees on either side. After about a mile we rounded a bend and then suddenly there it was, a real wow moment. It was like a fairy tale castle with several turrets. Johann advised us that the house had been built entirely out of local quarried rock. It was so impressive. As we pulled up outside the entrance to the house there standing to greet us were two extremely attractive women in their early thirties as well as two muscular men of a similar age.

'May I introduce Max and Fritz, they are both gardeners and handymen who keep the property in good repair, and this is Ingrid and Annaliesa, they are our two housekeepers.'

After shaking their hands, we then entered a magnificent hallway, all four walls were adorned with the heads of magnificent stags. 'All of these that you see here were shot on the estate over a good many years. Let me give you a guided tour of the house and then we will have lunch of suckling pig that the girls have prepared. I hope that neither of you are Jewish?'

'Mike and I are both nonbelievers,' Louise said, 'having such a variety of different religions in the world seem to be the cause of such strife resulting in untold misery. Germany's recent history is a testament to that.'

I couldn't help but notice the disapproving glances exchanged between Ingrid and Johann.

'Well then that has at least established that you are not Jewish and therefore have no problem with the pork, let us go and explore.'

The house was magnificent in every way. The furnishings, the carpets, the lighting and the paintings all complimented every room that we went into. Most of the paintings were by Otto Wagner, it was clear that he was extremely competent. The library was superb with floor to ceiling bookcases and a ladder nearby to assist in reaching the shelves that were too high. We finished our tour in the dining room.

There were three places set with beautiful crystal wine glasses at each setting. The meal was superb and was accompanied by a bottle of Austrian red Blauer Zweigelt wine, which Johann advised was produced just over the border.

The time was now nearing three thirty. Johann suggested that we make tracks for our night in Salzburg. We bade farewell to the four staff with Johann opening the front passenger car door for Louise.

As we were leaving the estate and turning onto the lane I said to Johann. 'I am a bit puzzled. My understanding was that Ottos wishes as to finding the heirs to his estate were delayed until the deaths of his housekeeper and gardener. As the gardener was the last to pass away two years ago, I was expecting to find the house and grounds in a state of disrepair. Who has been responsible for paying to keep everything in such good order?'

Johann shot me a look in the rear-view mirror. 'I believe that the upkeep and ongoing costs were deemed appropriate by the Committee of the organisation that Otto was deeply involved with. It is they who are meeting your expenses for this trip. It was a decision to keep the estate in good condition as a lasting legacy in remembering Otto.'

'What is the name of this organisation,' I asked.

Johann looking once more in his rear-view mirror. 'I am sorry that information I do not have.' And then with a contrived laugh. 'I am after all a mere chauffeur.'

'Where abouts is the farm?' asked Louise.

'I believe that the main farm buildings are a few kilometres away, although the house that you have just visited is on the estate. I have never been to the actual farm myself.'

'Would it be possible that we could visit the farm tomorrow or the next day?' I asked.

'My instructions were to show you the house and then for you to visit Salzburg and for me to collect you tomorrow at noon and return you to Munich for a final meeting with Herr Muller. I believe that your return flights to England have been scheduled for tomorrow evening.'

'Will you be returning to Munich this evening?'

'No, I will be staying in the same hotel as you. In fact, my room is the one next to yours. Don't worry, I will keep out of your way and will pick you up tomorrow. I will give you my card, it has my mobile phone details on it. If there is anything that you would like, then do not hesitate to call me.'

After booking into the hotel and settling into our room, again a lovely room. Louise and I decided that we would go out and explore Salzburg the City made famous by Mozart, its hilltop castle and of course the location for the film *The Sound of Music* starring Julie Andrews.

We found a coffee shop in Mozart Platz and took window seats looking out upon the square. 'Well Louise,' I asked, 'what do you think?'

'Hmm, there are a number of things that I have noticed. First of all, everyone connected with Dieter seems to be a pure Aryan or part of the so-called master race. I can understand there being one or two, but we have Johann, the six staff in Dieter's office and the four staff at the house, they are all so similar. Also, I get the distinct impression that they just require you to accept the offer, sign over the estate and disappear back home.'

'I agree with all that you have said. I feel that we are being managed and organised. Also, who is this organisation? Why have they invested so much money in tracing us and paying for our expenses in full?' There is so little information regarding Otto Wagner. Here is a suggestion Louise. Neither of us are due back at work for another five days, why don't we stay and make full use of our holiday time and carry out some research by ourselves?'

'I think that is an excellent idea. Without wishing to appear greedy, you may find that the offer of seven million euros is well below the real value. I'm with you Michael, let's go for it and conduct our own research.'

'We might as well begin now. You have your mobile and I have mine. The first thing that we know is that Otto Wagner was

Austrian and was born in 1889. For us, the search would be difficult, I suggest that we contact a leading Genealogists firm in Vienna.'

After scrolling through the internet where there were several such companies, we picked one that seemed to be the most prominent. I explained that we were looking for an Otto Wagner who was born in 1889 and who died near Berchtesgaden in 1952. The only other information that we had was that during the War he was in Berlin before transferring to a Panzer tank Corps and that he was taken prisoner by the British in 1944 and was repatriated in 1948.

I explained that money would be no object, but that time was noticeably short and that we needed a team on this and not just one researcher. I then requested that I speak with the head of the company. When he came on the line, I explained to him the urgency and again that money was not an issue. In order to show good faith, I confirmed that I would make an immediate bank transfer of five thousand euros on account.

That done, Louise and I looked at each other. 'What now?' Louise asked.

'First of all, I think that we should arrange for a car hire from tomorrow. Today is Tuesday, we have until Sunday before we must return to our jobs on Monday. I will phone Johann right now and advise him that there is no need for him to stay overnight and that he can return to Munich this evening.'

Johann answered the call on the third ring. 'Michael, how are you? I trust that you are both enjoying the splendours of Salzburg? I did tell you that it was a beautiful city.'

'You certainly did Johann and we agree with you it is a beautiful place to be. Just to advise you my friend that it is so beautiful that we have decided that we will stay here for a few days.'

There was a pause, and I could sense the disbelief in Johann's response. 'We would love to have you back another time Michael, but all of the arrangements have been made, I will pick you up tomorrow at noon and you have a meeting scheduled with Dieter for three in the afternoon. After the conclusion of business, I will drive you back to the airport.'

I sensed an edge to his voice. I put the phone on speaker so that Louise could hear what was being said. 'There's no rush Johann, it has taken two years or more to find us, so a little more time will be neither here nor there. We can amend our flights ourselves and keep in touch with Dieter.'

'I forbid it. I have my orders and they are to return you to Munich tomorrow, meet with Dieter, sign the papers and I will drive you to the airport.'

Louise then spoke in her soft, but firm feminine voice. 'Hi Johann, it is Louise. We have booked a whole week's holiday. It is our first time in Austria and Germany, I had no idea that this part of the world was so beautiful, it would be such a shame if we cut it short. We would very much like to visit Vienna whilst we are here. We did not realise the urgency that Herr Muller had attached to wrapping this up. I am quite sure that Michael would be happy to telephone him apologise and reschedule.'

'I will speak with Herr Muller, but I know that he is a fastidious man and gets very angry, when I say angry, I mean disappointed when his plans are changed. He is after all carrying out the instructions from his clients.'

Louise was not deterred. 'We would not wish to cause any offence to Herr Muller who has been extremely kind, welcoming, and courteous, but we would like to make the most of our trip. By the way, who are the clients that have engaged Herr Muller? I assume that it is the nameless organisation?'

'I will speak to Herr Muller and come back to you.' The phone abruptly went dead.

Looking at Louise. 'Well what do you make of that? How long do you think it will be before we receive a call from Herr Muller?'

'I reckon within thirty minutes.'

Louise's prediction was out by twenty minutes. Ten minutes later my mobile rang.

'Herr Muller, how are you? I apologise if our new arrangements have altered what you were hoping for. We really would like to see a little more of Austria and Bavaria before we return home.'

'Yes, I certainly appreciate what you are saying. Let me put a suggestion to you Michael. I will arrange for Johann to pick you up first thing in the morning, drive you back to my office, we can tidy up all lose ends. I can arrange for the money to be wired into your account immediately. We should be done and dusted by noon. We will arrange for a hire car, or I am happy for Johann to escort you until you return home at the weekend. We can make all of the arrangements.'

'That's most kind of you Herr Muller, but you will understand that there are things that we would like to do first by ourselves without the need to be chaperoned by Johann.'

'Listen to me Michael,' I could sense that he was struggling to remain calm and not appear to be aggressive, but he was failing. 'You will agree having seen the house and grounds that it would not be of any use to you. The organisation that I represent have agreed to increase their offer by a further five hundred thousand euros. If I may say so, you would be foolish not to agree.'

'Why are you reluctant to show us the farm estate?'

'My dear boy, I am not reluctant, I just assumed that it would be of no interest to you.'

'Anyone who is the beneficiary of a Will such as this, I am sure would like to have full disclosure and see exactly what and where everything is. Could you give us directions to the farm so that we may have a look?'

'You are making things exceedingly difficult. I will see what I can do and then get back to you.'

The following morning, we checked out of the hotel, took charge of our hire car and drove to Vienna. We parked up and went to a café near St Stephen's Cathedral. Suitably feed and watered we then took the open topped bus for a scenic tour of the city which also included stopping at Schonbrunn Palace that was once the main residence of the Habsburg rulers. We spent an hour there, not nearly enough before returning to the city centre and booking into a more modest hotel not quite to the same standard as the two hotels of the previous two evenings.

The following morning, Louise and I decided to visit the Vienna Opera House. During our visit we broke off to have coffee and cake in the café there. We had just taken our seats when my mobile phone rang. I had expected it to be Dieter Muller, but no, it was instead Hans Winkler the head of the Genealogists.

'Is that Mr Packham, I'm speaking to?'

'It is, indeed, Herr Winkler.'

'I am pleased to be able to give you an update as to what we have found.'

'Thank you, I am just going to put my phone onto record and speaker, please go ahead.'

'Otto Wagner as you correctly said was born in 1889. His birthplace was in the town of Eisenstadt a town south of Vienna and famous for its castle and for the church where Haydn the composer is buried. His father was a carpenter, and his mother was a nurse. In 1911, Otto who was a particularly good artist decides that he will move to Vienna.

'He was accepted by the Imperial Royal Arts and Crafts Faculty. We believe that it was in 1912 when he was doing a painting of the Vienna State Opera House that he met another painter undertaking the same task. Apparently, they got on quite well. His new artistic friend turned out to be none other than Adolf Hitler who was struggling at that time to sell his works. Hitler was hugely disappointed to have been rejected by the City's Academy of Fine Arts.

'In May 1913 Hitler decided to leave Vienna and move to Munich. A year later Otto also moves to Munich where he managed to find employment as an art teacher at a private city centre school. Otto somehow avoided being called up to serve in the military during the First World War and continued with his teaching.

'Our final piece of research so far has indicated that in 1919 Otto left his job and instead obtained a position as a clerk to Anton Drexler who was the founder of the DAP (German Workers' Party). The manifesto was based very much on anti-Semitic, nationalist, anti-capitalist and anti-Marxist ideas. We do know that Adolf Hitler had impressed Drexler with his oratory and was then invited to join the DAP which he did on 12th September that year. At the moment we are assuming that Otto and Hitler became reacquainted.'

'Thank you, Herr Winkler, that is remarkably interesting. I have recently learnt that I am the beneficiary to Otto Wagner's estate. Yesterday we saw the property that I have inherited. It is a magnificent property just outside the village of Bischofswiesen. The property is called *Schlachthaus* which Louise my partner who speaks German has advised me means Battle Manor. There is also a large farm attached, but as yet we haven't seen it. Is it possible that you could determine the provenance of *Schlachthaus*?'

'I will get my team to jump onto it straight away and give you a call when I have some news, hopefully at some time tomorrow.'

'That is much appreciated.' My mobile phone was advising me that I had another call. 'I will speak to you tomorrow. Thank you, bye, bye.'

'Hello this is Michael Packham.' Glancing at the number flashing I knew that it was Dieter calling.

'Michael how are you and Louise? this is Dieter.'

'Good afternoon Herr Muller, we are both fine and have had a most wonderful day here in Vienna. What can I do for you?'

'Everyone falls in love with Vienna, so no surprise that you and Louise are no different. My clients are applying a good deal of pressure on me and insisting that the documentation is all signed before you return to England. Now in order to help facilitate this, I am quite prepared to travel to Vienna and meet with you. Are you agreeable to that?'

'Herr Muller.'

'Call me Dieter, please.'

'Herr Muller, we feel that we are being rushed into signing a document when we are not in possession of all the facts. For example, we know nothing at all about the farm. Where it is. What income it produces. How many people are employed by the farm? Who has been responsible for the day to day running of the business?'

'Regrettably, I am unable to divulge the name of my clients, but I can arrange for you to visit the farm if you so wish?'

'Well, that would be good, at least it would give us some idea as to what is what. Would there be accounts available to show how the business is performing?'

'Let me text over the address details. Advise me when you would like to visit, I am assuming tomorrow? And I will arrange for the farm director to give you a full tour.'

'Okay, I am not sure that it will be tomorrow, we are enjoying our stay in Vienna. I do think that it would be wise for me to get a complete independent valuation. I feel uneasy that I would be selling to an organisation whose identity is being concealed.'

'I misled you when I said organisation. It is a consortium of several wealthy and powerful businessmen who like to keep their activities from the public domain.'

'Potentially then, this collection of individuals could be the Mafia, is that right?'

'My dear Michael, if this were the mafia, they would not be making such a generous offer. I will text over the address of the farm. Let me know when you plan to visit. Auf Wiedersehen.'

Chapter 4

My name is Otto Wagner, I am the only child of Ingrid and Joseph Wagner. My mother was a nurse whilst my father worked as a carpenter. We lived in the town of Eisenstadt. I had a happy childhood they were both good loving and tender parents. I was brought up as an extremely strict Catholic. As I grew into my teens, I began to think for myself and to challenge my own religious belief. I would have lively discussions with my parents. I respected that they were from a generation where traditional thinking was engraved into your being and that you accepted what you were being told.

Not me though. I was twenty years old, and I passionately believed that there was nothing wrong with sex before marriage (I had been involved in a brief intimate relationship with one of the female librarians where I worked). Also, mainly because of her, she had convinced me that a woman should decide for herself what should be done with her body. She was very much pro-abortion and convinced me too. My challenging the beliefs of my parents I could see was causing them a good deal of distress and upset. I loved them dearly and so as to avoid further misery, I secured a transfer to the Central Vienna Library.

My main interest when I was not reading and working, was painting. I was fortunate enough to win a place at the Imperial Royal Arts and Crafts Faculty. I realised at an early age that people liked my paintings especially the ones done in oil. My speciality was portraits. Maybe it was because of this that I was allowed to study part time whilst still working in the library and thus earning just enough to pay for my board and lodgings.

I also enjoyed sketching buildings and took an interest in architecture. I remember that I was sketching the Vienna Opera House in 1912 and got chatting to a fellow artist who was painting the Opera House. I discovered that he came from near Linz and that he was struggling to sell his pictures. I could see why. They were okay, but nowhere near the detail of my own. His name was Adolf Hitler. We became reasonable friends. In 1913 Hitler left for Munich and we lost touch.

A year later I moved to Munch and managed to get myself a job teaching art at a private school which had around 200 residential pupils. At the outbreak of The First World War, I was not inclined to sign up and told the headmaster that I would prefer to carry on teaching. I am not sure if it was because of the headmaster's influence somewhere, but I was not called up and so I continued to enjoy a comfortable life whilst many young men of my own age were being slain.

In early 1919 my school was forced to close, and I was unemployed. The situation immediately after the war for Germany was so bad, I was unable to sell my paintings. There was huge discontent in the country. There were so many small political parties. I had met a man whilst drinking in one of the Munich beer halls called Anton Drexler who had just established a very small political party called DAP better known as the German Workers Party. He was a powerful orator. He invited me to work as an administrator for him. I accepted.

By sheer coincidence later that year Adolf Hitler who I had not seen or heard of for eight years joined the party. I did not immediately recognise him at first, I was sitting at the back of the hall when Hitler took centre stage and started to read from an Anton Drexler's pamphlet called *My Political Awakening* which espoused views on anti-Marxists, anti-capitalist, and anti-Semitic ideas.

When Hitler spoke, he was like a magnate, you could not take your eyes of him. He spoke like no other that I had ever heard before. I was not a political person at all although I knew that I did not share the views of Marxists. When Hitler had finished speaking, I went and sought him out.

'Adolf, long time no see. I don't suppose you remember who I am?'

He looked at me for a second or two and then threw his arms up in the air and held out his hand to shake vigorously. 'Of course, I remember now, you share the same surname as my favourite composer, Richard Wagner. But you are not Richard, you are Otto. What are you doing here in Munich?'

'I was until recently an art teacher at a school. Unfortunately, because of the economic situation the school has had to close. I was lucky enough to have met Anton, who offered me a job as his assistant.'

Hitler then commented. 'Yes so many are now out of work. Anton Drexler has just put me in charge of propaganda. I very much endorse Anton's views.'

'How did you come to be in Munich?' I asked.

'If you remember Otto, when we met in Vienna my application for a place in the Vienna Academy of Art was rejected. This at the time was a huge blow to me. However, as I was interested in architecture, I applied to get into the Vienna School of Architecture. They would not accept me because I did not have a school leaving certificate. I had an option for military service, but I did not wish to be associated with the Habsburg Empire an empire that I despised.

'My father had died and so I inherited a small legacy which was enough to allow me to relocate to Munich. At the outbreak of war, I joined the 16th Bavarian Infantry Regiment. The war was awful. The needless slaughter of men. I shall never forget the mud and the thousands of dead horses. During the lulls in fighting, I managed to paint. At the time of the armistice, I was in hospital suffering from temporary blindness due to a British gas attack in Ypres.

'My being in the army meant that at least I had food and shelter and a small income on which to live. I was lucky that they appointed me to the Intelligence/Propaganda section. My activities involved making speeches to the troops advocating German nationalism and anti-Socialism. It is likely that I am going to be discharged soon. If that is the case, then I will work and try and promote the ideas of the German Workers Party. I remember

Otto, that you were an educated man and good with words, why don't you transfer to me and help with my writings?

'I will see that you receive payment for the work you will do. We have several patrons who are still wealthy and are so concerned that the Communists will take over Germany that they are prepared to bank role any political organisation that prevents this from happening. What do you say?'

'Well, that's extremely generous and kind of you Adolf. I think we should both speak with Anton first to establish that he is happy with losing me to you.'

'I don't foresee a problem. That is wonderful. I am the 55th member to join Anton's party although I have taken the number 555 in order to give the impression that we have more members than we actually do. The first thing that we need to do is to increase membership. Therefore, I appoint you as the Recruitment/Membership Secretary, Otto. You will be an asset to myself and to our Party. The first thing that we need to do is to get out there and get our message across and by doing so, increase substantially our appeal to the German people and increase our membership numbers. There is much to be done. There is so much hatred out there towards our government for signing the Armistice in November last year. I believe along with millions of others that we have been stabbed in the back. There is no doubt that it was the Jews in both the army and the government that had encouraged this surrender. After four years of German blood being spilt on the field of battle and for what? For our government to have signed the Treaty of Versailles which has blamed and is now punishing Germany for starting the war. This is all too much to bear.'

It was clear to me that Hitler was a deeply passionate orator.

The following day I turned up as usual at the shabby offices of The German Workers Party. Anton Drexler was already there and had no problem with me spending more time helping Adolf. I would still be working for the party.

The next couple of days were spent on formulating a strategy for attracting new members. It was essential that we publicised whenever Hitler and indeed Anton were speaking and ensured that most of our own members were in attendance.

It was decided that I would go along to a local beer hall and attend a meeting of the local communists giving the impression that I might be a possible recruit, and then to report back. When I arrived, there were many people, most of whom had been imbibing on the local beer. There was a lot of noise, and the atmosphere was full of smoke. I made my way to the back and stood next to a pillar on the other side was a young woman who seemed to be taking a keen interest in everything that was going on. Once the meeting got under way, I noticed that the young woman pulled out a notebook and started to take notes in shorthand.

There were four speakers that took turns in addressing the 200 or so souls tightly packed in. I would describe the speakers as being rabble raisers. It was in all honesty difficult to hear what each was saying because of the drunken behaviour of a large section of the crowd.

At the conclusion of the meeting many of us turned to leave. As I got to the exit door, I was pushed from behind which in turn made me stumble forward and push the person in front of me. The person in front of me turned around to see what was happening and I then recognised that it was the young woman who had been standing near to me.

'I am so sorry, it was a complete accident, my apologies again.'

'No need to apologies, I seem to get pushed and jostled every time I report on any of these political gatherings.'

'You are a reporter?'

'Yes. Like most men, you sound totally surprised to find that events cannot be observed and commented on through the eyes of a woman.'

'No not at all. It is refreshing. What paper do you work for?'

'I am a freelance journalist because women are still frowned upon. Indeed, in many countries' women are still denied the vote and therefore not given a voice into who they think should govern them. At least this changed last year for us German women.

But to answer your question, my articles mostly appear in the *Munich Post* newspaper.'

'Well, I for one am impressed and it is a pleasure to make your acquaintance. My name is Otto Wagner.'

She had a firm handshake which she held, and her eyes penetrated mine with a real intensity. I immediately felt this excited feeling in the pit of my stomach. A feeling that I had only experienced previously with my brief affair with Anna, a fellow librarian whilst in Vienna.

'Hildegard Krause, also pleased to meet you. I live only two streets away; would you care to escort me home and perhaps consider joining me for a night-cap?'

'Well, how could I refuse to escort a lady home. There is no need to invite me in though.'

As we started to walk it began to rain. After five minutes the light rain turned into heavy rain. It was true that Hildegard's flat was only ten minutes away. However, being an Autumn evening neither of us was wearing a protective coat and we both got drenched to the skin. When we turned the corner to the road in which she lived, she called out. 'My door is number 45, I will race you there.'

It took me by surprise, and she had a five-metre start, even so I was impressed at how quickly and smoothly she ran. It must have been a distance of ninety or so metres for I finished just behind her. We were both laughing our heads off. It was then that I noticed with the rain running down her cheeks, her perfect teeth and with her high cheekbones just how attractive she was.

Gasping for air and still giggling, she took out the key to the door of her flat and turned the key to open the door revealing a long hallway to the left of which was a staircase.

'We are both soaked,' she announced. 'You cannot go home like that; you will catch pneumonia. I have plenty of towels. I have a log fire that I can light, and we can dry your clothes in front of it.'

'I cannot possibly do that,' I said, with the image of my parents disapproving of any such behaviour flashing through my mind, particularly as the suggestion came from a woman.

'I am not inviting you to sleep with me, I have a couch that you can sleep on whilst I sleep in my own comfortable bed. I am just being practical. After all I am a woman! And besides, it would be good to have a late-night chat and get to know one another don't you think?'

She was clearly a woman who knew her own mind and I suspect usually got her own way. 'How can I refuse?'

'Please close the door behind you.'

And with that she bounded up the stairs taking two at a time.

We entered a wonderfully comfortable room. The floorboards were bear with a nice rug in the middle. In the front by the window looking out onto the street was an oak desk upon which was a typewriter. The room had a dining table and four chairs and to the side was a couch and one armchair which were placed either side of the fireplace. The fire was already made up and just needed lighting. Hildegard produced a match and in what was just a matter of seconds the fire had taken hold of the kindling wood and the small logs on top began to catch.

'Go to the room next door, that is my bedroom. In the cupboard you will find several large towels. Next to my room is the bathroom.'

'Well,' I say, bathroom?'

What I mean is, a toilet and hand basin. The water is cold I am afraid. When you have finished and dried off, in the far cupboard in my bedroom you will find some of my brother's clothing. You are a similar size. He keeps them here for when he occasionally visits Munich and his long-lost sister.'

I obeyed like an obedient puppy. I stripped off my clothes in her bedroom and took one of the large rough towels and made my way to the washroom. Hildegard was right about the water being cold in fact it was freezing. I dried myself vigorously with the towel which I found stimulating and restored me to some sort of normality.

When I returned to her bedroom, I discovered that my clothes had all been removed. I then opened the cupboard in the far corner and found a selection of clothes that suited me very well, including pants and socks. I put on a pair of grey trousers, a white shirt, and a warm knitted red jumper. I felt human again.

When I returned to the main room, I discovered a blazing fire in front of which was a clotheshorse, supporting my wet clothes.

'This will warm you up,' Hildegard said whilst handing me a glass of whiskey. 'If you excuse me, I will now also dry myself off and change into something warm.'

When she left the room, I wandered over to the desk in front of the window. There were several pages of typed copy all neatly arranged under different headings. The headings were German Workers' Party, German Social Party, German Socialist Party, National Socialist German Workers Party, German Freedom Party and finally National Socialist Freedom Movement.

Hildegard's notepad was lying open beside the papers. The heading read. 'Communist Workers Party – Address by Hugo Eberlein and Franz Mehring'. They were the speakers at the meeting that we had attended earlier. All of her notes were in shorthand, and so I couldn't read what she had written. My thoughts were interrupted when I heard the door behind me close. There stood Hildegard in a navy-blue dressing gown.

'Are you abusing my hospitality by spying on me?' The way in which she asked the question gave the impression that she was not in the least bit worried if I were. She had an air of a young woman who was assertive and confident and not afraid of anything.

'No, certainly not,' I replied with far less confidence, almost feeling like a naughty boy who had been caught out. 'You are clearly interested in politics and for a woman, it makes you rather unusual and may I say, remarkably interesting.'

'I am hungry, I am going to make myself a cheese sandwich, would you like one?'

'Now that you have mentioned it, I am feeling hungry, it has been several hours since I last ate.'

'Good. Top up our glasses, put a log on the fire and move back the clothes horse and sit down on the couch and I will bring over the sandwiches.'

I thought, this is the first time apart from my mother when I was very young, that I had ever been told what to do by a woman. Strangely enough, being told what to do by Hildegard, I found quite refreshing.

'Well now that you know what I do, what do you do? And why were you at a meeting of the Communist Party? I cannot believe that you are a Commi.'

'Certainly not,' I replied in horror. 'I have recently joined Anton Drexler and Adolf Hitler and work for them by researching and I suppose running around in general for them. Tonight, I was checking up on what our communist friends were up to and will report back tomorrow.'

'That's very interesting. And what did you think of this evening's meeting?'

'To be honest, I could hardly hear what was being said. There was so much noise.'

'I agree. But that seems to be the norm. So many of these meetings are being disrupted by opponents. My editor thought that it would be good if I attended these meetings as there was likely to be more respect for being a woman. Sadly, I must report that this is not the case. I wrote an article expressing my opinion that the communists in Munich had a hidden agenda. The following day when I was walking to work, I was approached by two thugs and pushed to the ground and told in no uncertain terms that if ever I wrote another article like that, then it would be my last. Intimidation seems to be everywhere now.

'Well, I will bid you good night Otto, there are two blankets on the armchair, you should be comfortable on the couch, my brother always seems to sleep well on it when he visits.'

I slept incredibly soundly. I am sure that Hildegard featured in my dreams, and I was not sure if I was still dreaming when I heard the dulcet sounds of her voice calling 'Wakey, wakey sleepy head it is time to get up.' And there she was.

'Go and have your wash, your clothes have all dried and I will fix us some toast and coffee.'

We ate breakfast and spoke about the depressing situation that Germany had found itself in. My mind was wandering though. I was captivated by this young woman. I am sure that my heart was beating faster than normal. I was deep in thought in wondering how I could somehow ask her out when I was aware that she was questioning me.

'Well?' she said.

'I'm sorry,' I stuttered. 'I missed what you said.'

'There, typical man, not listening. I said would you like to see me again?'

My heart leapt. This was a woman who was so self-assured. I had assumed that it was always the man who moved things forward, but not with Hildegard. I looked at her questioning face and realised how stunningly attractive she was.

'I thought you would never ask,' I blathered trying to sound amusing.

'Good then. I see that your man Adolf is due to speak this evening at the Hofbrau Keller. Shall we say eight?'

'I look forward to it.'

We then left the room, walked down the stairs and after she had locked the front door, she turned and gave me a quick kiss on the cheek before walking briskly towards the city centre.

I entered the office and Anton, and Adolf were already in discussion. 'Anything to report from last night?' asked Anton.

'It was quite a packed meeting, but it was difficult to hear anything because there was a lot of noise coming from the front section in the crowd.'

'Excellent, excellent, that would have been Ernst Rohm and his men.' Hitler observed.

'You mean that we deliberately disrupted their meeting?' I asked.

'Of course,' replied Hitler. 'It is essential that only our views are heard and that we are able to persuade members of other organisations to realise that we are the voice to be listened to.'

That evening I was early at the Hofbraukeller. I noticed that Ernst Rohm and a group of what can only be described as thugs were already there drinking. I had met Rohm three or four times and he was a person that I took an instant dislike to. This was compounded when after my last encounter with him, he propositioned me to go and spend the night with him. I had explained that I had a steady girlfriend, which of course I did not. Therefore, I was happy when Hildegard appeared, and I made sure that Rohm noticed her and I greeting one another.

'How lovely to see you Hildegard,' I said, taking her in my arms and kissing her fully on the lips.' To my great surprise she did not resist in any way. In fact, she put her arms around me and embraced me again just as I was pulling away.

'Well,' she said. 'I did not expect such a passionate welcome, I took you to be a shy bashful young man.'

'I am normally, you have no idea how you have helped me out here. I will explain later.'

'Does that mean that you did not mean it?'

'Absolutely I meant it, it was just sooner than I had expected, that's all.'

'Hmm.'

'I will see you after Adolf has finished speaking,' I said and gave her another kiss on the lips as we departed.

I stood to the side as Hitler nodded in my direction as he passed me and strode onto the platform. Ernst Rohm and his men started cheering loudly. Hitler then began speaking, slowly at first but gradually picked up pace and one had to admit he was galvanising. Then three or four people started to heckle at once, almost as though on a command. What did surprise me was the reaction of Rohm and his men. Without hesitation they roughly grabbed each heckler and unceremoniously evicted them from the venue. It was my job to count how many attended these meetings. To my reckoning there were around 111 including myself, Rohm and his thugs.

I met Hildegard afterwards. We were just discussing where to go when Anton Drexler appeared.

'Ah Otto my man, a successful start to the campaign don't you think? And may I ask, who is this lovely young lady?'

'May I introduce Hildegard Krause, Hildegard, this Anton Drexler leader of the German Workers Party.'

'A pleasure Miss Krause, Otto hadn't mentioned before that he had a girlfriend, especially if I may say, one so pretty.'

'Thank you, Herr Drexler, yes Otto is a very private man, we are devoted to one another.'

I nearly choked when I heard Hildegard speak these words. She was so naturally smooth and convincing.

'In that case it would be my pleasure if you were to join a few of us for a drink.'

'Thank you, Herr Drexler, that is exceedingly kind of you.'

We went to the back of the hall where Hitler was already in conversation with Rohm.

'And who is this?' enquired Hitler.

'My name is Hildegard Krause, and I am Otto's girlfriend.'

'Do you intend to support Otto in his work in promoting the cause of the German Workers Party?'

'I couldn't say Herr Hitler. After all we women have only recently been given the vote. Therefore, I will weigh up all options and make my decision on what I consider to be the best for Germany.'

'Well Fraulein Krause, I trust that Otto here will convince you that our policies are the best for our Motherland. At the moment there is mass unemployment, the population feel betrayed by our government of the Weimar Republic and morale is at rock bottom. The German Workers Party will change all that. We will get people back into work, reclaim lost lands and restore pride in being a good German.'

'May I enquire what you call a good German?'

'It is in essence, someone who will lay down their life for the Motherland. Someone who is born in Germany and is certainly not a Jew. The Jews have been responsible in no small way creating the situation in which we now find ourselves.'

There was no response from Hildegard and her face remained impassive. We stayed for another half an hour or so before we made our excuses and left. We walked home in total silence. When we entered Hildegard's room, she spoke for the first time.

'You know Otto, I have a sense about things. Call it a gut feeling or woman's intuition if you will, but I felt very uneasy in the company of both Rohm and Hitler. Although I am used to seeing meetings being disrupted by hecklers, this is the first time that I have seen them ejected. I followed them outside, ensuring that I stayed in the shadows and witnessed Rohm's hard men beat the hecklers viciously with sticks. It was awful to see. It would seem that the only way that they can succeed is through intimidation and violence.'

'It is important that we get heard.' I responded, trying to justify the actions that she had witnessed. 'Those hecklers I suspect were communists doing their best to disrupt and had not Rohm intervened then Hitler would not have been heard. Surely you do not wish to be governed by communists?'

'I certainly do not. There are so many small parties all trying to get our attention and our vote in order to put them into office.'

'Hildegard, last night before I slept on the couch, I read your reports that you had submitted to the *Munich Post*. It is clear to anyone who reads them, just how objective you are. You report faithfully the facts and finish with an honest appraisal of what you believe. I also have a gut feeling and that is that things are going to get tough, even dangerous for a while until a clear path has been determined. I believe it would be prudent for you to adopt a pseudonym for your reporting, ideally using a man's name. This will provide you with anonymity and ensure a certain amount of safety.'

'Thank you, Otto, that is very thoughtful of you. From what I saw this evening, that might well be a particularly good idea. How about if I use the name Leopold Bismarck?'

'I think that you are being provocative knowing full well the history behind that name.'

'Yes, I am, but there is no reason at all why there is not someone actually named after our former emperor. So, I will keep that name and let everyone guess. In the meantime, my woman's intuition has kicked in again. As soon as I turned around after you had fallen into the back of me last night, I looked straight into your eyes and felt an instant pang inside of me. Call it fate, but I felt an immediate connection and a longing. I am 30 years old and have had several relationships. None of which have been in the least bit fulfilling. But somehow, I just instinctively feel that you are the one that I have been waiting for. After just one day does that sound crazy to you?'

I didn't answer, I could not find the words. I reached out and drew her towards me in a passionate embrace that seemed to last an age. My fingers were running through her long fair hair, I was kissing her on the lips, her cheeks, her ears and down her neck. It provoked what seemed to be a perfectly natural progression when our carnal instincts took control. Without much thought we were hastily unbuttoning and unbuckling one another's garments and at the same time I was aware that Hildegard was pulling me in the direction of her bedroom.

It must have been around five the following morning that I stirred. I opened my eyes slowly and looked about me, it was dark, but I sensed the unfamiliar surroundings. Then I became aware of Hildegard's naked body tucked warmly into mine. She then murmured and opened her eyes. And then it happened once again. This time at a much slower pace. Enjoying one another and being aware of what brought pleasure to each other. Afterwards, we fell back asleep once more. It was around seven when Hildegard woke me with a hot cup of tea.

'How are you this morning lover boy?' she asked whilst at the same time stroking the hairs on my chest.

'I can say with the utmost certainty that that was the best experience that I have ever had.'

'Me too. We are the same age and yet it is for me wonderful to find a man that I can teach in the ways of sexual pleasure.'

'Well, I know that I am inexperienced, my only fling before was when I dabbled with a young librarian in Vienna. It is not that I have not found women attractive, I have just been very shy in asking them out.'

'No worries, we are going to make a great couple. Are you ready for breakfast?'

There was no going back after that. I thoroughly enjoyed being with Hildegard. She was such fun. A practical joker. I gave four weeks' notice to my landlord after which time I moved in with Hildegard. She continued writing her political sketches under her pseudonym Leopold Bismarck and I continued my role with the German Workers Party.

Hildegard was a very accomplished violinist. And so most evenings when we had spare time, I had returned to my favourite hobby of painting whilst she played the violin. I found her playing, thoroughly soothing, relaxing, and enjoyable.

I carried on my role serving Hitler and Drexler. It was now 1920 and our membership had grown to over 2,000. I was happy with my role and did not seek any kind of leadership or position of authority within the party. We now had a collection of 'thinkers' all bringing their ideas to the table. Amongst our members were Dietrich Eckart, Rudolf Hess, Hans Frank and Alfred Rosenburg.

I came into work one morning and found some very glum faces. Apparently, Hitler and Drexler had had a flaming row the evening before over policy disagreements. Hitler had stormed out and had resigned from the party. I sat in on the meeting that then took place amongst the leading protagonists. The conclusion was that the party needed Hitler. It was his fiery speeches that drew the crowds. Alfred Rosenberg then put it to Drexler that although he had been the founder of the party, it was Hitler who was now carrying the torch that had been lit by Drexler and that it was now time for Hitler to lead the party.

I could see that Anton Drexler was hugely disappointed, but he was also a pragmatist and appreciated the reality of the situation. Dietrich Eckart then proposed that Hitler be invited to rejoin the party as leader and that Anton Drexler became President. Everyone knew that this would just be a ceremonial position without any real influence, but Anton agreed.

A week or so later, Hitler returned as our leader. He announced that in his view we should change the name of our party because there were so many others with similar names and rename ourselves the Nazi Party short for National German Workers. Everyone agreed this could be a fresh start.

Within weeks the party membership had increased. One of the new members was no other than Hermann Goring who was a World War One flying ace. A hugely respected figure. It was agreed by the executive committee that the party needed to reach out to a lot of different members of society. And so, a twenty-five-point programme of policies were announced. These included:

- Farmers should be given their land.
- Pensions should be improved.
- Public industries such as electricity and water should be owned by the state.
- All German speaking people should be united in one country.
- The Treaty of Versailles should be abolished.
- There should be special laws for foreigners.
- Jews should not be German citizens.
- Immigration should be stopped.
- Focus on creating a strong central government.
- Government control of the newspapers.

I was tasked with typing the manifesto and then to arrange for the printing.

That evening I returned home, and Hildegard and I had a long discussion on what this meant. We both agreed that the hyperinflation that was ravaging Germany's economy needed arresting and that a strong central German Government was necessary. We also agreed that farmers should be given their land, that pensions should be improved and that the nationalisation of water and electric would be a good thing. Also, that the Treaty of Versailles which nearly all Germans considered to have been an act of retribution by the victors, should be abolished.

However, we were both in agreement to the parts that we felt very uneasy about especially the reference that Jews should no longer be German citizens and that the government should control the press.

It was 24th February 1920. The Nazi manifesto laying out the twenty-five objectives of the Nazi Party had been printed and distributed to our members. I had organised a meeting in the Staatliches Hofbräuhaus in Munich for that evening. Hitler would be the main speaker. I had predicted a gathering of around two thousand and this turned out to be the case. Hitler's oratory was so persuasive.

Hitler railed against the National Assembly who a year earlier had elected Friedrich Ebert of the Social Democrats Party as the first Reich President.

'The only good thing that the German National Party and we have in common is our rejection of the Weimar Constitution and the Treaty of Versailles. I agree that we should repeal the dedicated peace treaty and reacquisition all the lost territories and colonies. But we totally reject their aspiration to restore the Monarchy. This so called, National People's Party is no more than a coalition of The German Conservative Party and the German Fatherland Party with right wing elements of the National Liberal Party. We shall not allow it!' Hitler shouted. The applause and shouting were deafening.

1920 gave way to 1921. The Nazi Party membership was increasing daily. There was no doubt at all that this was due to Hitler's magnetism. Hitler had recently been elected as Party Chairman and leader. As a person who worked closely with him, I found that I was drawn to him like a moth to a flame. There is no doubt that I was in awe of him.

One morning I found myself alone with him. I generally would only speak in answer to a question or when required to do so. I plucked up enough courage to say, 'Herr Hitler, if you remember we first met as artists outside the Vienna Opera House. I have specialised in portraits. It would be an honour for me to paint your portrait.'

Hitler thought for a moment before replying. 'Yes I agree to that, but it must be a portrait of me addressing a large meeting. I need you to capture the intensity of my presence, for this you need to copy from a photograph.'

'Thank you, Herr Hitler, I will do my very best.'

I instantly regretted my suggestion for I had witnessed on several occasions the wrath of Hitler if someone had not pleased him or done or said something he did not agree with.

During this time Hitler had assembled a large group of unemployed young men and former soldiers and called them his Storm Troopers known as the SA. It was in reality the Nazis private army. They became known as the Brownshirts after their brown shirted uniforms. What disturbed me was that they were used extensively to break up the meetings of our opponents.

In the March of that year, I proposed to Hildegard. She was thrilled and immediately accepted. We were both 32 years old and felt passionately for one another the same as if we were two excited teenagers. Neither Hildegard nor I had spent a holiday together. In fact, we both seemed to work every day of the week.

Hildegard then suggested that we took a week off work to spend our honeymoon at some very good family friends of hers who lived just south of Salzburg. We had both been brought up as Catholics but neither of us were true believers. The following day I went to work and presented Hitler with his portrait. I was very pleased with it as I considered that it had caught the mood of Hitler in action. I was even more delighted when Hitler expressed how pleased he was with it. This was my chance.

'Herr Hitler, would you mind if I took one week's leave? Hildegard, who you have met, has agreed to become Mrs Wagner.'

'Congratulations Otto, I am certain that she will make an honest fellow out of you. Take two weeks off. After all, I cannot remember you missing a day.'

A month later, Hildegard and I were married at a small Catholic church just outside of Munich. There were only two witnesses, both who were colleagues of Hildegard's from the *Munich Post*. Hitler for our wedding present had made his Green Selve car available together with his adjutant Julius Schaub who chauffeured him around. I thanked Hitler very much and suggested that as I could drive then there was no need for Julius to take time off. To my delight Hitler agreed.

Chapter 5

After the service we celebrated with a glass of champagne (a present from Anton Drexler) with our two witnesses and the priest, before setting off towards the village of Bischofswiesen, which Hildegard explained was not far from the Austrian border. I had asked her several times who we were staying with, but she always just laughed, sometimes winked, and always tapped the side of her nose and said, 'You will find out soon enough my darling husband.'

It was a lovely sunny day. The mountains in the distance looked beautiful. We were in love. The birds were singing. It could not have been more perfect. Hildegard was acting as navigator and had a road map spread out on her knees together with some written directions. Eventually she instructed me to turn left. The name at the entrance said *Schlachthaus*. We drove for some way down a track which had splendid trees on either side and then rounding a bend of the track a large, beautiful house came into view. The first thing that I noticed were the turrets.

Hildegard then lent over me and squeezed the car's warning horn three or four times. She was laughing and laughed even more when two young women came running from the house to greet us. They were laughing and screaming with delight. As I stopped the car, Hildegard opened the door and leaped out with great athleticism right into the outstretched arms of the girls. They continued to laugh and hug one another, and all were speaking at the same time.

I got out of the car and stood by the rear until the girls had exhausted their greetings to each other. Hildegard then released the girls who were immediately respectful of my presence.

'Otto,' she said. 'Allow me to introduce my former charges, Leah and Eliana. As you can see, they are twins and were born in 1903 and so are both eighteen years old now, and I think you will agree are a couple of beauties.'

I held out my hand which they shook in turn. 'It is my pleasure and I agree with Hildegard, you are a couple of beauties.' Both girls giggled.

Eliana then said, 'Let's go inside and meet mama, papa sends his apologies, he is working on the estate but should be home shortly.' With that they all linked arms and headed for the house. I followed pulling our one luggage case.

After crossing the threshold, I heard another delighted scream, and I could see that Hildegard was hugging an older lady, who I assumed was the mother of the twin girls. After they broke off the lady approached me with a huge smile and with her open arms embraced me and gave me a kiss on each cheek.

'Congratulations, you must be Otto, we are so pleased that you have brought Hildegard back to us, even if it is for only a few days. I am Hannah Benowitz. Leah if you show Hildegard and Otto to their room, they can settle in. Abraham will be home within the hour and then we will have dinner. This evening I have cooked Vienna Schnitzel.'

Leah took the lead as we climbed a very impressive wide staircase, all the while excitedly chatting to Hildegard and saying how lovely it was to see her again. We turned right on the landing and entered a huge bedroom. There was a four-poster bed. The room led into a bathroom with a real plumbed in bathtub and a toilet. We both looked out of the windows and marvelled at the well-kept lawns with flower borders. Further on you could see a vineyard and into the distance the mountains. It was stunning.

'Well, we have almost an hour before the Master of the House returns,' Hildegard announced pulling me towards her and then skilfully unbuckling my belt. I lay on the bed, conscious that Hildegard had left and gone into the bathroom. I heard running water. She then poked her head into the room and said, 'The bath is big enough for the two of us, do you care to join me?'

As we sat in the bath, the water nearly to the top, facing one another, I said, 'Well now is the time for you to explain all.'

'Yes, I believe that it is,' she said. 'I was eighteen years old and my great love in life was playing the violin. I had been living and studying in Salzburg. Hence why I love playing Mozart so much. My parents bless them had supported me, but they could ill afford to continue. Dad was suffering from ill health and mum had to nurse him. I therefore was looking for a job. My violin tutor said that he had been made aware of a family across the border in Germany who had twin girls aged four years old. The parents were keen that they should learn the violin. They were looking for a music teacher cum nanny or governess.

'I told him that I had no experience with young children and would not be able to cope. He advised me that the parents were very loving, and that I would not be there to take over as a surrogate parent, but more to help with the girl's education. He thought that I would be ideal. So, he made contact and arranged for an interview.

'As someone who came from a very poor family, you can imagine how impressed I was when I first set eyes on this house. To me it was like a palace or a castle. Within minutes of meeting Abraham and Hannah I felt so comfortable. They were welcoming and after introducing me to Leah and Eliana, I could see that they were the most loving and devoted parents that any child could wish for. The two girls were absolute darlings, I immediately fell in love with them. Have you ever had that experience?'

'As a matter of fact, I have. It was the first time that I looked into your eyes.'

Hildegard chuckled and then continued. 'This was in 1907. I stayed for the next nine years. I left because my father had died and returned home for a short while. Three months later my mother died also. I sold their house and belongings and moved to Munich where I bought my present property. During my time as governess to the girls, it became apparent that Abraham was a very well-read gentleman. He was an avid reader of the news and each day when he had finished with the newspaper, I read and also caught up on what was happening.

'You will see tomorrow, but Abraham manages a large estate. He is a highly successful farmer. During the first two years of the war, before I left, things were grim for the inhabitants of the local village of Bischofswiesen. There were food shortages and many of the young men had been called to war. So, Abraham farmed his land and kept the villagers fed. No questions were ever asked. He provided eggs, potatoes, vegetables, milk and then chickens and lamb for eating. None of which he charged for. He had just enough surplus to sell at the market in Salzburg to provide sufficient income to keep going. As you can imagine, he is absolutely revered and adored in this area.

'I loved being with and teaching Leah and Eliana, I adored them both. For me it was not a job, it was a real pleasure. I taught them to read and write and importantly of course to play the violin. They are such willing pupils and are naturally gifted in everything that they do. After the evening meal Abraham would take the girls and study the Torah.'

'What's the Torah?' I asked.

'The family they are not orthodox Jews, but they have been brought up with Judaism. The Torah is the first part of the Jewish bible. It is the central and most important document of Judaism and has been used by Jews throughout the ages. It refers to the five books of Moses which are known in Hebrew as Chameesha Choomshey Torah. The girls can recite by heart nearly every passage. I don't know how they do it.'

The clanging of a gong from downstairs alerted us that it was time to go down and for me to meet Abraham.

We entered the dining room and there to greet us was Abraham. He embraced Hildegard kissing her on each check.

'It is wonderful to see you again and this time as a married lady. Once you had passed thirty, we thought that you were destined to live out your life as a spinster.' He then turned his gaze towards me and releasing Hildegard extended his hand with a very warm and firm handshake. 'Welcome to our home Otto. It is an honour for us to have you stay as our guests, particularly as this is your honeymoon. Please be seated and let us eat.'

After taking our seats, Abraham looked at me and said, 'If you will excuse us, we as a family always say prayers before each meal.' Without waiting for me to respond, Abraham and his wife and girls all bowed their heads whilst Abraham spoke in a language that I was not familiar with, but I assumed to be Hebrew.

The meal was one of the most enjoyable occasions that I had ever experienced. It was also accompanied by a red wine which was from their vineyard, called Blaufränkisch. It was such a medium smooth bodied wine with the flavours of black pepper and marionberry. I had never tasted such before. The entire family were delightful. Abraham was a man you instantly took to. He had a presence about him and yet you felt that he was very approachable, he exhibited no signs of superiority. Hannah and her daughters were fun and before we knew, two hours had passed by.

'Right then,' said Hannah. 'Let us get our musical instruments out and play. Do you play Otto?'

Before I had chance to answer Hildegard said, 'No, he is not a musician, but is a particularly good artist.'

'How wonderful,' said Eliana. 'Perhaps you could paint Leah and myself?'

'I can certainly do that,' I said, 'Of a matter of fact, I have just painted a portrait of Adolf Hitler, the newly elected leader of the Nazi party.'

'Hmm, I have my reservations about the Nazis, mind you I have reservations about all of them. Hopefully, we are tucked away down here and will be permitted to lead our lives in peace,' said Abraham.

Ten minutes later there they were in the drawing room. Hildegard and Leah on violin, Eliana with her viola, Hannah on Cello whilst Abraham was warming up his clarinet.

'I suspect from what Hildegard has said that it will be something by Mozart?' I enquired.

'You are correct,' replied Hannah. 'It is Quintet in A for Clarinet and Strings K581. Here goes, one, two, three.'

The sound was magical. I couldn't help but look at all five of them, they were so accomplished. But then for a few bars I just closed my eyes and absorbed the beauty of what I was hearing. It was the first time that I had ever heard any orchestral music played live. I regretted that I was unable to play. They continued to play compositions by Strauss and Beethoven and only stopped playing after around an hour and a half. It had been delightful.

The following morning, we enjoyed breakfast out on the terrace. Leah then volunteered to show me around the house. And what a house. There were so many rooms. Leah explained to me that the house was a fine example of Baroque architecture and was built in 1735 under the guidance of the architect George Bahr.

After mid-morning coffee a farm worker appeared with a horse towing an empty hay cart.

'Right then' said Abraham. 'Let us have a tour of the farm.'

Hannah and Hildegard stayed behind whilst I was joined in the back by the two girls. The tour lasted for about four hours. First, we visited the milking parlour, then the field where the chickens could roam. After that I was taken to the sheep area. Then to the vineyard and then a tour of the fields. It was truly a mixed farm. During the tour we stopped and loaded up eggs, milk churns, and vegetables. We even picked up several bottles of wine. At the back of the vineyard was a quarry which appeared to have an opening to a large cave. I was advised that the quarry was no longer in use, and nobody ventured down there as it was considered to be dangerous.

Finally, we went into the village of Bischofswiesen. What amazed me was how everyone acknowledged Abraham with genuine pleasure. Very impressive also was that he knew everyone's Christian name. On the way round the cart would stop and provisions would be dropped off to grateful inhabitants. The way everyone spoke it was as if one and all was considered an equal. Not once did the girls or Abraham patronise anyone when speaking. They were always cheerful and engaged in conversation inquiring about family members and in turn were asked who I was and where had I come from.

The next ten days flew by. Each morning after breakfast the two girls would pose while I painted their portrait. After each session they would beg me to let them see what progress I had made. But they were met with the same answer that all would be revealed when I had finished. Every afternoon, Hildegard and I would go for a walk. On two occasions we went into the village. I was amazed at how many people stopped to speak with Hildegard whom she seemed to know very well from her time as the girl's governess. In the evenings at the conclusion of our meal, the entire family would pick up their instruments and perform to an appreciative audience of one.

It was probably the happiest few days of my life. Family Benowitz were so hospitable, kind, and considerate. It had been good to experience rural life after the big city of Munich without the political strife which I now realised was a daily factor. Just before we left, I unveiled the painting that I had done of Leah and Eliana. They were both thrilled as were their parents. I did say that I could have painted it by just using one of the girls as a model and then added the second one to the side, they really were identical twins.

As we drove back, I was asking Hildegard how after she moved to Munich she had got into journalism. She explained that it had been through reading Abraham's daily newspapers, especially the political articles that it occurred to her that many of the reports were not objective. She also realised that they were all written by men. So, she approached the *Munich Post* and convinced them that having a woman reporter might give a different perspective. They were a little unsure but then agreed that she could go freelance, and they would pay her if and when her articles were used.

We both returned to our respective jobs on the following Monday. Everyone in the office was happy to see me back and asked where we had spent our honeymoon. I thanked Hitler for the use of his car which I must admit I had enjoyed driving very much. There was a lot of activity in the office.

Hitler was in a delightful mood because of the creation of the Hitler Youth movement. Also, apparently whilst I had been away, in Nuremberg Julius Streicher had become editor of a racist magazine called Der Stürmer.

Hildegard carried on reporting on the many political gatherings that were taking place in and around Munich. She was genuinely concerned on how many meetings by opponents of the Nazis party were being broken up by the Brownshirts and the speakers intimidated and threatened with violence.

A few weeks later, the editor of *The Munich Post* advised her that he had received threats from several political parties in relation to the articles being published by Leopold Bismarck which they did not like. It was hinted that his presses could be destroyed if the articles were to continue. Under the circumstances he advised Hildegard that they would not be printing any more of her articles. In other words, she was now unemployed.

As if this was not enough, Hildegard had been complaining of feeling unwell, particularly in the mornings. I convinced her that it would not do any harm for her to visit her doctor. Hildegard had always been healthy, and I had never known her to have been unwell. Upon returning home after a particularly fraught day in the Nazi Party Office which seemed to be attracting more and more people to it each day, Hildegard had already prepared our evening meal together with a bottle of wine given to us by Abraham.

After serving the meal, Hildegard opened the bottle of wine and poured two glasses and then said, 'I would like to propose a toast.'

'You have just lost your job and you would like to propose a toast?'

'Indeed, I would. I would like to propose a toast to the man in my life who is about to become a daddy.'

My heart leaped with excitement. I had never considered being a parent. We hugged and kissed one another whilst all the time laughing with sheer joy at the prospect. We concluded that Hildegard must have fallen pregnant during our honeymoon whilst staying with the Benowitz family.

'I will write and let them know our good news!' Exclaimed the excited mother to be of my first child.

Seven months later in the Spring of 1922 our son Helmut was born. This completely changed the dynamics of our family. We were struggling financially as my income from the Nazis was not as great as I had been led to believe, so Hildegard declared that she would teach the violin to pupils at our home.

By the end of that year the Nazi Party had 22,000 members. Incredible. I attended meetings and was sworn to secrecy as I took notes. Hitler and his associates planned to use Munich as a base for a march against Germany's Weimar Republic Government. The country was suffering from hyper-inflation. The aim was to overthrow the Bavarian Government first which was led by Gustav von Kahr.

On 8th November I was with Hitler who backed up by his stormtroopers interrupted a meeting in the Bürgerbräukeller Beer Hall in Munich where Gustav von Kahr was speaking. Kahr, General von Lossow who was the Bavarian army leader together with Colonel von Seisser who was head of the Bavarian police were then locked in a back room. They were forced to officially announce their support for the Nazis.

The following morning the Nazis led by Hitler and Ludendorff, marched into the centre of Munich. Unexpectedly the police and army confronted them, and shots were fired. I feared for my life and together with our supporters and SA we scattered.

A few days later, Hitler was put on trial and charged with treason. He was found guilty and sentenced to five years in prison but was eligible for parole in nine months. This suggested to us in the party that German judges and courts were also opposed to the government. The failed putsch emphasised that there was a great deal of opposition to the Weimar Government. The Nazi Party though was banned, and Hitler was prevented from speaking in public. During his time in prison, he wrote his propaganda book *Mein Kampf* (My struggle).

I was hugely fortunate to gain a job as an art teacher at a local school. The economy slowly started to improve. In 1925 Paul von Hindenburg was elected as President of Germany. Both Hildegard and I followed the changing political situation avidly.

It became clear to me after his release from prison that Hitler realised that he would never come to power by revolution and that he would have to use democratic means. He reorganised the party to enable it to take part in elections. I welcomed this because I felt that his extreme views especially those concerning Jews would not be accepted. There were other parts of the manifesto that I fully supported.

One evening in 1927, I had just put Helmut to bed. Hildegard was in the next room with a young girl who she was tutoring on the violin. There was a loud knock on the door. When I opened it, to my great surprise stood a smiling Adolf Hitler.

'Otto, I was hoping that you would be at home. May I come in?' Hitler embodied this magnetism, authority and entitlement and a sheer presence of forceful personality that it would be difficult to not grant whatever he wished for.

'I thought of you the other day Otto and I remembered how good you were at arranging the venues for me to speak at. Also, you were excellent at publicity. I have now engaged a man called Josef Goebbels as my publicist. He is based in Berlin. I would like you to work with him and under his guidance handle things here in Bavaria. You will be paid far more than you are at present in teaching art. What do you say?'

Before I had a chance to answer Hildegard walked into the room. Evidently the young girl's lesson had just finished. 'Herr Hitler, what a surprise, I would never have expected to have found you visiting our home.'

'I don't make a habit of visiting people's homes. Otto is a fellow Austrian for whom I have a good deal of respect. He is a fine administrator and right now this is someone that I need again especially as our membership is growing so rapidly. I have offered him an administrative position; you could say as my press secretary. It will pay considerably more than he is currently earning.'

'In that case,' Hildegard replied. I suggest that he accepts your offer. He would though have to give four weeks-notice to his present employer.'

'Of course, that is no problem. I look forward to you joining my staff in four weeks. We now have new headquarters, and it will be so much different from when you were last with me.'

With that we bade Hitler farewell. When we returned to our room I said, 'I am amazed that you have agreed for me to return to work for the Nazis, you saw for yourself how they bully people and indeed even beat them up.'

'I know dear, but things have changed. The Nazis are now pursuing a democratic path. You have been offered a well-paid job. Let us not gloss over our situation that we barely make ends meet. And besides the Nazis have struggled to win seats in the Reichstag. I believe that they have fewer than 50 seats out of 472. So, the chances of them coming into power and putting into force their twenty-five-point plan, I would suggest is most unlikely.'

Four weeks later, I arrived at the recently acquired new headquarters of the Nazis. The first person that I met as I entered was Rudolf Hess who was Hitler's deputy. I had always considered him a gaunt looking man, but he had always been friendly towards me.

'Ah, Otto my friend, how nice to see that you have re-joined us. Let me show you how the party has been reorganised since you were last here.'

On the wall was a huge pyramid drawing just like a Christmas tree. On the top was Hitler, beneath him were the SS, then the Leadership Corps, then the SA, followed by party membership and lastly Hitler Youth.

'My word,' I said, 'You have been busy.'

'For us to succeed in publicising our policies. We will show that Hitler is a strong leader. He has been given absolute control and all members must follow his directions. No dissent from this will be tolerated. This will be the way forward.'

'It is going to be difficult,' I said. 'The German economy is improving, most people feel more prosperous.'

'That is true at the moment,' replied Hess, 'but I have a feeling that this will not always be the case.'

That afternoon I met Joseph Goebbels. He was unbelievably persuasive. If it had been freezing outside, somehow, he would have convinced you that it was hot. He was a master of deceit. He gave me my orders and told me what he wanted before returning to Berlin. I was in charge down here in Bavaria and we would talk by phone twice a week or whenever Goebbels felt it necessary.

Up until 1929 the mood in Germany was increasingly optimistic. Although the Nazi Party was increasing its membership numbers, we were making extraordinarily little headway in winning the democratic elections. All this changed in October that year with the Wall Street Crash at the United States stock exchange.

This brought about a global economic depression. In Europe, Germany was worst affected because American banks called in all of their foreign loans at very short notice. These loans had been the basis for Germany's economic recovery from the disaster of hyperinflation. The loans had funded German industry and helped to pay reparations. Without these loans German industry collapsed, and a depression began.

Unemployment in Germany dramatically rose. Germans began to lose faith in democracy and looked to extreme parties such as the communists on the left and the Nazis on the right for quick and simple solutions. Ultimately the party that did better out of all this unrest were the Nazis. In 1928 we only had 28 seats in the Reichstag by 1932 we had 230 seats and were now the largest party.

I was amazed and I admit caught up in the excitement of what now seemed to be a runaway train. People were looking to the Nazis to bring back prosperity. Joseph Goebbels was a brilliant propagandist. He developed three main themes.

He portrayed Hitler as Germany's saviour. The man who would rescue the country from the grip of depression. He would portray the Jews as a threat to the economic future of the country and planted the thoughts that they were sub-human. Finally, he impressed the idea that the Nazis would create one German community that would make religion and social class less relevant to people.

During the next four years I only saw Hitler from time to time. Much of his time was spent in Berlin or criss-crossing the country speaking to audiences that were growing larger with each event. In April 1932 during the presidential election, Hitler came second with a vote of 37 per cent behind the popular President Hindenburg who had attracted 50 per cent. The following month, Chancellor Heinrich Bruning resigned, and Hindenburg appointed Franz Von Papen as his replacement.

After the July elections for the Reichstag the Nazis became the largest party. Hitler demanded that he be made Chancellor, but Von Papen remained. Everything was moving so fast now. Von Papen tried to win a majority in the Reichstag by calling new elections in November. Although we lost 34 seats, we still remained the largest party with 196 seats.

A month later Von Papen resigned. President Hindenburg then appointed Kurt Von Schleicher who was an army general, as Chancellor. In an attempt to split the Nazis, Von Schleicher invited a leading Nazi, Gregor Strasser to be his Vice Chancellor. Hitler was furious and forced Strasser to decline.

In January 1933, Von Papen and Hindenburg turned to Hitler and appointed him as Chancellor with Von Papen as Vice Chancellor. It was what Hitler had always wanted, but just a few years previously could never have expected. A year later in August 1934 upon the death of President Hindenburg it became apparent that the army supported Hitler. Hitler then combined the two positions of President and Chancellor into one office. This meant that only Hitler as head of state, could dismiss Hitler as the head of the government. On the day of Hindenburg's death all soldiers took the Hitler Oath, swearing unconditional obedience to Hitler personally.

Three days later I was summoned to a meeting with Hitler. I could not imagine what he would want with me, I was after all just an administrator. I felt very nervous. Hildegard told me not to be. She reminded me that I was one of the few people who had known Hitler for just over 20 years and from the humble beginnings from which he had come.

I was escorted into Hitler's office. Goebbels, Goring and Himmler were all present peering at a map on a large table. They all greeted me as though I was a good friend. In truth, I knew how much the three of them all despised one another and were continually trying to outdo each other in order to impress Hitler. They were not men that I liked. Hitler got straight to the point. A man with a lot to do and little time in which to do it.

'Otto my friend, the only way that we will be able to make Germany great again is by being a strong government that is not distracted by the views of others. By others I mean especially the Communist Party but there are others also who are seeking to derail and distract us. It is important that we remove them so that they may no longer be of any consequence and influence against us. To that end Heinrich Himmler here has built a camp just outside of Munich in the town of Dachau. The commandant of the camp is Hilmar Wäckerle he is in need of a good administrator. I am therefore going to give you the rank of an SS Sergeant Major and you will act as his logistical assistant. I am fully aware Otto, that you are not a soldier, but it is important that you have a rank of authority.

'It is unlikely that we will meet again Otto, but I valued your friendship when we first met in Vienna and of course you were a good organiser when you joined the German Workers Party, can you believe, thirteen years ago now? You served me well and you have played your part in helping me to achieve where we are now. But this is just the beginning. We will build roads and get industry and our great country moving again. There will be full employment and families will have bread on their tables again. But there will be pain before there is gain. There will be winners and losers. The winners will be those that throw themselves behind us, the losers will be those foolish enough to believe that they can oppose us. Thank you, Otto, you go with my best wishes. Please give my regards to Hildegard.'

And with that the four of them bent over the table and continued to study a map. I never said a word as I was ushered out. A secretary handed me an envelope.

'In here are your joining instructions as well as your rail passes to Dachau. Commandant Wäckerle is expecting you at nine tomorrow morning.'

I caught the train back to Munich and home. The three of us sat around the table at dinner and I explained that I had been given a new position approved by Hitler himself as the administrator at, I assumed, a detention camp at Dachau. In terms of money, it did represent a significant increase, although I would be required to wear the uniform of an SS sergeant major. None of us had heard of Dachau which apparently had only just been established.

The following day I arrived at the camp. I was surprised to see that it was surrounded by a high fence with barb wire on the top and that there were lookout towers with search lights and armed guards. The senior NCO at the gate demanded in a brisk and rude manner to see my papers. I fumbled around before withdrawing from my inside coat pocket, the letter of introduction that had been signed by Hitler himself. When he saw the signature, his entire demeanour changed. He quickly gave orders for the outer and the inner gates to be opened and advised me that he would escort me personally to the commandant's office.

There were lines of huts which I discovered were the living quarters of those who had been interned. It was predominantly men although there were some women there also. They all wore what appeared to be blue and white striped pyjamas. Upon reaching the commandant's office I was then handed over to a young secretary. I introduced myself and she then picked up a phone and spoke with Hilmar Wäckerle. She then escorted me a few metres, opened the door, and allowed me to pass through into a very spacious office.

'Good to see you again Otto. Who would have thought that you and I would ever have been working together? I believe like me, you were recommended by Heinrich Himmler.'

I remembered that Hilmar Wäckerle had been a member and like me was part of the failed Putsch in 1923. After that he had gone and managed a cattle ranch. Upon re-joining the Nazis in 1925 he had been influential in drafting the agricultural policy. I was in agreement that farmers should be given their farms.

'I am a little unclear as to the purpose of Dachau,' I said. 'Hitler told me that it was to house our opponents.'

'That's exactly right Otto. It is hugely important that we crush all opposition and that we can make Germany strong again.'

'How long are these individuals detained for?'

'As long as is necessary. The main groups here are political opponents from the nationalist parties and the communist.'

'What exactly is my role?'

'First of all, you have been given the rank of SS Sergeant Major. I realise that you are not a soldier and never have been, but it is important that you have authority. Your main job is to keep up to date records of everyone who is a guest here,' he said laughing. 'We will not tolerate any disobedience. All detainees are to be treated harshly.'

I decided to keep my head down, to observe but not to say anything. What I saw sickened me. Then on 25th May a school-teacher was beaten to death; his name was Sebastian Nefzger. The SS officers in charge claimed that he had committed suicide. However, an autopsy revealed that he was either strangled or had been asphyxiated.

The Munich public prosecutor then indicted Wäckerle and the SS officers involved on a charge of murder. Hitler, then issued an edict stating the Dachau concentration camp was not subject to German law as it applied to German citizens. SS administrators alone would decide on what punishments were appropriate.

The following month, Wäckerle was replaced as commandant by SS-Grupenführer Theodor Eicke. It soon became apparent how ruthless and cruel Theodor Eicke was.

The situation generally was moving very quickly. On 1st April, an edict was given to boycott all Jewish shops and businesses. This was followed a week later barring all Jews from working in the civil service or in university and state positions. On 26th April Hermann Göring established the Gestapo. An organisation, the very name when uttered brought fear and trepidation when the true purpose of that organisation was known.

On 10th May, there was a public burning of all books written by Jews, political dissidents and others not approved by the Nazis. On 14th July, a law was passed that stripped all Jewish immigrants of their German citizenship. It seemed to be one thing after another. On 15th September 1935 anti-Jewish racial laws were enacted. This meant that Jews were no longer considered to be German citizens and were forbidden to marry Aryans. Six months later on 3rd March came the news that Jewish doctors were being barred from German institutions.

Every night I used to return home, thoroughly depressed by what I knew was happening at Dachau. In the beginning it had just been political opponents, but now the net was being spread ever wider. Artists and thinkers were being detained along with Catholic priests. Many Jews were arriving daily. The only reason that they were there was because they were Jewish. It didn't make sense to me. There was a large site adjacent to the camp that was a training school for the SS. I feared speaking out for I had seen what had happened in the early days to some of the guards who had not expected to be part of such a cruel regime.

Hitler and his henchmen were very bold and took incredible risks. On 7th March 1936 German troops marched into the Rhineland. This was previously demilitarised by the Versailles Treaty. Two years late on 13th March Austria was incorporated and became part of the Reich. On 26th April it was decreed that it would be mandatory to register all property inside the Reich that was held by Jews. We could not believe that on 30th September a conference was held in Munich in which the governments of Great Britain and France agreed to German occupation of Sudetenland previously part of Western Czechoslovakia.

Each night Hildegard and I would discuss the worsening situation. I was aware whilst wearing my SS uniform, how people avoided me. Even neighbours who were once friendly, now kept their eyes averted. Helmut who was now sixteen was genuinely concerned about what was taking place. Several of his school friends who were Jews had been removed. All three of us expressed our opinions, but we emphasized to Helmut that our views must never be expressed outside of our home.

They were horrified when I explained that all prisoners underwent the same fate when they entered the camp, they lost their legal status, their remaining possessions were confiscated, their hair was shaved off, and they were dressed in striped clothes. They were allocated a number as well as a coloured triangle, which indicated what type of category they belonged to. The daily routine was filled with work, hunger, exhaustion, and fear of brutality from the sadistic SS guards.

We had a new commandant at that time SS Obersturmbannführer Alex Piorkowski. The impression that I gained was that each commandant was intent on appearing more macho and more sadistic than his predecessor. This was certainly true of Alex who had replaced SS Oberführer Heinrich Deubel.

As I was preparing to leave for home on 8th November 1938, Alex Piorkowski summoned me to meet with him. I entered his office and gave him the Nazi salute accompanied by 'Heil Hitler' which we were all obliged to do, an indication of our sworn allegiance to the Führer himself.

'Otto, this is just to advise you that I will need you to stay on site and not go home for the next couple of days from tomorrow, we are expecting a surge in detainees after tomorrow. You may have use of the guest house.'

I went home that evening and chatted to Hildegard and Helmut. Clearly something big was about to happen. It all became clear the following evening. The seriousness in which direction our country was moving in became clear on the nights of 9th and 10th November. This became known as Kristallnacht (night of broken glass) it was no less than an anti-Jewish pogrom in Germany, Austria and the Sudetenland. During that time over 200 synagogues were destroyed, 7,500 shops looted and over 10,000 Jews were sent to Dachau.

I was at my desk for sixteen hours during the day of 10th processing the names of our new arrivals. It was clear to me that they were mainly Jews. Another long day on 11th ensued doing the same as the day before. The following day I was checking through the lists again. I had always tried to have an efficient filing system and had put all detainees in alphabetical order. When rechecking the details of the newly arrived I came across two names that stopped me in my tracks. I felt as though I was hyperventilating.

One of the secretaries must have noticed and quickly came over and put her hand on my shoulder and said, 'Are you all right Otto?' Whilst in the office myself and the staff there were always very informal and courteous towards one another.

'Thank you, Gertrude, could you arrange for Oberaufseherin Meyer to see me please?'

'Of course.'

Oberaufseherin Meyer was the camp leader who supervised all the female prisoners.

Ten minutes later, I had by now moved into the interview office, there was a knock at the door and there stood Oberaufseherin Meyer.

'Sir, you wished to see me?'

'Indeed, thank you for coming Oberaufseherin. The day before yesterday amongst the female prisoners that came in and who are now under your care were twin girls Leah and Eliana Benowitz, is that correct?'

'I can confirm that they arrived in the early hours of yesterday morning. Two very attractive young women who have already caught the eye of several of the SS offices. I am certain that they will be found light duties so that they will be available to entertain the officers in the evening. You have an eye for beauty sir, and I am sure that our commandant will approve of your selecting these girls. One for him and one for you perhaps? Although I don't know how you can tell one from the other.'

Ignoring her observations which I found deeply offensive and sickening, I said, 'Please locate and bring these two women to me now.'

Almost an hour had passed before I heard the unmistakable sound of jackboots marching, and then coming to a halt outside the office. Oberaufseherin Meyer was ahead of the two girls who had been accompanied by two burly SS guards.

I called out from the office. 'Show the girls in, and leave the office, I will vouch that they will not try and escape, I will call you when I need you.' I had my back turned to the girls when they entered. 'Please close the door behind you on the way out Oberaufseherin.'

I stood there for a full minute without turning around in order to be certain that the girl's escort had left the building. I then put my finger to my lips as I turned around. Both girls stared at me with their eyes and their mouths wide open in shocked disbelief. I then walked to the door, opened it, and made sure that there was no one working in the outer office. The last time that I had seen Leah and Eliana was when Hildegard and I had stayed with their family on our honeymoon. They were 18 years old at that time, they were now 35 years old and were both very striking in appearance.

They stood tall and even here in this position they still exuded an air of confidence. I walked across to the window and pulled down the blind. I then went to both girls and hugged them at the same time. Their composure cracked and gave way to tears rolling down their cheeks. I also felt incredibly emotional.

I bade the girls to take the two seats in front of the desk. I then took my seat behind the desk and placed my head in my hands. I realised that I was shaking it from side to side as though in denial. All the emotion came out in the realisation that I was in effect a willing accomplice in the awful happenings that were taking place.

Looking at the two innocent, expectant, uncertain faces before me that were still in shock, I asked, 'What were the circumstances that lead to your being brought here?'

Leah answered, 'Our orchestra was giving a concert in one of the synagogues in the South of Munich. It was around nine at night the day before yesterday. Suddenly these stones and bricks were hurled through the beautiful stain glass windows. Then the doors burst open. It was terrifying. A mob of men appeared with lighted torches they spread out all over through the middle and along the sides. They were torching the fabrics and hitting the congregation with sticks and bare fists.

'People were screaming, there was much shouting. One of our elderly ladies who I believe to be in her eighties, turned around and looked at the mob right in the eyes. She was not going to be intimidated. One of the brownshirts with his swastika armband, just bludgeoned her around the head. She fell immediately to the ground, whilst on the ground several gave her a good kicking.

'My sister and I, although both first violinists and therefore in the front of the orchestra, quickly got up and made our way to the vestry where our instrument cases were. We returned our violins to their cases, picked them up and then left through the back door. All this was in under a minute. We made our way through the tombstones and out onto the street. There were so many people out. We could see that shops were being ransacked and the occupants were being rounded up and beaten both at the same time. Many of the perpetrators were laughing.

'Whichever road we turned down we found aggressive behaviour and then we heard someone call out, "Hey, they must be part of the Jewish orchestra," we both quickened our step to the point where we were almost running, but it was to no avail. We were both grabbed from behind. Strong arms pinned us back although we both managed to keep hold of our instruments. There were about six men all in Brownshirts, we knew these to be the S.A. better known as Storm Troopers. They were leering at us. One of the men grabbed the top of my blouse and tore it downwards and at the same time called out "Let us have some fun with these Jewish bitches," at that point I closed my eyes and went limp and fell to the ground, I fully expected us both to be gang raped there and then.

'But then a voice called out, 'Get back you thugs, what the hell do you think you are doing?' When I opened my eyes, there approaching us was a tall man of about our age in a black uniform with similar markings as you have on your tunic Otto.'

'Hmm,' I muttered. 'A member of the SS.'

'He clearly outranked our attackers because they all immediately stood to one side. He then asked the question were we Jews? We said nothing but nodded. He then issued a command that there was a truck at the end of the street and that we were to be taken there and put on it and then taken to the detention centre nearby. When we arrived in the camp, we could not believe what we were experiencing. The conditions inside were so crowded. Eliana and I had to share a bunk last night. We were told that we would have our heads shaven. It should have been yesterday, but I believe the camp was overwhelmed with so many in one go.'

Eliana looked at me and then asked, 'Otto, you were a friend of our family, what are you doing here as part of the S.S.?'

I felt at that time ashamed of myself. Like millions of other good Germans, we had not brought Hitler to power with the intention of destroying the Jews. The Jews were a big part of our economy and played a significant part in the very fabric of German life. I could not understand the vile hatred that Adolf Hitler and Heinrich Himmler had decreed for this section of our society. Indeed, I had seen that it was for anyone who opposed the regime.

'How are your parents Abraham and Hannah?' I asked.

'They were unable to attend the concert,' replied Eliana. 'Daddy had managed to buy us a flat in Munich and so we had not been back at their house for a couple of months. I have no doubt though that they are both worried sick. They would have heard what has happened and would have come to find us to make sure that we were unharmed. We are both totally shocked by what has happened.'

I stood up and left the girls and went to the small kitchen area that we had attached to the main office. I made three coffees and found a packet of biscuits. When I returned, both girls looked thoroughly distraught.

'Here,' I said. 'The biscuits are all that I could find in the kitchen.' I could see that both girls were extremely hungry. They had probably forgotten about their thirst and hunger through fear.

There was a loud knock at the door which immediately opened to reveal Oberaufseherin Meyer. There was a look of horror on her face when she saw the girls sitting down, eating biscuits and drinking coffee.

'Stand up you bitches!' she yelled. 'You always stand to attention whenever I am around.' Looking at me scornfully she then said, 'I will return these internees to their accommodation sir.'

'That will not be necessary Oberaufseherin, these girls should not be here, there has been a terrible mistake. They will for this evening stay in my room. I will explain everything to the commandant tomorrow when he returns from his trip to Berlin. I will take full responsibility and I commend you for doing your duty. Good evening.'

The Oberaufseherin gave both girls a withering look, before clicking both heels together and gave me the Nazi salute before about turning and leaving, clearly in a huff.

I then picked up the telephone, rang the guard room, and requested a motorcycle dispatch rider. When he arrived, I handed him a letter addressed to Abraham Benowitz. I had advised Abraham and Hannah that their daughters were safe and for him to stay at the estate until further news. The two girls also added a quick paragraph each to their parents.

The following morning, I woke up early. Fortunately, I had been given the private accommodation usually reserved for a high up official such as Himmler should he decide to visit and stay overnight.

This meant that there was a double bed, a bathroom and small kitchen. The girls occupied the double bed although I doubt if they slept well. I slept in the armchair. I went across to the mess hall. As I was the first there, I was able to help myself to three cooked breakfasts. I returned to my accommodation to find that the girls had both just got up.

I tried to sound more confident and optimistic than I was. 'Morning ladies, please sit down and enjoy your breakfast. Would you like coffee?'

They both nodded before Leah said, 'Otto what is going to happen to us? We are both so afraid. Two nights ago, we witnessed unbelievable scenes of destruction. The synagogue where we had been playing was being totally desecrated and was probably set alight after we had left.'

'Neither of you should be here. I am truly sorry for what has happened to you personally and what is happening generally in our country. I would think that the wider population including myself have been sleepwalking into this position. We have been misled by so much. I worked under Joseph Goebbels, I knew then that he was a master of deceit and propaganda. Unfortunately, now that he has complete control of the radio stations and the press, he can feed us whatever lies he wishes to.

'We cannot trust as fact what we now read or hear. Clearly, Himmler and Hitler are doing their absolute best to destroy the Jews. Once you have finished your breakfast, I would suggest that you would both benefit from a shower. Then just stay in the bedroom until I return. There is coffee in the kitchen for a drink.'

With that I left them, locking the front door behind me as I departed. I went to the general office where I discovered that Gertrude was already at her desk. 'Could be another busy day Otto, are you feeling okay now?'

'Yes, thank you Gertrude, I am fine. Yesterday when I was checking through the lists, I discovered two women who were friends of our family. Indeed, my wife Hildegard worked as the girl's nanny cum tutor for several years, I'm not sure how I am going to handle this when Commandant Piorkowski returns this afternoon.'

'Are the girls Jewish?'

'I am afraid that they are. They were detained two nights ago whilst performing at a concert in one of the Munich synagogues.'

'Well, all may not be lost,' Gertrude said.

'What do you mean? Do you have a suggestion on how I can get them back home and out of this hell hole?'

'Be careful Otto, people may be listening, but yes. A communique came in just a few minutes before you arrived stating that any Jew who could guarantee that they would leave the country are to be released.' Gertrude handed me the paper which I hurriedly read. Without thinking I gave Gertrude a hug and a quick kiss on the cheek. She blushed and smiled at the same time. 'I am glad that I have made your day,' she responded.

With that there was a loud knock at the door and in strode the Camp's Second in Command, SS-Sturmführer Robert Erspoenn closely followed by a mean looking Oberaufseherin Meyer.

'I understand that you Herr Wagner have given refuge to two Jewish bitches that were detained two evenings ago and were placed under the supervision of Oberaufseherin Meyer. I am commanding you to return these detainees immediately so that they can be processed and put to work as is required.'

I remained calm and took a moment before I replied. 'These women will remain in my custody until our Commandant Piorkowski returns later today.'

'May I remind you Sergeant Major Wagner, that I seriously outrank you and you will not disobey my orders, is that clear?'

'You are correct Sturmführer, you do outrank me. However, I was appointed to this position by Herr Hitler and Heinrich Himmler personally. Would you care for me to show you their letter of authorisation as personal assistant to the commandant? Indeed, this is the fourth commandant that I have served, whilst you I believe have only been here for three weeks. Now I suggest that you both leave and let the situation run its natural course.'

I could see that SS-Sturmführer Erspoenn was not accustomed to having his orders disobeyed and felt somewhat humiliated that it was in front of two members of camp staff. I was thinking that this is not a man to be crossed, be careful.

He thought for a moment whilst looking me straight in the eyes. 'Very well,' he said, 'I hope for your sake that our commandant agrees with you. Although I fully expect once I have advised him of your actions, that he will support me and that you will be charged with insubordination.'

With that they both turned to leave and as they did so, I clicked my heels, raised my right arm, and called out 'Heil Hitler.' They both immediately stopped and turned and responded in kind. Neither wished to have been accused of showing disloyalty to our leader.

Gertrude very kindly agreed to return to my accommodation and take some food for Leah and Eliana. I was feeling extremely nervous and uncertain. I had an uncomfortable feeling in the pit of my stomach. It was just after three thirty when Gertrude drew my attention and nodded towards the outside window.

The commandant's car had just entered the compound and was driving towards us. I kept a cautious eye on the car. As it pulled up outside the office, suddenly there to open the rear passenger door was SS-Sturmführer Erspoenn. He was in animated conversation for two or three minutes before walking off.

The commandant looked towards our office but then got back into the car and his driver took him to the commandant's house. It was over an hour before he returned to his office and summoned me before him.

'Now Sergeant Major Wagner, please explain yourself, I have been told some disturbing things by the deputy commandant that you have sheltered two young Jewish woman and on top of that, you have disobeyed orders from a senior officer and indeed, have been insubordinate. I hope that you can explain yourself, I would be extremely disappointed to lose your services.'

'Thank you, Herr Commandant. I have been here in my role for almost seven years now. You are the fourth commandant that I have served. I believe that I have carried out my duties as both the Führer and Herr Himmler had instructed me to do.'

'I cannot argue with you there Sergeant Major, but I have always felt that you have merely been keeping your head down and do not really believe in the cause or your oath that you swore to our Führer. I could easily test out my theory. If I were to bring before you a prisoner and told you to shoot them dead, as I have often found it necessary to do, in order to set an example and to keep order in our camp, I have my reservations that you would not carry out this order. Am I right?'

'I am an administrator and not a soldier Herr Commandant.'

'But you have the rank of sergeant major, do you not?'

'It was deemed that I needed to be put in uniform by the Führer so as to give me authority when moving about the camp. You would have noticed Herr Commandant, that I have never sought to use that authority in any way.'

'Hmm, that is true. Explain to me about these two Jewish women that you seem very intent on protecting?'

I quickly concluded that I would put all the true facts on the table. 'Herr Commandant, you have met my wife Hildegard on several occasions.'

'Indeed, I have, a fine-looking woman, a wonderful musician with very impressive qualities. You are the envy of many of the SS officers here.'

'That is kind of you to say so, Herr Commandant. Back in 1907 Hildegard applied for a position as nanny/tutor to twin girls, Leah and Eliana. Hildegard stayed there for several years and both girls became accomplished violin players. Just before our wedding in 1921, Hildegard had arranged our honeymoon. I had no idea where we were going until we arrived at this estate in Southern Bavaria very close to the Austrian border. Our hosts were Abraham and Hannah Benowitz the parents of the two women that are now in our custody.'

The commandant let out a low whistle. 'A family of Jews?'

'Indeed, Herr Commandant. They are the parents of the two girls who were snatched on 9th November whilst playing at an orchestral concert at a synagogue in Munich which like so many others has been destroyed. I can say without a second thought, that the time spent with that family has been the happiest time of my life.

'They own a farm. Abraham and his wife are probably the kindest people that I have ever met. They supply free of charge foodstuffs to many of the needy in their village. They have a real social conscience. If they were of Aryan stock, Germany would be proud of them and holding them up as a fine example of Germans helping out one another. Is it not the policy of our government to create one German community?'

'It is indeed Otto. I'm not sure how we can help you in your quest to free these two women, who are after all Jewish.'

'A communique came in earlier this morning Herr Commandant authorising that any Jew who could guarantee that they will leave Germany and go to another nation that is not under German control may leave the country.'

'Well, Otto, I would suggest that you have your get out clause and have been saved by the bell. You are a good man, Otto. Everyone likes you, including me. You are so efficient in your work and I and my predecessors have been impressed by your loyalty and organisational skills. I also know, as I suspect those commandants before me, that you do not share our methods at this place for dealing with those who oppose us.'

I thought it wise not to respond.

'This is what I suggest Otto my friend. I will make a staff car available to you. You may leave right away with the Benowitz women and return them to their home. As you know, I have been in Berlin for the last couple of days. I am going to give you some information that will not be in the public domain until tomorrow.'

I waited wondering what this could be.

The Commandant walked to his desk and sat down. He then pulled open a draw and took out a packet of cigarettes. He took one, placed it between his lips and lit it. Then taking a long draw he then made an 'O' shape with his mouth and exhaled, the result, a perfect circle of smoke appeared. It was something that I had seen him do many times. It was his party piece and caused much amusement. He studied the circle as it expanded and slowly dissipated before his attention returned to me.

'Tomorrow is 12th November which in years to come will be looked upon by the Jews as being another hugely significant date. A decree will be announced forcing all Jews to transfer retail businesses into Aryan hands. I am giving you this advice Otto because of Hildegard's connection with this family who clearly you both respect. For their own safety encourage them to leave Germany at the earliest opportunity.'

With that, he picked up the telephone on his desk and ordered a staff car to be brought to the office. 'I will grant you two week's leave Otto; I will expect you to resume your duties on the 25th. That is all.'

And with that we both 'Hail Hitlered' one another and I turned and left.

Outside the office stood a Mercedes-Benz 770 with the keys in the ignition. There was a full tank of petrol. There was no mistaking that it was an official car, with a huge Swastika painted on the drivers and front passenger doors. I got in and drove the 200 metres to the house where I knew the girls would still be. I unlocked the door to find two frightened young women anxiously waiting.

'I have some excellent news,' I announced. I am taking you out of here. First of all, as it is now dusk, I suggest that we spend the night at my home with Hildegard and Helmut, who you have yet to meet. Then tomorrow we will drive to your home. Before we leave, I would suggest that you use the phone there to ring your parents and advise them that we will be arriving at around noon tomorrow. I am just going to pop out and will return in a short while.'

It was amazing to see how the stress and fear had left their faces in a matter of seconds. They were their normal animated selves once more, displaying excited happiness as they started to dial. I left the building and walked over to the Detainee Property Store. Upon entering, I surveyed a scene of property being sorted into different piles. There was jewellery, money, coats and hats to name just a few. There was an NCO supervising the proceedings. He immediately came over.

'Herr Sergeant Major, I don't ever recall seeing you in here before. How may I help you?'

'Two days ago, two young women were mistakenly brought here. They are now to be released on the orders of our commandant. I have come to collect their property, namely two violins.'

'Ah yes, as someone who plays myself, I had a little play on them. I can confirm that they are both superb instruments. One moment please, I will fetch them.'

Leah climbed into the front passenger seat with Eliana in the back. They were both clutching their precious violins. We drove to the exit barriers. A cursory but puzzled look into the car by the guard who said nothing, before opening the inner gate and calling for the outer gate also to be opened.

We turned left onto the road for Munich and headed in the direction of my home and into the embraces of my family. All three of us let out audible sighs of relief.

Chapter 6

We pulled up outside my home at just after six in the evening. Surprisingly, no one had spoken a word during the journey. Both Leah and Eliana had fallen asleep. I was not surprised; they had had little sleep since they were taken.

I was very conscious when parking the official car outside our house. What would our neighbours think? And I was also concerned, given that all what was happening that the car might be badly damaged by disgruntled Jews or others, and there were plenty who did not agree with the policies that were being carried out by the Nazis.

As we entered the house, Hildegard, Leah and Eliana all burst into tears. The full emotions and the dreadful reality of the situation of what might have been had finally caught up with everyone. The three hugged each other for several minutes. I could feel my bottom lip quivering. Helmut stood respectfully back until the embraces were over.

Leah and Eliana, although twice Helmut's age, came and hugged him lovingly as though he were a brother that they had not seen in a long time. All five of us went into the kitchen and carried on talking whilst Hildegard prepared tea. There was little doubt that we all, including Helmut, now fully understood the seriousness of the policies that Hitler was pursuing.

After the meal was completed, Hildegard then suggested that the best remedy to forget all our troubles was to play music. I was so impressed and proud when I witnessed Helmut playing his violin so competently with the other three. They played several pieces specially composed for violins. Considering that they had never practised or played together before, it was excellent, and Hildegard was right, it had completely taken our minds off the awful reality of what was happening elsewhere.

We left our house the following morning. I was relieved after checking the car and looking underneath it, to establish that no damage or intent to damage us or the vehicle had occurred. Helmut did not join us as he was off to school. I felt distinctly uncomfortable in my SS uniform, but I realised that it was of critical importance that I carried if off with a display of arrogance and swagger that all members of the SS appeared to display.

I looked up at the name of *Schlachthaus* as we turned off the lane and onto the track that Hildegard and I had last driven down during our honeymoon. What a difference in circumstances now? I heard the gravel beneath the wheels crunch as I applied the brakes. There was no need for Hildegard to hit the horn this time to announce our arrival. I believe that Hannah or Abraham had been keeping a permanent vigil in anticipation of our arrival.

They opened the front door, but just stood there. They were fearful and I concluded also confused by the site of a Nazis car with an SS man at the wheel. Fortunately, Leah and Eliana had now opened the back doors and were running towards their parents. Yet again more tears. Both Abraham and Hannah embraced Hildegard. Abraham finally looked at me, but it was not in the same friendly manner in which we had said our farewells, several years earlier.

Abraham turned his back and walked briskly into the house accompanied by his two daughters. Hannah came over and gave me a hug.

'Otto, please forgive Abraham, the sight of any German military uniform enrages him. We were out of our minds with worry after what happened three days ago. We drove into Munich to where the girls had been playing. The synagogue had been destroyed. There was no one to ask for information. We had to be careful that we were not identified as being Jews. We will be eternally grateful to you for returning to us our beautiful daughters.'

'Thank you, Hannah, I have a good deal of explaining to do and I fully appreciate the hatred that Abraham must feel towards me at this time.'

Upon entering the hallway and then into the main body of the house, there was no sign of Abraham or Leah. Hildegard and Eliana were in the kitchen. Hildegard stepped forward and once again hugged Hannah.

'You know Hannah, I think that we could all do with a stiff drink,' Hildegard suggested.

'I agree,' Eliana said quickly reaching towards a kitchen cabinet and withdrawing four glasses followed by a bottle of Schnapps. 'This,' she declared, 'is homemade and will certainly bring a feeling of wellbeing, something that we could all do with right now!'

For the next hour or so, Hildegard, Eliana and Hannah busied themselves in the kitchen preparing our evening meal. When it was ready, Eliana went to the Library and advised her dad who was in animated conversation with Leah. Eliana must have been telling her dad and sister that the evening meal was ready.

But then I heard Abraham shouting. 'I will not share a meal with that man who has betrayed us all. All members of the Gestapo and the SS not to mention numerous others are our enemies and are out to destroy us!'

I looked across at Hannah, who I could tell was deeply embarrassed. The twins returned and said to their mum that it was best if the five of us ate and that dad would have his meal later. The meal was lovely, but no one enjoyed it. We had all lost our appetite. We ate in uncomfortable silence. After the meal, I asked to be excused. I went to our bedroom and changed out of my uniform and into civvies. I then made my way to the library.

I knocked twice and without waiting for an invitation to enter I went in. Abraham was sitting at an empty desk with his arms splayed out in front of him with the palms of his hands face down. His look could not have been more contemptuous. I was determined that he would hear me out.

With the library door opened, I called out to the four women in the dining room. 'Hannah, Hildegard, Leah and Eliana please come to the library, it is important that I talk to you all.' Abraham's face did not flicker, he remained unmoved.

There were two comfortable armchairs which Hildegard and Hannah took plus a three-seater settee on which the twins sat. The tension in the room was almost unbearable. I looked around at the expectant faces, although Abraham had now averted his gaze and was now focused on the back of his hands.

'I understand,' I began, 'how you must all feel seeing someone that you had previously welcomed into your home as a friend, now returning to your house as a member of the SS. It is a long story, and one which I will not detain you with. But I wish to assure the Family Benowitz that neither Hildegard or I are supporters of Hitler or the Nazi Party.

'I have ended up as an administrator in Dachau by pure chance and circumstances of my having known the Führer when he was a down and out artist in Vienna many years ago. Dachau is a terrible detention camp where unimaginable cruelty takes place daily. A place where every morning I do not wish to go. I go every day out of self-preservation and that of preserving the safety of Hildegard and Helmut.

'You would be right to suggest that I am unprincipled and indeed a coward. I am under no illusions that anyone who speaks up against this regime, even those who have considered themselves to have been good personal friends with the Führer are either thrown into prison or worse. And by worse, I mean eliminated. There is absolutely no loyalty from Hitler. He expects unconditional and total obedience from us all.

'I believe that it is fate, that I should have been at Dachau when your daughters were detained and taken there. I will spare you the details, but even on their arrival they had caught the attention of some of the SS Officers who appreciate the availability of attractive women such as your daughters. I do not wish to speculate what might have become of them. But one thing is for sure, it would not have been pleasant.

'My being there Abraham and the fact that I was able to convince the commandant that they did not belong in Dachau and were in fact family friends of Hildegard, who I realise holds her in high esteem, was extremely fortunate for Leah and Eliana.

'The camp commandant has given me the use of the official car for two weeks. I feel sickened every time I put on and wear that SS uniform. But on this occasion, it has resulted in being the passport out of Dachau for your twin daughters.

'None of us know for certain what the future holds. But the present spate of decrees does not look good for anyone who is Jewish. I was permitted to remove Leah and Eliana because of a decree that was issued yesterday permitting detainees from Dachau to be released providing that they could guarantee that they will emigrate from Germany.'

Abraham clapped his hands in despair. 'You mean that my daughters will have to leave Germany, the country of their birth and go and live in a foreign country? What right did you have to give such an undertaking?'

'The alternative Herr Benowitz, does not bear thinking about.'

'He is right dear,' Hannah said. 'We should look at this as Divine Intervention. This is the will of God. It was him who placed Otto there in order to save our dear girls.'

Abraham placed his face in his hands. I could hear him speaking once again in Hebrew and so I deduced that he was offering up a prayer. When he stopped, his shoulders began moving up and down, we all realised at the same time that Abraham was crying. It was pitiful to witness this strong, kind, loving, thoughtful and generous man in such distress. The reaction of everyone including myself was to gather around him and give him words of comfort. His two daughters were hugging him. We were all wiping away the tears.

After a moment or two he appeared to regain his composure and put both of his hands in front of him with the palms facing outwards in a signal to us all to stop, and step back. He then pushed his chair back and stood up and turned to face me. We all looked at him nervously, as if not sure what he would next do.

He held out his outstretched right and with his left clasped me on the shoulder and pulled me toward him. For a man who was now 56 years old, I could feel how incredibly strong he was. This gesture was all too much, and we all began to cry with tears streaming from our emotionally filled eyes.

Fleetingly, I thought of my camp commandant and what he would have thought if he had seen me now. I would have confirmed all of his fears that I was a German who did not share the rhetoric that the Jews were the cause of our financial woes and that it would have been impossible for me to cause anyone physical harm.

Abraham then recovered his composure, breaking off from our embrace, then said, 'Now where is that schnapps?'

We all laughed and then proceeded to go downstairs to the kitchen. Once our glasses had been fully charged, I suggested that we adjourn to the living room as there was some important news that they needed to hear. Once everyone was seated, I began to speak.

'I have been the administrator to four camp commandants at Dachau over the past five years. It has been impossible for me not to have knowledge of what has been going on there. Predominantly our prisoners, for that is what they are, are from the Jewish community. But not all. My own countryman, the last fascist chancellor of Austria before the Anschluss, Kurt Schuschnigg is at present a detainee.

'Well known German politicians such as Leon Blum, Theodor Duesterberg and Leopold Fifi are amongst our prisoners. Last week the emanant scientist Sonderaktion Krakau from Krakow University arrived. We also have distinguished writers such as Heinrich Eduard Jacob, Franz Roh and Jura Soyfer.

'When I first arrived, it was mainly communist prisoners such as Alfred Andersch, Emil Carlebach and Oskar Müller but now it is I regret to inform you, mostly Jews. These include Bruno Bettelheim, Jakob Ehrlich who died in May of this year. And can you believe the German World War One Veteran and Entrepreneur, Ludwig Kahn who came in on the same night as Leah and Eliana?'

I could tell that my listeners were all stunned. 'We have had absolutely no idea as to what is going on. You have shocked us with these well-known names. When a person who is so famous and respected such as Ludwig Kahn has been imprisoned, it makes me realise just how ruthless the Nazis are and just how vulnerable we are here,' Abraham observed.

'You must remember,' I continued, 'that Goebbels, I am ashamed to say, who I worked with, is a master of deceit and propaganda. He has full control of all the media. Hence you will only read and hear what he deems as being appropriate. You will never be regaled with true facts.

'You would have been aware that there has been a steady escalation of measures all aimed at undermining and blaming Jews for the current state of Germany. Earlier this year with the boycotting of all Jewish businesses followed by laws barring Jews from the civil service, universities and state positions. What happened three days ago with Kristallnacht was the worst and a clear indication of the violence that has now been encouraged by the Nazis.

'I am afraid that I have even worse news. Yesterday before leaving with Leah and Eliana, I was informed by the camp commandant who had just returned from Berlin, that today a decree will be announced which forces all Jews to transfer their businesses into Aryan hands.'

No one spoke. I could see that they were in shock and were trying to comprehend what I had just announced.

'I don't understand,' Abraham eventually said. 'Are you telling me that we have to give up all in effect what is ours? This farm was established by my grandfather. I am the third generation and when I have gone, my daughters will be the fourth. It is my hope that they will both marry and produce at least one heir between them so as to continue. No! No!' he shouted, 'this is absolutely outrageous, it must not and will not happen!'

Again, no one spoke for several seconds. The enormity and the seriousness of what I had reported was beginning to sink in. I was pleased that the next to speak was Hildegard.

'It is important that we recognise the true situation as it really is. There is little doubt that for whatever reason, Hitler,

Himmler and the Nazis are determined to marginalise anyone who is Jewish. I would say, after listening to the accounts that Otto has regularly described to me, that it is worse than that. It is possible that they are trying to destroy Judaism, and this is just the start. There seems to be no holding them back.

'The most important thing for the four of you, is your physical safety. Otto has confirmed that the reason why Leah and Eliana were permitted to leave yesterday was because Otto had given his assurance that they would both leave Germany. For your lives to be saved, you Abraham and Hannah, however abhorrent and unjust all of this is, you must also depart to a foreign country.'

Hildegard paused and I could see the four faces were absorbing the true implication of her words. Then she continued. 'Abraham, Hannah, do you trust Otto and me?'

They both spoke at the same time, with Hannah giving way to Abraham to speak. 'With what has happened over the last twenty-four-hours and the danger that I now realise Otto has potentially exposed himself to in the saving of our daughters from who knows what then of course we trust the both of you.'

Hildegard then continued. 'Not any of us here knows what the future will hold. Right now, it is looking uncertain for everyone, but especially if you are Jewish. Hitler has stated that he wishes that the Reich lasts for a thousand years. You will recall that the leaders of the Roman Empire had similar aspirations. I suspect that Hitler's dreams will end up very much like that of the Roman Emperors, they will not bear fruition. But the fact is that none of us know.

'What is certain is that your property and business have to be transferred into Aryan hands. You will now have to trust Otto because you have no other choice. I suggest that you transfer your business and this house into Otto's name.' Hildegard, quickly put up her hands to prevent all four of the Benowitz's who I could see were about to protest. 'Before you say anything,' Hildegard continued, 'because I can see that you are all appalled by this situation and no doubt consider that it is a contrived betrayal of your friendship but let me assure you it is not. I gave this a lot of thought in bed last night after Otto told me what today's decree would mean. To me this is the only option available to you.

'We have absolutely no interest in stealing your property and assets for our benefit. This way, we can temporarily look after this house and your farm until the day that we all long for, when this regime will fail, and democracy will be restored permitting you and many others to return to the country of your birth.'

Eliana was the first to speak. 'Mama, Papa, these are not words that any of us would have wanted or have expected ever to have listened to, but these are extreme circumstance in which we find ourselves. I reluctantly agree with Hildegard's assessment of where we are, the state of the country, the reality for our own personal safety and her suggestion for registering the property in Otto's name.'

This time an even longer silence. I would say, an uncomfortable silence. And then Abraham looked up and said, 'Let us have another schnapps.'

No one laughed this time. The mood was now sombre. Leah replenished our glasses. I was not normally a drinker of alcohol, but the effects of the warm comforting glow in the stomach that followed a swallow of schnapps could not be denied.

Abraham after downing his schnapps indicated to Leah that he wanted a refill. A moment or two later of what appeared to be contemplation, Abraham then continued. 'So, I agree that it is possible that the four of us could leave for perhaps America. I do have a cousin living in Montana who farms cattle. There are three Jewish families in our village that I am deeply concerned for. I see no future for them here in Germany and like us, I fear for their safety. We need to persuade them also to leave.

'The next thing is that we employ several of the villagers on our farm. As well as that we supply produce to help many of the poorer families who are unable to afford to buy for themselves. What would happen to them?'

Clearly Hildegard had given much thought to the situation without consulting me to ascertain my thoughts.

'I would think that this could be a reason for Otto to resign his position at Dachau. He could explain that this estate has been transferred to him. He could stress the importance that this farm continue in the effort to supply food to the Reich.

'I realise, that Otto knows nothing about farming, but I do remember when we spent our honeymoon here that you introduced us to your foreman Christian Schmidt, if he is still here, then he could teach Otto all that he needs to know. We would ensure that the status quo remains the same. By that I mean that those who work here would continue to do so and supplying the needy of Bischofswiesen would continue.'

Everyone appeared to be deep in thought, weighing up the various options until reluctantly they all agreed that Hildegard's plan provided the only solution to the awful dilemma that they were all now facing.

My mind was now racing, I said, 'Look, it is essential that we act at full speed. We must make use of my being part of the SS and ensure that it is used to our advantage. I have little doubt that with today's proclamation about transferring Jewish property to Aryans that it will be no time at all when someone in the Bavarian State will view this as an opportunity for themselves and will stake their claim. It is important that we leave first thing in the morning in order to complete the transfer.'

The conversation between the six of us carried on until the early hours of the morning. We then retired to our rooms, although I doubt if much sleep was achieved. At around nine in the morning, Abraham and myself departed in the official car, with me driving wearing my full SS uniform. I noticed as we drove through the village that those inhabitants who we passed looked very shocked when they realised that it was Abraham in the front. But he tried to give a wave and a smile of reassurance.

A long queue had already formed outside the property registration office of Munich's Town Hall when we drew up. There were several Storm Troopers who were acting as marshals. The line of course, as expected was made up of Jews all looking fearful. I got out of the car and slammed the door behind me and with as much arrogance as I could muster, I marched to the front of the line with Abraham closely behind. I immediately pushed myself in front of an elderly Jewish man who was in the process of handing over some documents.

I ordered the clerk to retrieve the relevant papers. Abraham signed the deeds of both the house and the farm over to me. I then signed as the authorised new owner. I ensured that my full rank was recorded as that of being in the SS. One copy stayed in the town hall records department, whilst we took the second. I then strutted back to the car, on the way trying to show as much distain as I could for the Jews in the queue for the benefit of the watching Storm Troopers.

I have little doubt that they were all puzzled by seeing Abraham in the passenger seat. On the journey home, I expressed my sympathy and sorrow to Abraham. He looked absolutely wretched although I could tell from our conversation that he was in the process of planning what should happen next.

When we arrived home, Abraham sent out word that he needed to see his foreman, Christian Schmidt. By the time that Christian had arrived, I had changed back into civilian clothes. Abraham led Christian into the dining room where Hannah, Leah, Eliana, Hildegard and I were sat around the table. He could not have been in any doubt that something serious was happening.

Abraham introduced Hildegard and I, who he remembered from our previous stay. Abraham then went on to explain the entire set of circumstances that had brought us to this point. He emphasized that I was a current member of the SS and that both Hildegard and I were not supporters of the terrible things that were happening. He made Christian swear, that he would never divulge this information that had been given to him in complete confidence.

When the meeting was finished, we all stood up. Christian expressed his sorrow for the circumstances in which the family now found themselves, but grateful that he could continue to look after the farm and gave an assurance that he would teach me everything that he knew. He then shook us all by the hand, receiving a special hug from Hannah, before replacing his cloth cap and with shoulders slumped left the house. On the way out,

Abraham instructed Christian to arrange for the three Jewish families in the village to be brought to the house later that evening.

That evening the three Jewish families who all knew one another and were good friends, arrived together. All of them betrayed signs of suffering acute nervousness. They had never been summoned before to Abraham's who was in effect "The Lord of the Manor" but as Hildegard and I had previously observed, a much-respected man.

The three couples had eight children between them, their ages ranging from five years to fourteen years old. Abraham explained the critical situation that he believed all Jews were now at. Hannah interspersed with the occasional words of reassurance.

Abraham divulged that he and his family had reluctantly decided to leave Germany and hopefully resettle in America. He emphasised that in his view any Jew remaining in Germany was in severe danger. Life as everyone had experienced just two or three years before had now changed, whereby Jews were now seen as outcasts.

All three families lived in houses that were rented. Abraham said that he would if they were in agreement, take the families to Munich where they could apply together for the relevant paperwork. He stressed that he and his family were departing in just a few days and that he would help financially.

Clearly this had come as a total shock. Abraham suggested that they went into the library and discussed the situation. He made it clear that these were his wishes to see them safe but that if they did not choose to take his advice, then that was their choice alone and he would respect their decision.

It was just over an hour before the families came back in to join us. Like family Benowitz they had looked at all the different scenarios and came to the conclusion that the course of action suggested by Abraham offered the best chance of survival. Abraham then advised the families that I was a member of the SS, and then briefly explained my circumstances. It was agreed that he would take them to Munich the following day and that I should follow in the official Nazi car to help speed up proceedings.

By the end of that day, all four families had been issued with their travel documents. It was agreed that all four families would leave together. The farm owned a lorry. Abraham suggested that all four families travel in this taking Christian with them. They would cross the border from Germany and into Belgium at Aachen and then drive onto the French port of Calais. Christian would then drive the lorry back. From Calais a ferry would take them across to Dover in England. They would then head to London and to see the American authorities in order to obtain the necessary visas to enter the United States of America.

It was decided that this would happen in seven days' time. This would give enough time to make all necessary arrangements and for everyone to leave their homes in an orderly manner. The day before they were due to leave, Abraham called me into the library. He told me that he wished to show me something.

We left the house and headed towards the quarry. When we arrived, Abraham took me inside a cave. He lit a lantern and we walked on for about twenty metres until we came to a rock face and could go no further.

'Otto,' he said, putting his hand on my shoulder, 'there is something that you should know. Despite appearances not all of us Jews have been passive and unaware of the possible dangers ahead. During the past eighteen months a network has been set up which has involved bringing many items of value from different parts of Bavaria and Southern Austria here. These have included Old Masters, and many antiquities for safekeeping from our synagogues.

'I have been amazed at the wealth that has been entrusted to me to safeguard. Everything was brought here under the cover of darkness. Hannah and my daughters know nothing of this. The only other person to know is Christian Schmidt who I trust implicitly and was my co-conspirator.'

'Where are they hidden?' I asked looking at the rock face.

'You cannot see!' exclaimed Abraham.

I took the lantern and examined all the facing surfaces and sides.

'If they are here,' I remarked, 'then they are incredibly well hidden.'

'I am pleased that you have said that Otto. You have reaffirmed my belief that the treasures are undetectable to the human eye. Right here in front of you, we have poured two metres of concrete to seal the entrance. All of the valuables have been entombed just like in Ancient Egypt. We have taken great care to ensure that the concrete is an exact match of the quarry stone.'

The following morning Christian drew up outside driving the Opel Blitz three-ton lorry. He had collected the three Jewish families first. They all alighted at the house and came inside. Hannah had prepared a huge breakfast for everyone. The children appeared to be extremely excited by what they considered to be an adventure. Their parents were not quite so sure. When everyone was seated Abraham said prayers. Afterwards he said, 'Not exactly the last supper, but I suspect the last breakfast.'

When breakfast was over, those travelling, all took turns to visit the bathroom. Afterwards, we gathered outside. Again, our emotions took hold as we started hugging everyone in turn. Then to my surprise Abraham invited the two youngest children and their father to join him in the driver's cab and announced that throughout the journey all of those on board would spend time riding up front.

'What a considerate human being this is?' I thought.

Once the luggage had been securely placed on board which included three violins and a clarinet, everyone clambered up into the back. The tailgate was secured from the inside by Christian. With that the lorry moved off, with everyone waving. Hildegard and I continued to watch the lorry until it rounded the bend and moved out of sight. It felt eerily quiet and unnatural that it was just the two of us left. Without acknowledging it, I suspect that we both knew that they would never be returning.

CHAPTER 7

Hildegard and I returned home to our house in Munich. We explained everything that had happened to Helmut. He was a mature and yet sensitive young man. I could tell that he was upset by the circumstances that had led to our friends having to leave Germany. He assured us with I thought, confidence and conviction that he would be able to live in the house by himself.

Although he had never introduced us to her, we were aware that he had just started dating a girl called Paula who was the only cellist in the orchestra that Helmut had now become very keen on playing in. We said our goodbyes and returned to the estate. We promised to phone one another on a weekly basis.

Two days later I drove back into Dachau. The gates were opened for me even before I had pulled up. I returned the car to the compound and then sought a meeting with Commandant Piorkowski. I explained to him everything that had taken place and how it would be of benefit if I left Dachau and attended to the farm for the sake of the Reich. I also added that he had correctly observed that I was not a soldier and being at Dachau would not be something that I would choose.

He smiled wistfully and then said, 'Well Otto my friend, it seems even although you do not approve of the Nazi policies, you have benefitted from them, and I imagine are now a very wealthy man. You have now become some sort of Feudal Lord. I congratulate you. You have a lovely wife in Hildegard, and it is as much for my admiration for her that I agree to release you in two weeks' time from your duties here.'

'Thank you, Herr Commandant,' I replied. 'I will do my best to serve the Fatherland.' I was thinking how is it that someone who is so utterly ruthless and cruel, could also have a kind side to him. I had met Commandant Piorkowski's wife and his young son and daughter, all of whom he adored. I had met them though, at a reception in Munich. I did wonder if Mrs Piorkowski was aware of her husband's work.

After two weeks I was ready to leave. Gertrude came and gave me a hug and a peck on the cheek and made it known that she was very sorry to see me leave. According to her, I was the main reason why she came to work each day. It is funny, being a happily married man, how I had not picked up on signals that I now realised were pretty obvious. I told Gertrude that I would miss her too, which was true and gave her another hug before leaving this hellhole for the final time.

We settled into our new way of life. At first the locals were very suspicious of us. Christian, I realised was giving us a good press. Also, Hildegard started giving free violin lessons to several of the village children. They would be brought by their parents to our home. Whilst waiting in the library we would offer the parents a glass of wine from our own cellar. They soon all began to relax and enjoy their weekly visits, it became a social evening for them.

Christian was an absolute diamond. He was passing on his knowledge of farming and the running of the estate that he had acquired over many years. We became very close friends. He and his wife Ursula were often our dinner guests. We felt extremely humble when they reciprocated. It indicated that they were completely at ease and had accepted the situation however sad the circumstances. Ursula was a fine cook. We looked forward to our meals with them. Ursula and Hildegard, like Christian and I became close friends.

Under Christian's guidance we continued the same routine of delivering supplies to those villagers most in need. The dreaded Gestapo visited us twice. When I explained that I was ex SS and that I had a letter certifying my release as an administrator from Dachau authorised and signed by Obersturmbannführer Alex Piorkowski, they accepted this and left us alone.

It was now early March. We had received two letters from Abraham. He explained that they had only just arrived in New

York and were intending to stay with his cousin in Whitefish, Montana. However, their daughters had decided to stay in London and had both been able to obtain employment with the Bank of England and it seemed were exceedingly happy.

Hildegard always had the radio playing in the morning whilst preparing breakfast. It was now 15th March 1939. The programme was interrupted by a special announcement informing listeners that the German Army had marched into Czechoslovakia and occupied that country which would now be governed by Germany. We both looked at each other. Apparently, no action was being taken against this move by either France or Great Britain.

There was a lot of activity, particularly in recruiting personnel for the armed services. Both Hildegard and I were concerned that the military build-up was for a sinister purpose. We therefore thought it a good idea, if we rented out our property in Munich and had Helmut live with us. I could find him work on the estate. He was reluctant to do this because he now had a steady girlfriend from the orchestra. We convinced him that he could travel back at weekends to see her. Just like I had, Helmut took to farming very quickly and enjoyed the rural life and the health-giving aspect of working outside.

On 23rd August came the news that the Foreign Ministers of Germany and the Soviet Union, Joachim von Ribbentrop and Vyacheslav Molotov had signed a document that was officially called the Treaty of Non-Aggression between Germany and the Union of Soviet Socialist Republics. Hildegard and I were both very sceptical about this knowing full well how much Hitler and Stalin distrusted and disliked each other.

Just one week after signing the Non-Aggression Treaty, the armed forces of Germany invaded Poland. Over nine million radios had been sold cheaply in Germany at the behest of Joseph Goebbels so that he could indoctrinate the listeners with his propaganda. These people's receivers could only be tuned to the Nazi station. Listening to foreign stations was banned. But we had been left a radio by Abraham that we could tune into foreign stations including the BBC.

We were aware of Britain's final ultimatum letter to Germany, delivered at nine a.m. on Sunday 3rd September. The Foreign Secretary Lord Halifax had written it, stating that unless Hitler's troops withdraw from Poland, Britain will fulfil its obligations to Poland. The demands were dismissed.

We sat in the kitchen glued to the BBC broadcast band. We didn't have to wait long. Neville Chamberlain the British Prime Minister addressed the nation at eleven fifteen a.m. In a five-minute broadcast he announced that as Hitler had failed to respond to British demands to leave Poland, then Britain was now at War with Germany. Hitler's bluff had finally been called.

We were aware that it was not just Britain that we were at war with, Germany was also facing the armed might of the Commonwealth and France. The BBC was our only source to obtain accurate information as to what was happening. We discovered by listening to these broadcasts that the situation was changing rapidly. On 15th September it was announced that the Soviets and the Japanese had signed an armistice on the Manchurian border. The commentators concluded that this would free up Soviet troops to move to the west. And so, it was proved. Two days later Soviet troops entered Poland and advanced to the demarcation line that had been agreed with Germany.

In early November, Helmut visited his girlfriend in Munich. When he returned, he reported that there were rumours that an assassination attempt on Hitler's life had been made on 9th. He had been addressing a large audience in a beerhall but had left fifteen minutes earlier than expected. A bomb placed behind a pillar not far from where Hitler had been speaking went off killing eight and wounding sixty.

There were many Germans such as Hildegard and I who were thoroughly depressed at what was happening. We were peace loving and did not wish to go to war. Most Germans felt that the Versailles Treaty had been the root cause for many of our country's economic woes that Hitler had exploited. Several of the men in the village had now been called up. Helmut, Christian, I and two others avoided the call up owing to our status as essential agricultural workers.

We were astounded by the speed of the developments. After six weeks of heavy fighting on 10th May 1940, German forces occupied the Netherlands and Belgium. We were all stunned by the news that France had surrendered to German forces after a battle lasting just 46 days. The French army had always been considered as the most powerful in Europe. Our troops occupied Paris on 14th June.

On 22nd June there was great media coverage in Germany given to the armistice between Germany and France. The instrument of surrender documents were signed in the same converted wagon-lits, or railway sleeping car, in the forest of Compiegne, north of Paris. This was the same carriage and same venue that the French had used to accept the surrender of Germany at the end of World War One.

By the end of April 1941, German troops had occupied both Yugoslavia and Greece. Then after five days of severe fighting German forces captured the Mediterranean island of Crete. There was a real sense of euphoria in Germany. A feeling of invincibility that no one could stop Hitler. His vision of creating a Master race was looking more and more likely. Every day, Jews from Germany and the countries that it occupied were being rounded up and taken off, although many did not know where to or what their fate would be.

The biggest shock of all came with the announcement on 22nd June that an operation code named Barbarossa had commenced with German troops attacking the Soviet Union. Hitler had broken his word and the agreement that Germany would not attack the Soviet Union. The three of us, over dinner that evening speculated if Hitler had now bitten off more than he could chew.

The German army's speed in taking Soviet territory appeared almost unstoppable. By 2nd October German forces were preparing to take Moscow. It was a hugely significant day for Helmut also, when he received a telegram ordering him to report for training for a role in the Luftwaffe, north of Berlin. Our luck at avoiding the call up had run out.

The three of us had our final family meal that evening. It was all very sombre. Hildegard was especially critical of Hitler and kept repeating that she wished the assassination attempt in 1939 had been successful. Three men from the village had already lost their lives in the battle for France. Helmut was extremely subdued and hardly spoke. The following morning, we said our goodbyes. I believe that the three of us sensed that this was our final time together.

We learned on 7th December that the Japanese had attacked the American fleet at Pearl Harbour and that the United States was now at war with Germany and Japan. We both thought that this was the beginning of the end. There was no way that Germany could now be victorious fighting against, Great Britain, the Soviet Union and the United States amongst others.

Because of Helmut's agricultural skills repairing farm equipment he had been selected to train and then work as an aircraft mechanic. His letters remained quite upbeat.

We learnt from the BBC that the German city of Lubeck had been carpet bombed on 28th and 29th March 1942. The war was now coming to Germany.

The bombing resulted in a huge loss of civilian life. Everything according to the Nazi propaganda being dispensed by Goebbels painted a rosy picture. The German forces would soon be victorious with the conquest of the Soviet Union. Hildegard and I knew that this was not the case.

We exchanged letters regularly with Helmut, his spirits seem to have improved. As an aircraft mechanic we felt sure that Helmut would survive the war. At least we as parents so far, unlike so many others had been spared the horror of their offspring being sent into battle.

The German public because of the propaganda fed by Goebbels, were anticipating the news that Moscow had fallen and that the rest of the Soviet Union would fold very quickly. Weeks of waiting then turned into months, with still no announcement. Then on 19th November, the BBC announced that forces of the Soviet Union had mounted an offensive northwest of Stalingrad and had broken through the German lines trapping the 6th and 19th German army (250,000 men) in the city.

One week later we received a letter from Helmut advising that he had been selected and transferred for pilot training. That was our very last communication with our dear son. A little over a month later in January 1943 we received a telegram from the Air Ministry advising us that Helmut's Junker fighter plane had been shot down whilst on a mission for the battle of Stalingrad. The telegram concluded that we should be proud of Helmut as he had sacrificed his life in the service of his country.

We were both devastated. It was as though a light had been extinguished in our lives. Hildegard became thoroughly depressed. She stopped going out. She discontinued with her music lessons for the village children and did not even play herself. She couldn't bear to listen to the radio. She ceased cooking our meals and began smoking cigarettes, something that she had never previously done. Most of her time was spent in the bedroom with the curtains closed. I became extremely worried. Ursula came around several times, but Hildegard refused to see her.

It was now mid-February. I returned home at around six in the evening after Christian and I had completed milking the cows. I was tired and also feeling down. I entered the house and was surprised when I walked into our bedroom not to find Hildegard there. I instinctively knew that something was wrong. I ran into every room calling her name. I then ran outside and checked the two outbuildings and the garage. No Hildegard. I was becoming frantic. I remembered thinking of the advice that my own father had given me when he said, 'have nothing to do with panic,' much easier said than done.

I collected my powerful torch from the hallway and then ran into the garden.

The beam of light from the torch was frantically searching and penetrating the darkness. And then, there she was, suspended from a tree one metre off the ground. I let out a manic shriek like that of a distressed animal that had been caught in a trap. I quickly took the knife that I always carried for work, from my trouser pocket and cut through the rope.

Hildegard had chosen to stand on the wooden seated swing that we had put up for visiting young children to play on. This had allowed her to pass her rope over the hanging bough supporting the swing. After looping the rope around her neck, she had just jumped off the swing.

I held her tightly as the knife cut through the last frayed strands. I didn't want her to fall. I quickly released the rope from her neck and placed my fingers there in the forlorn hope that I might find a pulse. I knew there would be no pulse. Hildegard's body was cold, and I suspect she had been hanging there for several hours. I was on my knees, cradling her head in my arms and sobbing uncontrollably. I lost all track of time, but it must have been well over an hour before I could bear to move.

I lifted her in my arms and carried her into the house and placed her on our bed. I was struck by how peaceful and serene she now looked. The pain of losing our only son had been all too much. As I sat there, my eyes were drawn to an envelope that I had missed seeing when I had come into the bedroom earlier.

One of Hildegard's many interests had been calligraphy, her handwriting was a thing of rare beauty. Whereas most of us wrote merely as a means of conveying our thoughts, she had turned handwriting into an art form. It resembled Harlow Solid Script. Her writing was an exercise in total symmetry. The envelope was simply addressed to *My Darling Otto*.

My Darling Otto – You are the man that I have adored for these past twenty-two years. Life with you has always been such fun, even during these last few difficult years. You have been a wonderful lover, my best friend and confidant. You are also the kindest and most considerate of humans. I know how it must have been a struggle for you when you were appointed by the Führer to work in Dachau. I am consoled that you never took part in any acts of cruelty or worse whilst there. I realise now that millions of us have been complicit in assisting Hitler to have become the total dictator that he now is. We both shared a gut feeling that he would not be good for us, but never imagined that he would end up as Chancellor and President.

You can take solace from the fact that you saved the lives of Leah and Eliana. And although all of Abraham's assets have been transferred to you, it was better that they were than to someone else. As fate would deem, you were responsible for saving the lives of Abraham and Hannah and the three families who as we know are now safe and beginning a new chapter in their lives.

You have been a wonderful father to Helmut. I blame Hitler for Helmut's death and the destruction of our country and the misery that he has caused millions of people to suffer. You and I have never truly believed in God and the afterlife. I am though, now hoping that we are mistaken and that I will be reunited with Helmut soon and that one day the three of us may be together.

In the meantime, my darling you must carry on. So many people in the village depend on your generosity just to keep them alive. Thank Christian and Ursula for being such good friends. You are only 54 years old Otto, please remarry and make another woman as happy as I have been. Gertrude one of your camp secretaries I know was sweet on you.

I am so sorry Otto that I have proved to have been so weak when you and others are so strong. But I just have no will left to carry on with no end to our misery in sight. I have loved you so much my darling. Take care. Love Hildegard xxx

I waited until the following morning before contacting the relevant authorities. Everyone was exceedingly kind. Christian and Ursula suggested that they stay at my home until after Hildegard's funeral. The funeral was held some days later in the village church. A church that we had seldom attended. I believe that the entire village turned out to say farewell. I realised then how popular and much loved she had been. Father Benedict conducted an appropriate service.

I carried on running the farm with Christian and two others for a further six months. I decided that I needed to move away. I sent a message to Herman Goering in the hope that he would remember me and offering my services as an administrator in the Air Ministry. To my surprise he responded and offered me a job at headquarters as well as sending his condolence for the loss of Helmut.

It was arranged before I left for Berlin that Christian, and Ursula would move into our house and run the farm as efficiently as they always had. 'You, Christian,' I said before leaving, 'are in total charge. Carry on as if you were Abraham.' It was now mid-June 1943.

I reported to the Luftwaffe Headquarters as directed and began my job as an administrator. I was tasked with keeping tabs on the production of aircraft, this also involved the development of a new weapon that the hierarchy was sure would win Germany the war, it was called the V2 rocket and was being developed by a brilliant engineer called Wernher Von Braun.

It became apparent to me that Germany was losing the war. The prospect of being taken prisoner by the Soviet Union who would be targeting Berlin filled me with horror. I decided then that I would prefer to die in battle. I then requested a transfer to the army and found myself allocated as a Panzer tank radio operator. I had the rank of Private Soldier.

I then found myself quicky in action as our 5th Panzer Army made its way through France and finally in August 1944, we were defending our lines around the Normandy town of Falaise. We were under the command of Field Marshal Walter Model, who was well respected by those who served with him. The fighting was ferocious. I am not sure how many Allied tanks we had destroyed, we were up against mainly the British Cromwell tanks that were inferior to the firepower and armour plating of our Panzers.

Then suddenly there was a crashing sound, and our tank came to an abrupt halt as if hitting a brick wall. The temperature inside became instantly unbearable. I was the farthest crew member from the front. Immediately the gunner sitting in front of me was swearing and cursing a stream of obscenities, quickly opened the hatch and climbed out followed by the gun loader, I followed next, quickly glancing as I did so to the front where the commander and the driver remained motionless in their seats.

As my head came through the hatch, I was greeted with a wall of flames, our vehicle was seriously on fire. The noise all around was deafening. I jumped to the ground and rolled over several times. My two colleagues stood up and began to run back towards our lines, they had only managed a few steps each when they were both felled, I assume by enemy bullets. The noise was so deafening it was impossible to distinguish different sounds.

I lay still for several minutes and then I began to crawl forward on my stomach before sliding down into a ditch. It was exceedingly difficult to see, but I realised that I had stumbled on to a dead body. I immediately froze, not sure what I should do. Then when my night vision had cleared, I looked closely, and could see that the corpse was a dead Tommy. Without consciously thinking, I rolled the corpse over and with great difficulty removed his great coat. I then discarded my own head gear and tunic and with much effort managed to put on the newly acquired great coat.

I continued to make my way along the ditch without encountering any more dead Tommies. It was extremely muddy, after a hundred metres or so, the ditch flattened out a little and I realised that it would soon no longer afford me any cover. As I peered back towards my own lines, I made out the silhouette of a German infantryman with rifle in hand. Without thinking I stood up and called out. I had never experienced such pain before, the soldier must have thought that I was the enemy and fired.

I opened my eyes very slowly; it was if the lids were stuck together and were gently being unglued. At first, I was having difficulty in focussing but gradually my vision cleared, and I could see above me there was green canvas. My ears were still filled with a ringing sound that must have occurred when the shell hit our tank. I imagine that I was on some sort of stretcher because without warning two men appeared and with one at the head and the other at the foot, they lifted it up and carried me through into another tent. Then a face loomed over me.

He was dressed as a surgeon with rubber gloves a mask, a hat, and an apron which I noticed was bloodstained. With his fingers he opened and examined my eyes with a small torch. I then heard him announce that I was alive and that it would appear judging by the blood that I had been shot in my left shoulder. He then issued a command to someone out of my sight, to remove my coat and strip me down to the waist.

I felt two pairs of hands very gently rolling me over onto my right side whilst they removed my arm from the great coat. Then all hell broke loose.

'For fuck's sake Don look who we've got here! A fucking Nazi no less.' Then looking straight into my eyes, I saw for the first time a face full of hatred and scorn. He was so wound up that he was spitting out the words, I feared that he was going to punch me in the face as he continued. 'You fucking Nazi bastard, you were trying to kill us all and we were being shot at by your fucking friends as we rescued you!'

Before he had chance to continue, he was interrupted. 'Thank you, Corporal, who do we have here?'

'A fucking Nazi, that's who we've got here sir!'

'Thank you, men. I would hope that if ever you had the misfortune to be wounded in battle and were found by the enemy, that like us now with this patient, they would take care and look after you. All civilised nations whilst at war are governed by the Geneva Convention. Friend and foe when injured are accorded the same respect. Thank you Corporal, you and your colleague have both performed your duty.'

I looked at the man hovering above me and I could see by his startled reaction that I surprised him when I spoke in perfect English. 'Thank you, sir, I empathise with the sentiments just now expressed by my rescuers. I feel that we have been turned into a nation of Barbarians.'

'Unfortunately, war brings out the very worst in people,' he replied. 'Let us not dwell on that, what has happened to you?' Answering his own question. 'Ah, I can see what has happened to you, you have been shot in the left shoulder. I am amazed that you have not lost more blood, perhaps it was the great coat that saved you. The good news for you is that at first glance this does not look serious. I am going to carry out what is called an arthroscopic procedure. If successful you should be back as normal in just three or four months.' There were two female nurses present. 'I regret,' he continued 'that we have little in the way of anaesthetic and so this is going to hurt.'

He was not wrong there. The pain was excruciating but subsided greatly when he had located and carefully removed the bullet which he dropped into a tin bowl with a clang. 'Well, that's not one of ours,' he said. 'Your friends must have thought you were trying to defect to the winning side.'

During the procedure he had been continually asking me questions about my life, my family and where I came from. It was apparent that he was a kind, considerate man who genuinely was asking questions because he was interested in the answers. I thought, how is it that we are at war and fighting one another?

It did not make sense.

'Well, that's you done,' I heard him say. 'Good luck, I hope that you will be able to return to your home and resume a better life in the not-too-distant future. Next.' I heard him say and he was gone and with that I was being moved to another tent which was in effect a field recovery ward. I asked one of the nurses the name of the surgeon, she replied that his name was Major McKee.

A month later I was shipped over to Portland in Dorset and then onto a place called Devizes in Wiltshire. This is where prisoners of war were processed before being dispersed to various parts of Britain. Several weeks later I was sent to a Yorkshire town called Malton, and to camp number 83. For the best part of four years, I worked on the land. My experience of running the estate back home and what I had learnt from Christian was soon recognised and I was given a more senior role in managing the farm. We were, under the circumstances very well cared for. There was little hostility from the local inhabitants.

CHAPTER 8

It was in June 1948 that I was informed that I was free to return to Germany. I felt very nervous, unsure of what I would find. I boarded a train in Calais and after several changes I arrived at Munich. It had been three years since the German surrender. The four allies, Britain, France, the United States and the Soviet Union had governed Germany through the Allied Control Council. There were tensions mainly involving the different ideologies of the Soviet Union and the others.

On that very day when I was travelling home, the Soviet Union had blockaded Berlin. The only way for food and supplies to reach the inhabitants was by air. A concerted effort by Britain, the United States and France commenced with planes flying supplies in, twenty-four hours a day.

The journey back to Bischofswiesen took me three days. The aftereffects of war were to be seen everywhere. Bombed out buildings and piles of rubble still awaiting removal.

The bus chugged to a halt, and I apprehensively got off not knowing what to expect. I trudged alone down the track to the former home of Abraham Benowitz. As I approached the front door, I could not help but to glance to the right at the tree where Hildegard had so sadly ended her life. I clasped the iron door knocker and knocked twice.

I heard a dog bark and then approaching footsteps from inside. The door opened and to my absolute delight there standing in front of me was Ursula. She let out a squeal and we both simultaneously moved into one another's outstretched arms and tightly hugged each other. Emotion came to the fore once more with me trying to restrain the tears but Ursula showing no signs of such inhibitions.

Schwarzer, their German Shepherd dog was as excited as we were. He was jumping up and down, furiously wagging his tail whilst continuing to bark. 'Look,' cried Ursula,' Schwarzer still remembers you. Come inside, I will go to the farm and fetch Christian, I will only be ten minutes.'

As soon as I crossed the threshold, I set down my suitcase and went on a quick reconnaissance, familiarising myself with a house that I had left five years before. None of the rooms had changed. On top of the staircase there hanging was the picture that I had painted of Leah and Eliana with their violins. I felt a knot in my stomach. Just then I heard the front door opening.

Christian quickly removed his cloth cap and stepped forward to shake my hand and to clasp me around the shoulder. We were both caught up in the unexpected circumstance of my returning without warning.

Ursula then ran a hot tub for me to soak in. Christian handed me a glass of schnapps before I went into the bathroom. It dawned on me that this was the first bath that I had experienced since leaving the house for Berlin. How I enjoyed it. I lay there in a contemplative mood inevitably thinking about Hildegard and Helmut. My mind then turned to Abraham, Hannah, Leah and Eliana. I wandered how they were all doing.

Ursula had prepared and cooked a wonderful roast pork dinner. 'Pork?' I queried.

'Yes,' Christian replied, 'shortly after you left for Berlin, we were visited by a Nazi official from the department of agriculture. Germany was conscious that it had to maximise every square inch of available land. Pigs don't need a lot of room, so we now have around 200 at present in the field that we grew wheat in during your last year. Every year we rotate to another field. It is amazing the increase in crop yield that results following on using the field that was used for pigs the previous year.'

'If Abraham had still have been here, then that would have been the final insult for such a religious man,' I said.

For the next hour or so, I briefly explained what had happened to me and in return heard about the plight of those in the village. Sixteen young men had been taken and lost their lives. I felt depressed and despondent, although I knew that I shouldn't be. The wicked regime had been defeated and we were now at the start of a new beginning. I embraced Ursula and Christian and retired to bed.

Ursula and Christian, out of respect I imagine, had not taken the main bedroom for themselves after I had departed, but instead one of the guest rooms. I climbed into the bed and pulled up the covers. This was the most comfortable bed that I had been in since I had left five years previously.

I was awoken with a slight knocking on the bedroom door. Ursula entered carrying a breakfast tray. 'Good morning Otto,' she cheerfully said. 'You have slept for just over twelve hours, you must have been exhausted?'

I sat up whilst Ursula drew back the curtains. A shaft of sunlight penetrated the room, and I could hear the birds singing. I thought to myself, 'Otto you have survived. You must stop feeling sorry for yourself and make a new start and above all, maintain the legacy of Abraham by helping others.'

From the day that we had entered *Schlachthaus* and got to know Ursula and Christian, they had become so close as almost for me, to regard them as my brother and sister. Ursula was three years older than me, whilst Christian was now sixty-four, five years my senior.

I ate my breakfast and then after spending time in the bathroom, which I now realised was one of life's pleasures that we all took for granted. The feeling of being clean and having clean teeth, I would from now on, look upon with appreciation. The same I thought after changing into my clean clothes. It is not until you are without these things, and I include being fed, that you realise just how much these things are accepted as being almost our right and never considered for what they truly are.

For breakfast Ursula had boiled me two fresh eggs from our own hens. The crusty bread that accompanied my breakfast, she had baked herself overnight. The marmalade also was what she had made. During my journey home from England, I had witnessed many beggars whose only concern for the day was to avoid hunger. I stood up bringing myself to my full height.

I cannot say if it was the spirit of Abraham, but I suddenly felt full of resolve.

Christian was in the kitchen eating a sandwich, which for him was his lunch. 'Otto, my friend,' he said. 'You look refreshed and ready to go.'

'Once you have finished your lunch Christian, I would like you to take me on a tour of the farm and bring me fully up to speed with what the situation is now and what took place during my absence.'

After Christian had finished his lunch, we went outside, I was surprised to see an ex-US army jeep, which Christian advised me had been discarded as being broken down. He had recovered it and repaired it to full working order.

I said, 'Is there anything that you cannot do?'

Christian turned the ignition and threw the vehicle into gear, and we were on our way. When we arrived at the farm buildings which housed the equipment and storage facilities, Christian introduced me to two recently employed farm hands, Frederick and Willey. They were both in their late teens and had mercifully avoided being called up. I vaguely remembered them as boys from the village. We stood and chatted, and they appeared to be so grateful that Christian had given them the chance of employment and a regular income. They were also pleased that I had survived the war and was now back.

We continued on our journey visiting all the livestock. There was now a herd of just over two hundred Murnau-Werdenfels dairy cattle. In addition to the cattle, there was a flock of one hundred and four Bavarian Forest sheep. These, Christian advised me had proved to be a sound investment. They didn't need too much looking after, the ewes produced a high percentage of twins, the meat was good, and the fleece normally weighed around 3.5 kilograms. with the rams and 3.00 kilograms with the ewes.

The last field that we visited was where the chickens roamed. There seemed to be too many to count. The breed was Ausburger which were here before I left. I remembered that they were a dual-purpose breed, with good meat qualities. The hens I knew laid approximately 180 white eggs each year.

Finally, we finished at the quarry. Christian pulled up in front and switched off the ignition. We sat there for a moment or two, neither of us speaking.

I then turned and spoke. 'Christian, the day before Abraham left, he confided in me that a network had been set up which involved many items of great value being brought to this place. Over a period of time how you and he under the cover of darkness, stored these items inside the tunnel and how when completed you sealed the tunnel with two metres of concrete, taking extreme care to ensure that the concrete blended into the wall could not be detected.'

'Yes Otto, Abraham confided in me that he had told you just as we said our goodbyes. You and I are the only ones to know of this. When the items were brought to us, we always took delivery of them inside the barn. Those dropping off the items had no idea where they were being hidden. Even my wife Ursula has no knowledge of what took place.

'Last year we were visited by the members of the State Bavarian Police. I was surprised to see that the Chief of Police himself was present. He advised me that it had been reported that a huge stash of stolen artefacts had been brought here during the early months of 1938. Naturally, I acted with total disbelief and denied all knowledge. The Chief Inspector produced a Search Warrant, that I noticed had been signed by himself. He then ordered a full search.

'I could not believe how thorough they were. Every nook and cranny were looked into. Floorboards were pulled up, cavity walls were inspected, the house attic was given a thorough going over. The farm buildings were almost pulled apart. Then a systematic inspection of all the fields, using amongst other things, metal detectors, I imagine to locate a possible burial place.

'Of course, their efforts yielded nothing. The very last thing that was looked at was the quarry. This did cause me a good deal of anxiety. Pneumatic drills were called in and where Abraham and I had cemented the entrance, because it was a flat vertical surface this is where the drilling began. They removed about one metre of rock inside before concluding that it was just part of the quarry. They drilled and tried excavating other parts, but all with the same negative result.

'They were here for just over five weeks, so clearly they were convinced that the information that they had received was accurate and believable. In the end the Chief of Police came to me. I was shocked when he grabbed me by the lapels and pushed me against the wall. He made it abundantly clear, that should it be found that I was lying and what they were looking for was discovered, then he personally would ensure that I would never again see the light of day.'

'Who do you think tipped them off?' I asked.

'I have no idea. The treasures came from far and wide, including Vienna. It could well have been one of the priests trying to curry favour and I imagine there would also be a substantial financial benefit to whoever provided information that would lead to the recovery of the hidden items. Every item was meticulously recorded and logged from where it had come from. There is a ledger sealed inside the cave along with the items.'

'Abraham was a fine judge of character Christian. He knew that you would never betray him or break your pledge. I have nothing but respect for you. I admire your steadfastness and your loyalty.'

At the conclusion of the evening meal, we adjourned to the living room accompanied by a bottle of the estate's red wine. After we had toasted one another, Ursula asked the question that I had been expecting. 'Otto, you were away for almost five years and never once did you write. In times of war, we don't subscribe to the maxim 'that no news is good news'. So many parents have no idea the fate of their sons especially those that fought on the Eastern Front.

'Many were killed, sadly as you can relate to, but thousands were taken prisoners by the Soviets and are still prisoners and few people know who they are. It is terrible. It is so distressing as a parent constantly hoping that your son may still be alive.

'We felt much the same about you. We were both worried sick Otto, a simple letter would have meant so much. Every day, I would check the post in the blind hope that you had written and that you were safe and well. Fortunately, yesterday when you unexpectedly arrived, our sheer relief and pleasure at seeing you again, overcame our shock and anger. It is wonderful to have you back home where you belong but the pain and worry that you have caused us could have been prevented.'

'Sorry is of course such a tiny, but important word. I knew that you would be concerned and yet I selfishly ignored your pain. This was not deliberately done to cause you stress and anguish, I am truly sorry for my inconsiderate actions. Once I became a prisoner of war and was sent to the north of England, I worked on the land with my fellow prisoners. The production of food for the very survival of Britain, with so many men away fighting the war, was essential.

'Not since I was a librarian in Vienna had I found such peace of mind. Here I was, no conflict, no violence. I am being housed, okay I admit nothing like what I was used to whilst living here with Hildegard, but I was fed and had no responsibilities or worries. My mind was completely uncluttered. I then considered that I wished to forget my past. The two personal tragedies that I had suffered, one can never eradicate from one's mind.

'I seriously considered staying in Britain or else to emigrate to the United States. But then just a few weeks ago I was advised that I would be repatriated. It was then that I was hit with a feeling of guilt that I was breaking my word to Abraham. I remembered that I pledged that I would maintain his legacy by helping as many of the villagers who need our support. It was then that I realised that my lack of concern and actions towards the two of you was unforgivable. I am truly ashamed of myself. You have been such steadfast and loyal friends, that I have completely let you down. I really am so sorry; it was thoughtless and unkind of me.'

Silence followed. Then Ursula said, 'Anyone for another glass of wine?' I opened my arms as she came to replenish my wine and gave her a hug. 'It's just as well that you have returned.' She continued, 'just three weeks ago, the Chief of the Bavarian Police, the one who had authorised the detailed search of the estate gave us another visit. This time it was to inform us that as you had not returned, it was presumed that you had been killed in the battle of Normandy and therefore all of your assets would pass over to the State.'

Christian after taking a sip of his wine, then spoke. 'I then produced the letter of authorisation that you had given me the day before you left. It was a conditional will. The condition being that it would come into effect only when it was proved that you were deceased. And as you had instructed, we had this certified legally by a firm of attorneys in the Austrian city of Linz. The will stated that in the event of your death, you had left the entire estate to Ursula and me.

'I could see that this came as a shock to the Chief of Police. He then challenged me as to why you would leave such an estate to someone who was little more than a farm peasant. I replied that I really didn't know and that perhaps you liked us.

'He was clearly incredibly angry at these unexpected circumstances. Now that you have returned, then the status quo has been restored.' After a short pause, Christian then carried on. 'I began working here for Abraham's father in 1900 as a sixteen-year-old. Indeed, Ursula joined three years later and that was when we first met. This farm and house are all that we have known. Now that you are back Otto, it is now time that Ursula and I retired. Abraham and Hannah paid us well and we have enough savings to see us through to the end.'

This was the last thing that I had expected to hear. Somehow, I had assumed that Christian and Ursula would always to be part of the estate. It could not be denied that they had both been invaluable to Abraham and Hannah. They were part of the family.

I thought for a moment, and then I said, 'For all that you have done over so many years, you deserve to retire happily. The problem that I have is, who can replace you?'

Ursula shot Christian a quick glance before picking up her wine glass and taking a sip, perhaps a signal for Christian to continue, which he did.

'We would not leave you Otto, without ensuring that you were in safe hands. In your absence I employed a gardener, Frank Meyer, he is twenty-five years old. I have huge confidence that I can train him to manage the estate in the same way as I have. There is also a lady called Tanya van der Leyen, she is twenty-four years old, single and has recently moved to Bischofswiesen from Salzburg. She has been working as a maid for the Louden family on the outskirts of the village, but they have decided to sell up and are moving to Stuttgart. Therefore, in two months' time she will be looking for a new position.'

I sat there in thought, gazing at the flames from the open log fire. Ursula then picked up from where Christian had left off. 'If you are in agreeance Otto, we will give you six months' notice. That will give us enough time to fully train Tanya and Frank.'

'That is very kind of you both and I am grateful for your thoughtfulness. A quality that I wish that I shared with you. Please engage the pair, I trust your judgement fully with this. I don't believe that any arrangement has been set up for a pension of any kind for you. I will arrange before you leave that you are in receipt each week half of what you would have been earning had you still been employed.'

And with that we continued chatting for the rest of the evening until finally retiring to bed.

One-week later Frank joined Christian as his deputy estate manager, part time gardener. This was followed eight weeks later with the arrival of Tanya van der Leyen. As neither owned their own property, it was deemed beneficial if both lived in the house. There were after all, several spare bedrooms.

The six months as I had thought quickly came and went. On the final day of Christian and Ursula's employment, I arranged for Tanya to cook a lavish meal with the help of Frank, in honour of my two departing friends. It was a joyous occasion. I imagined beforehand that it would be very solemn and that tears would be shed as we said our uncomfortable farewells. But how wrong was I?

The entire evening was just full of laughter. Just before my two honoured guests left, Christian produced an envelope out of Ursula's handbag.

'Otto,' he said, 'this is the copy of your will, signing the estate over to us, should you not return from the war. We are exceedingly pleased to say that you have returned and that this document is now null and void. Please find someone who is worthy to inherit the estate and who will continue to honour the principles of Abraham.'

As they were leaving, I reminded them that they were to dine with us, by us I meant Tanya and Frank, who already I had become fond of, every couple of weeks. With that I waved them off and returned to the lounge for a nightcap. For me, the will I had written would remain in force and that Christian and Ursula would remain the benefactors. I now realised that a new chapter in my life was about to commence.

CHAPTER 9

I was surprised by how seamless the transition from Christian and Ursula being replaced by Frank and Tanya was. The previous incumbents had imparted all their knowledge to two willing recipients who were eager to please.

It was three months later. I was in the library which I also used as an office, when Tanya knocked at the door to advise me that a Herr Adenauer, Chief of the Bavarian Police force had called to see me. I asked Tanya to show him in, I was curious to see what this man looked like and what the reasons were for his visit.

He entered the room with the demeanour of me being his long-lost friend. He shook my hand warmly, gripping it tightly. When he stood back, I asked him if he would like a schnapps.

'A schnapps?' he exclaimed. 'I have never been known to turn down the offer of a drink my dear fellow.'

I poured the drinks. There were two armchairs in the room, I invited him to sit in one, whilst I took the other, the one nearest the door.

'I am puzzled Herr Adenauer as to what I owe the pleasure. I believe that you and your small army of men spent five weeks here tearing the place apart during my absence.'

'I regret Herr Wagner that we were in receipt of some false intelligence.'

'What intelligence was that?'

'We had received information that during the early part of 1938 a network of religious zealots, mainly Jews, but also some Catholic priests had looted their churches and had transferred the items for safe keeping to another place. Our informant convinced us that it was here. As you have been made aware, a search was carried out, but absolutely nothing was found.

Sadly, our informant is no longer with us, he tragically had an unfortunate accident.'

'What sort of accident?'

'He was a Catholic priest. It would appear that he took a walk in the hills near to where he lived. He must have slipped and hit his head on a rock.' Winking at me, he continued. 'If you know what I mean?'

I took a sip of my drink. Purposely, I remained silent and let the Chief of Police continue.

'I understand from our research Herr Wagner that you were a friend of the Führers and that you became one of the founding members of The German Workers Party. Indeed, you were a member before Hitler joined.'

I continued my silence.

'Then you became an administrator or perhaps nowadays we would say personal assistant to the Führer. You arranged his diary, his speaking engagements and typed out his speeches. And then in 1933 at the request of our Führer, you accepted the position to help establish the first concentration camp at Dachau. I would think an immensely proud moment for you?'

I said nothing.

Undeterred, Herr Adenauer continued I believe in the hope that he would impress me by his knowledge of my life. 'And then my friend, because of the polices brought in by Himmler and the Führer, you hit the jackpot and managed to nab for yourself this valuable and profitable farming estate owned by the Jewish businessman Abraham Benowitz.

'You resigned from Dachau and concentrated on making loads of money running your newly acquired enterprise. Then surprisingly, you left this and joined the Air Ministry in Berlin before leaving in order to train as a radio operator stroke assistant driver of a Panzer tank. The last record that we have, is that of your involvement in the heroic battle in defending Normandy from the Allied Forces. we assumed that you had given your life for the Fatherland.'

He stopped and looked at me. I am sure he was hoping that I would congratulate him on the accuracy of his account. Instead,

I said, 'I was wounded in the Battle of Normandy and was subsequently held for almost four years as a prisoner of war. This could have been fate, for it saved me from joining the millions of other dead Germans who had needlessly been slaughtered on the altar of one man's and his cohorts' egos.'

In an instant I surveyed the palpable change in Herr Adenauer's attitude. This was a man who clearly was not used to having anyone express views directly to him which were contrary to his own beliefs. His insincere smile was replaced with a tight-lipped anger which I could see he was having difficulty in restraining.

I continued before he had chance to comment. 'The British authorities I found whilst in their custody to be both honourable and efficient. We were all told, and I had no reason to doubt them, that a little time after the cessation of hostilities, the authorities of each German State such as Bavaria were sent a complete list of all Germans who were the Guests of His Majesty King George VI. Therefore, I would suggest Herr Adenauer that you knew full well that I had not perished like so many others.

'I put it to you, that you saw an opportunity to take over the former Benowitz estate that was legally transferred to me for yourself. How unworthy for a man in your position? But then unfortunately for you, I had made a contingency will in the event of my death in favour of Christian and Hannah Schmidt.'

A period of what seemed like, prolonged silence ensued. I could see that he was struggling to regain his composure, which he achieved brilliantly like a skilled actor.

'Nothing like that Herr Wagner. I and others are very pleased that you have survived and are now back efficiently managing once more this estate.'

'What others?' I asked.

'An organisation was created after the war to assist many of your former colleagues who had escaped retribution. Many of them had to assume new identities and are now working in menial jobs.'

'You mean like peasant farm workers such as Christian Schmidt who you couldn't believe was the new owner of an estate that he had been running successfully for years?'

'My apologies, I misjudged the capabilities of Herr Schmidt. No, there are several hundred of struggling members who were totally loyal to the Nazi Party.'

'This may come as a shock to you Herr Adenauer. First of all, the war is now over. Fortunately, Hitler is no longer with us, and his cancerous policies died when we were defeated. And secondly, I like millions of others did not support or actively agree with what was going on. We realised all too late, much to our shame which will be with us until the day we die.'

'I would be very careful if I were you Herr Wagner. You would be surprised by just how many of your former colleagues feel that the Germans are the Master Race. They would be most upset and disappointed to hear now of your treachery.'

'You mean that I could also have the misfortune of falling over whilst on a hill walk and hit my head on a nearby rock? I promise you Herr Adenauer, I will watch my step. Now if you are done, I will escort you to your car.'

I was understandably very cautious and nervous of what might happen after Herr Adenauer's visit. I did not wish to frighten Frank and Tanya, so I told them to look out for anything unusual.

It was about a year later when the tragic news of Christian and Ursula's suicide was revealed. According to the coroner, they had made a pact to die together by connecting a hose pipe to the exhaust pipe of their car and then via the boot of the car drilled a hole for the hose pipe to pass into the interior of the car and then to run the engine. They had left a suicide note on the dashboard.

All five of us had enjoyed a wonderful evening together several days before, during one of our fortnightly get togethers. They were as happy as I had ever seen them. Christian had found a new hobby of bee keeping. We were the recipients of his bees' hard work, when he would on each visit bring a jar of delicious honey. Ursula had thrown herself into several village projects.

I attended their funeral along with the rest of Bischofswiesen, they were an extremely popular and well-loved couple. I looked around at those in attendance all of whom I knew. Except for two well-built muscular men who made no attempt in concealing themselves. I approached them after the service.

'Good afternoon gentlemen,' I said. 'I don't recall having seen you before?'

'You are correct Herr Wagner,' said the taller of the two. 'We read about this tragedy and just wished to come down and pay our respects.'

'That's very kind of you. Will we see you again?'

'Not if everyone does the right thing, you won't.'

'I understand,' I said. 'Now if you will excuse me, I have business to attend to.'

Upon arriving home, I poured a glass of schnapps and took it into the library sat down in the armchair and considered what my next move should be. The beneficiaries of my will were no longer alive. I realised that I was the last surviving member of the Wagner family. There were no siblings, cousins, or children. Quite a chilling thought. It was also clear that there was some ex-Nazi organisation that had already disposed of a priest as well as my two good friends. Clearly, they were to be taken as a serious threat.

The following day I advised Tanya and Frank that I would be travelling to Munich for a few days before taking a week's holiday to be spent in the north of England.

My first port of call after arriving in Munich was to the City's library. I spent a couple of hours researching the backgrounds of the different law firms in the City. I finally found what I was looking for. I left the library and made a telephone call from the booth outside. I arranged an appointment for the following day at ten a.m. with a long-established law firm called Muller and Schneider.

I arrived a minute or two before my appointment and was met by a young man in his late teens. 'Good morning Herr Wagner, I will show you into my father's office.'

There to greet us was a man in his fifties who had the looks of an academic professor. A full head of wild white hair with glasses that made him look very studious. 'Good morning Herr Wagner, I see that you have already met my son Dieter. I understand that you wish to prepare and for us to witness your Last Will and Testament?'

'I do. It is a simple will. I am the legal owner of a farm estate and large house that was transferred to me in November 1938 under a decree forcing all Jews to transfer their retail businesses into Aryan hands. The previous rightful owner was a gentleman by the name of Abraham Benowitz. I have continued to run the estate in the manner in which I hope that he would have approved.

'I have no direct descendants to inherit my assets. However, there is a man, an Englishman who saved my life in 1944. I believe his name was Major McKee, he was a surgeon in the British Army Medical Corp and served in France during the invasion of Normandy.

'There is a caveat. I have two loyal employees who live on the estate. A Miss Tanya van der Leyen and a Mr. Frank Meyer. It is my wish that they stay in the house for the rest of their lives. Upon the death of the last survivor, I would wish you to invoke my request and discover and identify Major McKee or his own descendants as the beneficiary of my Last Will and Testament.'

'We can certainly do that for you. Of course, tracing this Major McKee would involve an unknown expense, I assume that we can reclaim this out of your estate?'

'Yes sir, you may. Also, I would be grateful if you would send a copy of this will to Herr Adenauer who is currently the Chief of Police in Bavaria.'

'Could I enquire why?' asked young Daniel.

'I believe that Herr Adenauer is connected with an organisation that assists former Nazi members who managed to avoid justice after the war. I was a member of the SS, but I have never shared the brutal doctrines of the Nazis and therefore have no desire in any way to assist Herr Adenauer and his organisation.

If you could prepare my will today, then I will call in tomorrow and sign it off.'

'We will gladly do that for you Herr Wagner.' Gunther Muller then stood up and held out his hand that I shook. 'My son Dieter will show you out. Until tomorrow Herr Wagner. Good day, sir.'

After signing the documents, the following day, I then caught the train bound for Paris and then onto Calais where I boarded a ferry to Dover. I made my way to London and then onto Yorkshire where I visited my old prisoner of war camp at Malton. I didn't seek anyone out; it was just a sentimental journey.

Afterwards I made my way into the ancient market town of Wetherby, a town in West Yorkshire which is situated on the River Wharfe. I had made an appointment with a firm of solicitors for the following morning. I found a hotel in the town and stayed for several days relaxing by doing a painting. It is an area of outstanding natural beauty.

Tanya and Frank were pleased when I arrived back. There had been no problems. They asked me about my trip to England. I told them how beautiful it was and showed them the painting that I had completed whilst there. The painting, I explained was a scene of a typical High Street found in most English towns.

Everything ticked along nicely up until 1951. The estate was making a good profit and we were still taking care of a good number of the villagers who depended on our help. My two best friends were Tanya and Frank, who were both extremely efficient at running the estate and the house.

It was in December that year when I started to feel unwell. I was suffering from back pain and had digestive problems. Also, I was losing weight and was looking jaundiced. Tanya nagged me to visit the doctor, remarkably this is something that I had never had to do previously. I realised that I was unwell and after several tests I was advised that I had pancreatic cancer and that there was nothing that could be done.

The burial of Otto Wagner took place on 6th March 1952. Tanya and Frank carried on living and working until their deaths, Frank's being the latter in 1997.

Daniel Muller and Ernst Schneider had now taken over the law firm set up by their fathers, who were now deceased. In accordance with the requirements of the will of Otto Wagner, they appointed staff to carry on and run the estate until the descendants of Major McKee could be located.

Daniel Muller also wrote a handwritten personal letter that he posted to an address in Berlin.

Chapter 10

The following day Louise and I left Vienna and drove west until we reached Salzburg. We decided to stop just outside the city at a restaurant for lunch before continuing onto Bischofswiesen. We drove past the entrance to *Schlachthaus* and into the village itself. We parked the car and then walked through the village. It was a pretty place with a village square around which were several shops, a hairdresser, one café and a bit further along was a tired looking restaurant. The square was dominated with an impressive church.

It is strange how when most people go to new places, even if they are not religious, how the church somehow always becomes a building of curiosity that you end up having a look inside. And this we did.

The huge oak door creaked loudly as we slowly pushed it open. We were greeted by the unmistakable smell of a church interior. At the back was a baptism font, two rows of pews ran either side of an aisle that led to the quire that separated the presbytery and sanctuary. Behind and above the altar was a magnificent stained glass Lancet window depicting the crucifixion of Christ.

There was a metal shelf with several candles glowing. There was a donation box and unlit candles. I put a ten euro note in the box and Louise and I took a candle each and lit it. We offered up our private thoughts.

When we stepped back, I said to Louise. 'And who were you thinking about?'

'Me? I said a little prayer for Otto Wagner, and you?'

'Mine was in memory of grandad McKay.'

Our thoughts were interrupted by the church door squeaking open. Upon being closed it revealed a man who was clearly the priest of the church. He put some prayer books onto a shelf near the entrance and then made his way towards us.

'Good afternoon and welcome to the church of the Virgin Mary, you must be visitors? We are a relatively small community and I know everyone.' Extending his hand towards Louise, he introduced himself. 'I am Father Benedict, pleased to meet you.'

'Louse Johnson, Father and this is my partner, Michael Packham.'

'What brings you to Bischofswiesen?'

Father Benedict was a man who looked priestly and kind. I would have estimated his age to have been in the early seventies.

'Just recently Father,' I began, 'I unexpectedly received a letter from a law firm advising me that after extensive enquiries, it would appear that I am the new owner of *Schlachthaus* and the farm estate. It was left to my grandfather by the owner, Otto Wagner, who died in 1952 with no surviving relatives. Did you know Herr Wagner?'

The Priest looked at us both for a moment or two and appeared to be in deep thought. And then finally he asked. 'Are you in a hurry right now? I would like to invite you back to my home for tea. I live with my sister and can recommend her fruit cake.'

'We would love to,' responded Louise. 'It would be good to know about the village and perhaps you could shed some light on the life of Otto Wagner?'

'My home is behind the church; I have to walk through the cemetery to get there. On the way I can show you where Otto is buried.'

We walked along a path for about sixty metres before cutting across a corner to the far perimeter. We stopped in front of a grey granite headstone. In gold lettering were the words, Otto Wagner 1889–1952. Underneath were the words, 'A much loved man by all who knew him.' The two plots next to Otto had similar headstones. One was for Tanya van der Leyen, deceased in 1995 and the second to Frank Meyer, deceased 1997.

'Tanya and Frank,' I said, 'they were the housekeeper and gardener at *Schlachthaus* were they not?'

'They were indeed,' responded Father Benedict, 'and the two plots next to theirs belong to the husband-and-wife, Christian and

Ursula Schmidt who died together in 1949. Ursula was the house-keeper whilst Christian was the estate manager for many years whilst loyally serving the previous owner, Abraham Benowitz.'

'How did Christian and Ursula die together? And why did Abraham sell the estate?' Louise asked.

'Ah, here we are,' Father Benedict said as he opened the gate leading onto a short pathway that led to the front of an old-world cottage.

As he opened the front door he called out. 'Elizabeth, we have company.'

Almost instantly a lady who could not be mistaken as being anything other than Father Benedict's sister bustled into view busily wiping her hands on her apron.

'Let me introduce Louise and Michael, who I suspect are English, although I have to commend Louise on speaking excellent German.'

'We are English,' I replied. 'I understand more than I can speak, but yes Louise is fluent.'

After shaking our hands Elizabeth returned to the kitchen. The three of us then entered a very cosy front room.

'Sit yourselves down and make yourself comfortable.' Father Benedict said. 'To answer your questions Louise, Christian and Ursula died of carbon monoxide poisoning. The official verdict was that they had both committed suicide, although I and others had serious reservations about that. With regard to Abraham and the estate, this was not sold to Otto, it was a forced transfer in respect of a decree in 1938 that all businesses registered by Jews, must be transferred to Aryans.'

Before either of us could answer, Elizabeth appeared holding a tray containing a pot of tea with four bone china cups and saucers and a freshly baked fruit cake.

'As it so happens,' she said, 'by coincidence, both Benedict and I are very fond of the English Breakfast tea. Milk and sugar anyone?' We both confirmed milk but no sugar.

Louise then spoke again. 'Father Benedict, what do you mean that there was doubt over the deaths of Ursula and Christian?'

'This couple had worked for many years at *Schlachthaus*. They had served Abraham, where Christian was the estate manager and I might add a very efficient one at that, whilst Ursula was the family's cook and housekeeper. When Otto took over, they continued in their roles. They retired six months after Otto returned from his incarceration as a prisoner of war in England.

'They gave six months' notice and used this time in order to train both Frank and Tanya and pass on all relevant knowledge for a seamless transition. In retirement, they were very happy and threw themselves into different village projects. Only two days before their deaths, they had attended mass and were their normal cheerful selves. They were members of the local council and had confirmed that they would be at the meeting the day after their deaths to discuss a new children's' playground project. They simply loved life. They would have been the last people that I could imagine who would have taken such a drastic course of action.

I then said, 'Well Father Benedict, if it was thought that they had not taken their own lives, how did their lives end?'

'We cannot prove it of course, for there is no evidence. But foul play was suspected.'

'You mean they were murdered?' said Louise.

'Two weeks after they were buried, Otto came and saw me. Let me say straight away, that Otto was a fine, upstanding, decent, honest man, I will explain why in a moment. But Otto confided that he had made a will and had left everything to the Schmidt's. Apparently, on his return to Germany and shortly after moving back in and taking over the estate, he was visited by the Bavarian Chief of Police. It would seem that this individual was representing an organisation whose membership consisted of people that this country is not particularly proud of.

'I might say that before Otto told me this, he had confessed to me that he had been a member of the SS during the war and asked for forgiveness. However, Abraham, just before his enforced exile had told Christian the full story of Otto's background.

'It would appear that yes, Otto was a founding member of the Nazi Party, but both he and his wife Hildegard, although supporting some policies that they thought would benefit the recovery for Germany, they were appalled by Himmler and Hitler's hatred and destruction of European Jews. By not making their views known, was a source of great regret. They were also realists that to have done so would have endangered them and their young son Helmut.

'God works in mysterious ways. Had Otto not been an administrator at Dachau, then it is highly likely that both Abraham's daughters would have perished. Otto's wife, Hildegard before she met Otto had been the girl's tutor for a number of years and was considered part of the family.

'When the decree was announced that all Jews must transfer their property to Aryans it made perfect sense to transfer it to Otto and Hildegard. Otto gave his word that should circumstances ever change and that Abraham returned, then Otto would transfer the estate back. Otto's view was that he was just looking after the estate for Abraham. Also, he gave his word that he would continue supporting those villagers that were struggling to buy food.

'The police chief was very unhappy when he learnt of Otto's arrangement. He tried to convince Otto that as a founding member of the Nazis and being an SS member that he should support the members of this organisation, many of whom were finding life difficult. This was because, I suspect that many had changed their identities and concealed what their roles had been during the war.

'The police chief was aware that Otto had no relatives. We believe that by removing the Schmidt's that Otto would then agree that there was no one else that he could justify in leaving his estate to and that the organisation would be the beneficiaries. As you both well know, Otto did not succumb. He wrote a new will, I had no idea who the beneficiary was, but he had also included an addendum that the will was not to be executed until the passing of Tanya and Frank, who were permitted to carrying on living and working in the house and on the estate.'

'Why do you think he did that?' Louise asked.

'I believe that he thought that time is a great healer. He would have figured that Tanya and Frank who were both healthy and young would probably live for a further forty or fifty years. By this time, it would not be unreasonable to think that certainly that Herr Adenauer the Chief of Police, would have passed on and perhaps the organisation or the requirements of these ex-Nazis would have all but disappeared.'

'But you don't believe they have?' I asked.

'It is sad to say that there is a substantial right-wing element in our country who believe that the policies pursued by the Nazis would have made Germany great and that they still believe in the ideal of Germans being the Master Race. The reality is that Germany is a great multi cultured country surrounded by former enemies who are now our allies and that we are now at peace. And that is how it should be. But the threat is still there, and those that still share that belief need funding. Having an estate such as *Schlachthaus* would provide a good revenue stream. I cannot work out the connection between your grandfather and Otto. Why did he leave his estate to an Englishman?'

'More tea and cake anyone?' Elizabeth enquired.

Our cups were refilled, and we all indulged in a second slice of wonderfully delicious fruit cake.

'In short, my grandfather, who was an army surgeon, saved Otto's life by removing a bullet from his shoulder during the battle of Normandy. Both Louise and I, although clearly delighted that we are the potential beneficiaries of such an unexpected windfall, nevertheless feel uneasy with what has been happening. There is a certain amount of pressure being applied on us by the law firm in Munich who are representing as they call it, a consortium of businessmen. Initially they did not wish us even to come and view the estate. They made an offer of seven million euros.'

'That has now been increased to seven and a half million euros, darling,' added Louise.

'Surely, it is not worth that amount?' observed Elizabeth, before taking another mouthful of fruitcake.

'That's a good point Sis,' remarked Father Benedict. 'I am not into real estate, but I would have thought that five million would be nearer the true value.'

'Then why should they offer us more?' enquired Louise.

'There has always been a good deal of speculation that before the outbreak of the war, a horde of treasure was hidden on the estate. Just after the war, Christian told me that a search of virtually everywhere lasting for just over five weeks was conducted by the Bavarian chief of police.

'It is also interesting to note, that after Frank Meyer died, the estate was then placed into the hands of a Law Firm called Muller and Schneider from Munich. They obtained the legal requirements to carry on running the business until such time as the beneficiary of Otto's will had been located. We in the village welcomed this. The estate does employ two men from the village who work as farm hands but also because Abraham's wishes of supporting the needy had been continued right up until Frank's death.

'Regrettably though under the stewardship of the new custodians, this benevolence and act of kindness ceased. I went myself to see the new estate manager, a man called Heinrich Merkel, just in case he was not aware of what had happened for many years previously.

'I try not to speak negatively or unkindly of anyone, but Heinrich Merkel was a man I instantly took a dislike to. His manner was brusque and dismissive. That is being kind to him. In truth it was rude and hostile. He made it abundantly clear that they were aware of what had taken place for many years and were appalled by what had happened. He emphasised in no uncertain terms that they were running a business and not a charity.

'There are now four people living permanently in the house. Two women and two men. The two men especially look more like security guards than gardeners, although the gardens I have to admit looked very well cared for. There has been a noticeable increase in security where up until Frank's death there was none.

'The entrance to the driveway of *Schlachthaus* is now controlled with an electronic gate and a surveillance camera. It is apparent that significant digging activity has taken place in the fields. It would appear that every field is being systematically excavated in turn to a depth of around two metres. This would suggest that they have solid information that the horde of treasure is buried somewhere on the estate.'

'That is very interesting Father Benedict, Louise and I are spending the night there, and tomorrow we are having a complete tour of the estate which will be conducted by Herr Merkel. Do you have any knowledge what happened to the Benowitz family?'

'Abraham and his family as you are probably aware did not worship at my church, they were Jewish. They were though religious and very supportive of their synagogue. I never received any letters from Abraham. I did hear that he had moved to the west coast of the United States with Hannah and that his two daughters had decided to stay behind in England. That is all I have, I am sorry.'

Elizabeth, then surprised us by speaking. 'Life under the Nazis was terrible. So many were being persecuted, not just the Jews, Catholic priests, academics, gypsies, disabled folk, indeed anyone who they thought either opposed them or was not fit to be called a German. During the war, we heard rumours about this camp near Munich at Dachau. We could not believe, or we refused to believe that it was almost a factory of death. The stories, that detainees were being gassed and then their bodies burned was horrifying. The tragedy is, that many who lived near Dachau knew but turned a blind eye.

'After the camp was liberated, the local population who had claimed that they were unaware of what was happening, were taken by the United States Army for a tour of the camp. There was such revulsion by the Americans and disgust that the locals did nothing. Gradually as all of Germany was conquered it then became clear as to the full extent of Himmler's persecution of the Jews especially when the full range of these extermination camps became known.

'So many lost their lives because of their beliefs. Amongst them were Titus Brandsma, a Dutch priest and philosopher, Bishop Jan

Maria Michal Kowalski and Bernhard Lichtenberg a German Roman Catholic priest just like Benedict here. Doing their best to serve God and their communities. It is good that some survived and gave testament of what had happened including Adam Kozlowiecki who later became a Polish cardinal and Oskar Mullera a well-known communist. After all these years, us Germans who lived through it still feel great shame.'

'It was not your fault,' said Louise. 'The main thing is that we are now all friends. There is a saying that I very much believe in and that is, that no matter how long you nurse a grudge, it will never get better. So, we have all moved on and are better for it. The act of forgiveness is a wonderful quality.'

I glanced at my watch and realised that we had exceeded our expected time of arrival for our meeting with Heinrich Merkel. We thanked Benedict and Elizabeth and I promised that I would keep them advised as things developed.

We pulled up at the wrought iron gates of the estate. I pressed the intercom and a lady's voice answered. 'Hi Michael, this is Ingrid, I will see you in a few minutes.' And with that the gates slowly opened, and we drove through and on towards the house.

When we pulled up outside, Ingrid was there waiting for us. 'Louise, Michael how nice to see you both again,' and surprised us by giving us both a kiss on each cheek. 'Come on in. Heinrich sends his apologies, but he has without warning been called away to an important meeting in Bonn. He should return by midmorning tomorrow. I will take care of you during your stay. Max and Fritz together with Annaliesa have left for their annual leave. Let me show you to your room.'

We entered the hallway for a second time with the adorning stag heads looking down on us once more. Although it was only three days since we were last here, we now viewed it differently. To all intense and purpose this was ours now and we took more notice of the surroundings.

'This is your room,' Ingrid confirmed. 'It is the master bedroom which overlooks the rear gardens and then onto the mountains. Is it not a beautiful sight?'

'It certainly is,' confirmed Louise. 'Do you know any of the history of this house and the estate?'

'Annaliesa and I were employed just over two years ago, to keep the house tidy and to cook for the estate workers. I have no knowledge of the estate's history.'

'What are the responsibilities of Max and Fritz?' I asked.

'Fritz is the partner of Annaliesa. The boys have several jobs, keeping the gardens in good order, odd jobs and security.'

'May I enquire who your employers are?' I asked.

'It is an organisation out of Berlin, called The Brotherhood. It is like a big club and in order to be employed you have to be a member.'

'What sort of club?'

'It is I suppose a political organisation where the members agree with the central policy which is to make Germany great again and to stop all immigration which is causing great harm to our country.'

'But Germany, very much like Great Britain is now a multi-cultural society and I would have to say, we are better off for that.'

'That is your view, Michael, but it is not one that I share. I believe that the majority of crimes committed in Germany are by people who were not born here. It is our view that Germany must be a country that is for Aryans. In other words, thorough-bred Germans.'

Louise I could tell was shocked to hear this from a relatively young woman. Without waiting for us to comment, Ingrid announced that dinner would be served in around one hour and that she had cooked especially for us, Shepherd's pie. She then left and returned to the kitchen. We then both decided to take a shower and to change.

'I thought,' said Louise, as she was drying her hair, 'that it was fortuitous that we should meet with Father Benedict and Elizabeth.'

'Yes, I agree, disturbing revelations. Of special concern is the deaths of Christian and Ursula and indeed the priest before them.'

We made our way downstairs and into the dining room which was just set for two. 'Are you not joining us, Ingrid?' Louise asked.

'No Louise, I am here to serve only. Would you care for some wine?'

The Shepherd's pie, which I have to say is one of my favourite meals was delicious and this was followed not surprisingly by Black Forest Gateau.

'Are you able to give us a tour of the house Ingrid? On our first visit, it was all a bit overwhelming, and I don't think that we took much in.'

'Yes of course, it would be my pleasure.'

We did a whole tour of the house. This time I took special interest in the various paintings that hung on the walls in several of the rooms. The first painting that caught my eye was of two lovely looking young women who were clearly twins with their violins. There in the bottom right-hand corner was the signature 'Otto Wagner, 1921'. I asked Ingrid if I could remove the picture to see if there was any information on the back. She agreed. On the back was a typed-out note. 'Leah and Eliana Benowitz'.

It was apparent that Otto Wagner had been an extremely talented artist. The painting of the girls was the only human life picture. The rest were landscapes I suspect of the estate, except for one. A picture that we both instantly recognised was that of the Vienna Opera House. Then there was another painted from the driveway, giving the first view of the property that we were now at.

Our assumptions were confirmed when we stood in front of a painting that this was the view from out of the bedroom window which we had been allocated that evening. It showed the magnificent gardens below and then stretched out across meadows until in the distance were the mountains.

They were all excellent paintings. The telephone began to ring in the hallway. Ingrid excused herself and went downstairs to answer it.

The last painting that we almost missed seeing because it was tucked away in the far corner of the library caught my attention because it was out of character with the others. This was a scene from an English town. It was as though Otto had painted it whilst standing at the top right-hand corner of a busy street and had decided to just paint the shops and premises on the opposite side, gradually tapering off towards the bottom of the street.

Otto's trademark signature appeared in the right-hand corner along with the date 1950. It was not an overly large picture, and I was able to take it down by myself and look at the back. Again, there was a type of written note, this time it read *'This is a painting of great significance'*.

'It is good,' remarked Louise, 'but I find it strange that it is so unlike all of the others. What do you think he meant by the painting being of great significance?'

I looked very closely. The first premises had the signage Carmichael's Family Solicitors. Next to Carmichael's was Woolworths and then Timothy Whites, Sainsbury's, Marks and Spencer and finally Lloyds Bank. It didn't quite seem right somehow. The town where Louise and I lived and indeed most High Streets, consisted of mostly independent shops, interspersed with national chain stores such as Sainsbury's and Boots the Chemist. This painting I suggested to Louise is not from an actual town scene but has been painted from Otto's imagination.

We heard Ingrid finishing off her telephone call with 'Okay Heinrich, will do, see you tomorrow.' We then made our way downstairs.

Ingrid was surprised that we had taken so long viewing the paintings. 'Otto was a fine artist, wasn't he?' I would think that the paintings are quite valuable,' she suggested.

'That was Heinrich on the phone, he hopes to be here a little earlier than expected tomorrow to give you a tour of the estate. I am advised to tell you that Dieter Muller also will be coming down to see you at around two tomorrow afternoon with some very good news. I understand that your flights are scheduled for nine tomorrow evening back to London?'

'They certainly are,' I responded. 'It has been a lovely few days, which both Louise and I have enjoyed very much. I think that we would like to take a stroll before we turn in, if that's okay with you Ingrid?'

'Of course, Michael, would you like me to come with you?'

'That is kind of you Ingrid, but not necessary, we will be staying close to the house. The gardens are very extensive, the sun set will be in about thirty minutes, is it possible that we may have a bottle of Champagne and two flutes? It would be lovely to enjoy a sundowner.'

'We don't have champagne as such, but we do have a much loved and popular sparkling wine that is produced from the estate's own grapes. It is pink, I think you will enjoy the taste, one moment please.'

We stepped out through the French doors and onto the patio. Me clutching the bottle of wine with Louise holding the crystal glass flutes. It was so peaceful. The only sounds were all natural. The birds were singing, and in the field at the end of the garden some new borne lambs were bleating. It was warm and still.

It was a formal garden with paths crossing at regular intervals. There were all manner of flowers and shrubs, Capability Brown would have been satisfied with this design. We continued walking about two hundred metres to the far-right hand side where there was a walled garden. As we passed under the stone archway, an ornate fountain with three statuesque mermaids came into view, with water pouring from the vases that each was holding. The sun that was now turning a deeper orange was dipping down towards the mountain peaks and in fifteen minutes would be lost to our view.

'Isn't it just wonderful?' Louise remarked. There were four benches facing north, east, south and west facing the fountain. We went and sat on the west facing bench.

Louise then held out the two champagne flutes at arm's length and I proceeded to fill them. The bubbles were certainly lively as they popped into the air above the rims of the flutes.

'Well?' said Louise. 'What shall we toast to?'

'I would like to propose a toast to Mrs Packham.'

'Your mum?' Louise responded with a note of incredulity.

'No, not my mum, although she would have been over-joyed to have been here to welcome the new Mrs Packham to our family.'

There was a fleeting moment when I could see that Louise was processing what had just been said and then a broad grin from ear to ear and finally a yelp of delight that was then replaced with spontaneous laughter. She quickly put the flutes down on the seat and flung her arms around my neck and kissed me fully on the lips. We clung tightly to one another.

When we broke from our clinching, Louise looked at me and then said, 'I don't wish to be presumptive and assume what I heard was not what I thought it was, so, over to you, my man.'

I reached into my trouser pocket and pulled out a small box. I looked at Louise and then said, 'Shall we sit?' We both sat and faced one another. With the small box in the palm of my hand, I opened the lid to reveal a ring which held particular personal significance for me.

'Miss Louise Johnson, would you please accept my invitation to become my lawful wedded wife?'

With laughter, she replied, 'Yes and yes, nothing would make me happier than to become Mrs Packham, but are you not going to go down on one knee with your proposal?'

'I believe in total equality and that we will always be equal my darling, that is why I sit here and am looking directly into your eyes.' And then I handed over the ring.

Louise took the ring and slipped it on. It was a perfect fit. 'This is lovely Michael, it looks antique?'

'It belonged to my grandma Estella who passed away in 1987. She of course was the wife of my grandad, David McKay. The reason why we are here.'

'It is absolutely beautiful. It is so lovely to have this family connection. I promise you now Michael that we will have a life that is filled with fun, and I hope two or three children. I will aim to be the wife that you deserve and a good mother as I know also that you will be both a superb hubby and daddy.'

With that we both clinked our glasses and took sips of our sparkling wine, arm in arm we continued our walk around the walled garden. A few minutes later the sun ducked behind the mountains and out of view. We extended our walk for another thirty minutes or so, by then dusk was giving way to darkness and the bottle of fizzy had been consumed.

'You both look as though you have won the lottery, observed Ingrid when we returned. 'Although I suppose by inheriting the estate in a sense you have. Have you decided to accept the monetary offer?'

'No, we haven't given that a thought,' Louise said whilst thrusting her left hand prominently showing the ring finger in front of Ingrid. 'I am delighted to say that I have just received a proposal of marriage, one which I am ecstatically happy to have accepted.'

'That's wonderful,' replied Ingrid. 'Let me be the very first to congratulate you both. Would you like another bottle of that wine?'

'It was certainly of high quality,' I said, 'although I had better be careful, as William Shakespeare had observed, too much alcohol provokes the desire, but affects the performance.' Both women giggled.

'With that in mind,' Louise said. 'Could you make us two coffees and bring them into the library please?'

'Of course, I will see you in a few minutes.'

We went into the library and looked into the game's cupboard and to Louise's delight there boxed up was one of our favourite games, *Rummikub.* Ingrid brought in the coffees and then wished us good night. We played four games and decided at two games all that would be a good time to stop. While Louise was gathering the tiles and returning them to the box before placing it back in the game's cupboard, I walked over and examined once more the painting of the English High Street.

Louise joined me and we looked at it for several minutes. 'I feel as though I am missing something,' I said.

'What you are missing,' Louise said with a tug at my sleeve, 'is making love to your fiancée.' And with that we left the library and entered our bedroom.

Our love making that night was so touchingly gentle. It truly was made in the spirit of love and not lust. It was the best experience that I had ever had. We both laid back looking up at the ceiling whilst our rapid breathing gradually slowed down and returned to normal. We remained like that for two or three minutes.

Louise then said, 'You are deep in thought, I hope you are not having second thoughts?'

I smiled and said, 'No, no second thoughts. No, the painting in the library is what I am thinking about. It has occurred to me that there is only one independent business in that painting, all the others are nationwide concerns such as Woolworths and Timothy Whites. The first and therefore most prominent in the painting was Carmichael's the family solicitors. I know that it is a longshot, but when we return home, I am going to see if there is a Carmichael's solicitor, I expect there may be a few and make contact with all of them.'

They both turned to one another, kissed, and fell asleep in one another's arms. Had they have inspected the painting on the wall above their heads and turned to look at the back, they would have seen a tiny listening device. In a small room beneath one of the turrets in the west wing, Fritz was sitting with headphones on and a tape recorder on the table in front of him. Together with Max and Annaliesa, they were not on leave as had been suggested by Ingrid but had been taking turns on listening in on Michael and Louise.

After breakfast and just before ten, the sound of a vehicle crunching the gravel outside could be heard as it came to a stop. Without knocking, in walked a brute of a man. He was about six-foot, four inches tall and weighed in at around eighteen stone. He looked incredibly strong. He had piggy eyes, thin lips and a three-inch scar across his right cheek. He wore a scowl and looked extremely hostile. I immediately thought of Father Benedict and his first impression of meeting Heinrich Merkel.

In a gruff, guttural voice he said, 'Good morning, I understand, God only knows how, that you have been left this estate, there must surely be a huge mistake. Why on earth would a German soldier loyal to the Reich leave such a property to a solder from the enemy?'

It was Louise who responded, as he had not indicated that he wished to shake our hands and introduce himself, Louise did it for him.

'Good morning, you must be Herr Merkel?' extending her hand, she continued, 'I am Louise, and this is my fiancé Michael Packham, who has as you have confirmed inherited the estate. When Herr Wagner made his Will, we were not at war and therefore no longer enemies. I believe Herr Wagner left the estate to a man who had saved his life. I assume that you have been instructed to take Michael, the new owner, and I guess, therefore your new employer on a tour of the estate. Shall we go now?'

Ingrid looked horrified at what had just occurred. I suspected that later on she would feel the full force of Heinrich's anger borne out of the humiliation of having been spoken to by a foreign woman who was a good deal younger than him.

The vehicle was to my surprise a British Land Rover. There were two front passenger seats besides the driver. It was clear that Heinrich wasn't going to volunteer any information. We had to ask for every detail and were met with little in the way of useful facts.

We viewed the farm buildings, very impressive. The farm still had pigs, chickens, dairy cows, and sheep as well as arable including a south facing vineyard on one of the hills. It was certainly all of 2,000 acres. In one of the fields a JCB was digging deep into the ground. Looking at the field it appeared that a track of around twenty foot wide and about eight feet deep was being dug. To the side of these were other tracks that had been refilled.

Our guide offered up without being prompted, that it was rumoured that a Roman settlement had once been there, and they were excavating to see if this was the case. On the way back to the house we passed the quarry. It was clear that Heinrich was not intending to stop. I tapped him on the arm and pointed to the quarry. Clearly annoyed he turned the vehicle and drove toward the quarry stopping a few metres short.

'This,' he said, is where the stone for the house and the farm buildings came from. Many of the village homes were constructed out of the stone quarried from here. No one goes there anymore; it is far too dangerous.'

With that Louise opened her door and started for the entrance and then I quickly followed. Heinrich like a spoiled child digging his toes in, refused to leave the vehicle. We walked into the centre of the quarry. It wasn't massive.

There was a cave in front and to the side. We walked in for about twenty metres, but it became dark, and so we did an about turn and walked back to towards the vehicle.

Louise in a low voice said, 'I am not in the least bit interested in looking at the quarry, I just wanted to piss off Heinrich, have you ever met before such a repulsive creature? Why would anyone wish to employ him, I have no idea?'

Approaching the front of the house, there stood a brand-new top of the range Mercedes-Benz CL 600. I thought, wouldn't it be nice to own a car like that. Then I thought, 'well hold on, I might well soon be able to afford a car like that.'

We entered the house and there to greet us in total contrast to his estate manager was a smiling, charming Dieter Muller. He came across like an avuncular uncle.

'Michael, Louise how wonderful to see you both? I understand from Johann that you enjoyed visiting both Salzburg and Vienna?'

'We did, Herr Muller,' I responded.

'Good to hear. Let us go in and have something to eat. I hope that Ingrid has been taking good care of you?'

'Perfectly so,' I said. Before I could continue, my mobile phone rang. I recognised the number as Henry Winkler's the genealogist. Quickly thinking, I put it onto speaker and said, 'We engaged a company to carry out some background research you may be interested to hear what they have found? Herr Winkler, thank you for calling, do you have any further news?'

'I do Michael, it is not a lot, but you did ask me to find out the provenance of *Schlachthaus*. This property was owned by three generations of the Benowitz family. As you probably can work out for yourself with regard to their name, they were Jews. In

1938 a decree was issued that all Jews had to transfer their businesses into the hands of Aryans. This property was transferred over to Otto Wagner, who we believe from our research was a member of the German SS.'

'Herr Winkler, this is Louise speaking. So, what you are saying is that Otto Wagner did not purchase this asset at market value? Putting it crudely he stole it or had it gifted to him under severe duress. Would that be correct?'

'Yes, my dear, that was the order of the day, hugely regrettably and it caused a good deal of unhappiness.'

I then asked, 'Herr Winkler, do you know what happened to Abraham and his family?'

'We are working on that at this very moment, I believe that we may have some promising leads. I will contact you when I have further news. Goodbye to you both.'

Dieter, Ingrid and Heinrich had stood there listening intently. The scowl on Heinrich's face was now even more pronounced. Ingrid had turned a little paler, but Dieter quickly regained his composure and said, 'Ingrid, please bring our tea and cake into the dining room.'

'Certainly, Herr Muller,' replied Ingrid as she quickly busied herself.

Louise and I sat on one side of the table with Dieter and Heinrich on the other. Dieter then opened up his brief case and produced several legal documents.

'I have some good news for you both,' he continued. 'The consortium of businessmen have increased their offer by a further five hundred thousand euros making a new total of eight million, I think you will agree, very generous, No?'

'That certainly is most generous. What concerns me though, is why the consortium that you represent who I assume are all astute businessmen would wish to pay substantially over the market price? It is puzzling.'

'It is a generous gesture on their part to conclude business. The price certainly is at the high end, but they see this location as having so much future potential especially with holiday makers.

Now I have the papers here if you would care to sign, the money will be transferred immediately.'

Louise looked at me and then said, 'Herr Muller, Heinrich took us on a tour of the estate this morning. To be frank we were unimpressed by his hostile attitude and lack of information, if he is an example of the type of person that you represent, then we would rather not deal with them. So far, we have been given few details about the running of the estate. There has been no sighting of the last three years of accounts. It is apparent that this has been a deliberate act of non-disclosure which has made us feel uncomfortable.

'You heard what Herr Winkler reported? This farm estate belonged to Abraham Benowitz, and it was taken from him by a law which people today would find repulsive, unacceptable and unlawful.'

Ingrid entered the room pushing a tea trolly upon which was a tea and coffee pot, milk, sugar and cake. Without a word, she just placed everything on the table and left.

'With regard to Herr Winkler's call. What he has reported to you was false. Abraham sold the estate to Herr Wagner for a fair price because he had sensed that war was coming. And rather than defend the Fatherland he took his family abroad somewhere.'

'But Abraham was a Jew, and the Jews were being persecuted Herr Muller. Also, how could a man in Otto's circumstances possibly have had the money to have purchased such an estate?'

Just then there was a knock on the door and Fritz entered. 'Ah Fritz my dear fellow,' Dieter said looking somewhat surprised. 'I thought that you were on vacation?'

'Good afternoon everyone. I was but I cut it short and returned a few moments ago. Could I have a word in private with you Herr Muller?'

'Please excuse me, help yourself to the refreshments.' Dieter Muller then stood up and left the room followed by Fritz.

We decided not to make small talk with Heinrich but spoke to each other about what work we had to do when we returned to our jobs.

Fritz took Herr Muller outside. 'Herr Muller forgive me for interrupting your meeting, but I think you will consider what I am about to say of importance.'

'Get on with it man,' Dieter Muller responded irritably.

'Last night it was my turn to listen in on our guests. Earlier that evening, Michael had proposed to Louise, and she had accepted. As you can imagine, when they came to bed, they were, how shall I say, very loving towards, one another, I must confess that being a good heterosexual man, I found I was myself being aroused and thought what a lucky bastard Michael was to have captured such a fine-looking woman as Louise.'

'Get on with it man, I'm not interested in your feelings,' snapped Dieter.

'Forgive me Herr Muller. But after their exertions they began talking about the painting which is hanging in the library.'

'Which painting? There are several!' snapped Dieter once more, unable to conceal his irritation.

'It is the one that features the main street of an English town.'

'Yes, I know the one, an unusual departure of Otto's who normally painted landscapes of the German countryside. So, what of it?'

'They apparently had studied the picture for some time and also concluded that it was unusual. It provoked them to take the picture down and to see if there was anything on the back. There was a note on the back which read *This picture is of great significance.*

'They continued to consider these words and concluded that it was an unusual painting that did not represent a true scene but was painted out of Otto's imagination. Apparently, there was only one independent business, a solicitor by the name of Carmichael's. All the other premises were national companies which would not have been so.

'Therefore, Michael indicated to Louise, that when they return to England, that he will research all solicitors with the name of Carmichaels to see if there is a link. This morning Annaliesa went onto the world wide web and discovered a firm of solicitors in the Yorkshire town of Wetherby. This firm was founded in 1928 by a man called Zachariah Carmichael. It is now being run by his son George Carmichael.'

'Hmm.' Dieter Muller stood pondering what he had just heard. 'You have done well Fritz. What you have told me, may well be the answer to our current problematic situation. It is feasible. We know that Otto was a POW in Yorkshire and that he returned to visit England shortly after the deaths of Christian and Ursula. Give Johann a ring and tell him that I wish him to fly to England this evening, I believe he may be able to fly to either Leeds or Manchester. I need him to arrange and meet this Mr George Carmichael. Thank you Fritz.'

Dieter Muller returned to the dining room with a spring in his step and was clearly upbeat. 'Ah, well I have just been speaking with the consortium and they have indicated their wish to withdraw their offer of purchasing the estate from you. Congratulations you are now the official owners of the estate. It will take a few weeks for the administration side to be completed, but in the meantime, we are happy to run the business on your behalf until such time as you make your own arrangements. Are you happy with that?'

'Thank you, Herr Muller. We are overwhelmed at the moment with our new situation. So, the more time that we have, the better.'

With that, Herr Muller stood up, shook our hands and wished us a pleasant journey back to Britain and assured us that if there was anything that we needed not to hesitate to get in touch. And then he was gone. Quickly following on his heels, without saying farewell, was Heinrich Merkel.

Louise and I exchanged uncertain looks. We could not fathom out what had just happened. We went to our room, packed up our things, thanked Ingrid and drove to Munich Airport for our return flight home to Gatwick.

Chapter 11

'Johann, this is Dieter Muller, where are you now?'

'Good evening sir, I am in the departure's lounge for my flight to Manchester, which leaves in one hour.'

'It will be around ten when you arrive. Book into a hotel and give me a ring in the morning and I will give you your instructions.'

'Thank you, sir, I will speak with you tomorrow. Good night.'

'Come on Louise, we should just be in time to check in.'

'I'm coming, I'm coming.'

'London Gatwick sir?' Enquired the lady at check-in.

'Phew, yes, what a rush? We are at terminal one, aren't we? I thought we were in danger of missing our flight,' I said.

'You made it with five minutes to spare. And yes, this is terminal one. Any luggage?'

After checking in we then went through Customs and headed towards our departure gate.

As we made our way towards our designated gate, Louise suddenly gripped my hand. 'Look,' she said, pointing through the glass of another departure lounge where the passengers were in line with their boarding passes. 'Isn't that Johann Ballack?'

There was little doubt that it was him. Johann was a man who stood out in any crowd. I glanced up at the destination sign of the departure lounge. 'It would appear that Johann is off to Manchester. I wonder what he will be doing there?' I muttered. 'You might have thought that he would have mentioned it.'

'You know,' said Louise, 'I haven't felt comfortable with anyone that we have met apart from Benedict and Elizabeth, in connection with this inheritance.'

'Me neither,' I replied. 'I think that we both share common instincts.'

Once we had entered our departure lounge, Louise then took out her laptop.

Her fingers were tapping the keys like a concert pianist playing Chopin's Minute Waltz. I could see that she was busily scrolling down different pages. Eventually she stopped and pointed.

'Ah ha,' she said. 'I think I may have found the significance of Otto's painting. Here, look, Michael. George Carmichael, family solicitors established 1928. We are both at work tomorrow, I will ring them from there.'

The following morning, a Monday, I left at seven forty to begin my shift at A&E. Louise left half an hour later for her estate agents, eager to share the news of her engagement.

'Is that you Johann?'

'Yes, sir, this is Johann.'

'I will email over to you all the details and paperwork that you require. It would not surprise me, if Otto had not left instructions with Carmichael's to thwart us in obtaining ownership. Make an appointment as earliest as you can, hopefully sometime today. I will send over a guidance of what you have to say. Have you got that?'

'Yes sir, thank you.'

'Good morning Carmichaels Solicitors,' a cheerful voice answering the phone confirmed.

'Yes, good morning Mam, my name is Johann Ballack and I have just flown in from Germany. Is it possible that I might be able to make an appointment to see George Carmichael today?'

'I will gladly make you an appointment, but it will not be for today as Mr Carmichael is at present on a walking holiday near Heidelberg in Germany. He will be back next Monday. He has two appointments already, the first available will be at eleven, is that okay with you?'

'Damn nation,' Johann uttered under his breath, and then in reply said, 'It doesn't need to be Mr Carmichael himself; I am sure that another partner will be able to assist.'

'I am sorry sir, but it is a sole practice. Mr Carmichael is the only solicitor. Could I have brief details about the matter you wish to discuss?'

'Just say that it is in connection with a will involving an estate in Bavaria.'

'Thank you, Mr Ballack. We look forward to seeing you next Monday at eleven.'

'Good morning Carmichael solicitors,' the receptionist answered who had just dealt with a previous caller.

'Good morning, I am ringing on behalf of my fiancé Dr Michael Packham, he is busy in A&E this morning. Would it be possible to arrange an appointment with Mr Carmichael?'

'Of course, when would you like to see him? Mr Carmichael is on leave now and will be back in the office next Monday.'

'Next Monday will have to do then,' replied Louise. 'A morning appointment would be more convenient.'

'Mr Carmichael's first available appointment would be at noon. Could you tell me briefly what it is in connection with?'

'It involves a Last Will and Testament of a German called Otto Wagner.'

There was a pause at the other end, and then. 'Make it twelve fifteen.'

Louise replaced the receiver and thought for a moment or two. 'Why did the receptionist change the time?'

It was Friday afternoon at two. The A&E department was quiet, and my boss Dr. Wilkinson let me go early knowing that I was travelling up to Yorkshire the following day and would not be back until Tuesday. I wondered if there was any news about the whereabouts of any of the Benowitz family and so I decided to call Henry Winkler the genealogist in Vienna.

The female answering my call, I could tell was feeling harassed or stressed out. I asked if I could speak to Henry Winkler. There was a pause, and then she advised me that there had been a fire-bomb attack two evenings ago which had completed destroyed their offices and that Herr Winkler who was working at the time had been severely burned and is now in intensive care with life threatening injuries. She advised me that she was answering calls from clients at a temporary office. I felt numb when I replaced the receiver. I decided against telling Louise, I didn't wish to alarm her.

I waited for Louise to return from work on Saturday morning. We ate the lunch that I had prepared. We hugged and kissed one another before I got into my Ford Focus to begin my four-hour drive to Wetherby. After an uneventful drive I arrived at my pre-booked Bed and Breakfast. It was a family run business run by a charming couple who were delighted to have people staying at their establishment.

The following day I took a stroll. My only knowledge of Wetherby was through the racecourse. I would like to think that my only vice is that of the weekly flutter on the horses. I never place a bet of more than a few pounds and I usually break even. It is an interest that I enjoy. I do remember my dad saying to me 'that the only people who make money on horses are those that follow the horses with a bucket and spade,' wise words indeed.

I discovered to my delight, that Wetherby was a small market town with the River Wharfe as a good focal point. I had decided that I would do a reconnaissance and locate Carmichael's. I entered the main street and in no time at all, there it was. It was unmistakable from the painting of Otto's. The office front was exactly the same, although I suspect that all other premises and their fasciae had changed many times since 1949. I was very pleased to see that there was a café directly opposite that opened at eight in the morning.

The following morning, I thanked my hosts for a pleasant stay not before I had eaten a full English breakfast with all the trimmings. I parked just outside the town centre and walked to the café arriving there at just after half past eight.

As someone who had been brought up always to tell the truth and never to lie, I felt a pang of guilt when I entered the café and said to the waitress that I was an undercover police officer on surveillance because we were looking for a possible criminal who might be visiting Carmichael's that morning. The waitress became quite excited when she thought that her café might play its part in solving perhaps a drug bust in Wetherby, where apparently 'very little happens.'

I picked up the café's copy of that days *Yorkshire Post* and pretended to read it whilst keeping an eye on Carmichael's. I didn't have long to wait. Ten minutes later an elderly gentleman arrived at the same time as a young woman who I assumed was his receptionist/secretary. I was on my third cup of coffee when the unmistakable figure of Johann came into view walking with great purpose. He was looking at a scrap of paper, which I assumed was the address and looking up at the different signages. Finally, he came to the one he was seeking. He looked up briefly, pocketed the note and then entered.

'Good morning sir, I'm Alison, Mr Carmichael's secretary, and you must be Mr Ballack.'

Johann responded with one of his best smiles that he always kept for the ladies. 'Thank you, Alison, I am Johann Ballack from Germany. I must say, what a lovely town Wetherby is? Have you always lived here?'

'I am a native born and bred; I have never travelled outside of Yorkshire.'

'Really? that does surprise me.'

With that Alison came from behind her desk and went over and knocked on George Carmichael's office door. 'Nice legs,' thought Johann before being ushered in.

'Good morning Mr Ballack, or should I say Herr Ballack? What brings you all this way to our sleepy part of the world?'

'Thank you, sir,' Johann said taking a seat. 'I am the messenger of a very well-respected Law Firm in Munich, Muller and Schneider. My mission here today involves an estate in Bavaria which was owned by a man called Otto Wagner. Herr Wagner sadly passed away in 1952 at the age of sixty-three. His last Will and Testament left his estate to an Englishman by the name of McKee. We believe that this was in recognition that McKee had saved Herr Wagner's life during the war.

'Muller and Schneider obtained legal authority to run the estate whilst they pursued exhaustive enquiries to locate this McKee. Forty-eight years have now passed and regrettably no descendant of McKee has been found. Therefore, the Statute of Limitations owing to the time that has passed has been applied for in the German courts.'

George Carmichael was a doughty typical Yorkshireman. He loved his cricket and had been the opening batsman for his village team for many years. His batting average when he retired from the game twenty years ago was nineteen runs, the average time spent accruing these runs at the crease was around two and a half hours. He was considered by many to be an obdurate but well-liked man. One who would not be hurried along.

'The question is, Herr Ballack, what brings you to my office?'

'Well sir, we believe that Herr Wagner visited Wetherby in 1949 and may have seen, I guess it would have been your father, Zachariah and perhaps left a document which would help establish our credentials.'

George Carmichael without saying a word, took out and started to fill his pipe before lighting it, sending a cloud of smoke into the air. It was as though he was framing his response.

'I can confirm what you say is correct, Herr Ballack. Otto Wagner did call in and see my father who as you may have ascertained by his name, was a well-respected member of the Jewish community here in Yorkshire. It may be because of my father's religion that Otto deliberately sought him out. You say that you have been searching for this beneficiary called McKee for almost fifty years now, is that what you are saying?'

'That is correct sir.'

'I am surprised to hear that, because I took the trouble to read the will earlier this morning that Otto had left with us. There was an addendum which I must say I am surprised that you are not aware of in which he has requested that two of his loyal staff a Tanya van der Leyen, and a Frank Meyer could stay at the property until they died. Only then would his will become pertinent. Do you know when these individuals died? Of course, if they died perhaps in the nineteen fifties for example then your Statute of Limitations would apply. Before I can hand over and carry out the wishes of Otto Wagner, I will have to ascertain when the two forementioned passed away.'

Johann had always been a person who had got his way, very often this was achieved through violence and intimidation. George Carmichael presented him with a situation in which he could do neither. He was quite simply perplexed and unsure of what he should do next.

Johann, then stood up and said, 'I believe sir that your actions could be viewed as conspiring against the wishes of Otto Wagner in denying this estate be passed to the rightful custodians. I would think that is likely that Dieter Muller who is a heavy weight lawyer in Munich compared with you working in a small parochial town will shortly be in touch. Good day sir.' And with that Johann stormed out of the office not even glancing at Alison on his way out.

It was at ten minutes to twelve, I was on my fourth cup of coffee and desperate for the loo but dare not in case I missed Johann exiting from the solicitors. The front door of the office suddenly opened, and Johann slammed it behind him as he set off in the direction that he had first appeared. I noticed that he had now put his mobile phone to his ear.

At exactly twelve-fifteen I entered the offices of George Carmichael. The receptionist who introduced herself as Alison advised me that she would let Mr Carmichael know that I had arrived. When she returned, she offered me a cup of coffee? I politely declined, thinking that that was the last thing that I wanted now as I had no need for any more caffeine. It was a further ten minutes before George Carmichael's office door opened.

'Mr Packham? My apologies for keeping you waiting. I just had to check up a few facts, please come this way.'

Thank you, sir, a pleasure to meet you.'

'Now how may I assist you?'

'A few weeks ago, I received a letter from a firm of solicitors in London called Hildreth and Watkins.'

'Ah yes, I am familiar with that firm. Daniel Watkins is the surviving partner. It is a very well respected and long-established law firm based in the Gray's Inn district, where for a Yorkshireman, rents would be considered outrageously extortionate.'

'I agree with you there. The letter was an invitation to visit him because it was possible that I might be the beneficiary of an estate in Southern Germany.'

'Would that be in Bavaria?'

'That's very perceptive of you. To cut to the chase, my grandfather was an army surgeon with the rank of major during the Second World War. In July and August of 1944, he was the surgeon in a field hospital just outside the French town of Falaise. An important battle took place there, which fortunately the Allies won, and this opened up the route to Paris and beyond.'

'Yes, the history of the Second World War has always been of interest to me,' George Carmichael observed.

'It would appear that my grandad saved the life of a German soldier who had been a Panzer tank radio operator. According to Daniel Watkins, Otto Wagner, the German soldier in question was survived by no living relatives. He therefore left his estate to Major McKee. That was a problem because my grandfather's name was David McKay and not McKee.

'It took two years involving research from a company of genealogists, with I understand two or three false leads, until they finally traced me as being the possible beneficiary. Therefore, we were invited to Hildreth and Watkins. Once there Daniel Watkins asked me several questions the answers of which confirmed to him that I was the person that they had been seeking. Four weeks later I received a letter from a German law firm called ...'

'Would that have been Muller and Schneider?' enquired George Carmichael.

'Well yes, how would you have known that?'

'Continue on my dear boy.'

'We, and by we, I mean my fiancée, Louise and I travelled to Munich to meet Herr Muller. At first, he seemed very genial.

He was quite insistent that we accept an offer from a consortium of businessmen for seven million euros.'

'That's a lot of money, I could buy the Headingly cricket ground for that.'

'Both Louise and I thought it strange that such a sum of money should be offered and that it was presumed that we would accept. We said that we would like to view the estate. Herr Muller reluctantly agreed. The estate is a mixed farm of about 2,000 acres and I would imagine very profitable, although we were shown no accounts. We had questioned how it was that a private soldier in the Germany army could own such a huge estate.

'It was by pure chance, or good fortune, you might say, that whilst visiting the village by ourselves we bumped into the Roman Catholic priest of the local church called Father Benedict who took us to his home where he lived with his sister, Elizabeth. It was whilst having tea we found out much of what we were seeking.

'The estate had been in the hands of the third generation of a Jewish family called Benowitz. The husband and wife, called Abraham and Hannah had twin daughters, Leah and Eliana. When the twins were about four years old their parents engaged a tutor cum governess to educate their girls. The person they engaged was a lady called Hildegard. She was a gifted violinist. She became part of their family and also taught the girls the violin to a very high standard. This pleased Abraham and Hannah who were also accomplished musicians.

'Hildegard left the girls when they were in their late teens and moved to Munich. She next saw the family Benowitz in 1921 when with her new husband Otto Wagner, they spent their honeymoon there. Hildegard worked as a newspaper journalist, quite unusual for that time. Otto had become involved in the Nazi Party. Apparently, he had first met Adolf Hitler back in 1912 in Vienna where they were both artists.

'Hitler then appointed Otto in 1933 to be an administrator in the newly erected and first concentration camp, called Dachau.

Hitler deemed that Otto should wear the uniform of a member of the much-feared SS. It must be stressed that Otto did not share the doctrine of his fellow SS officers.

'In 1938 a decree came out that all Jewish property should be transferred into Aryan hands. Hildegard together with Otto visited Abraham and suggested that it be transferred to them. They made it clear that it would not be a permanent transfer and that if Abraham were able to return and conditions permitted, then the property would be transferred back to him.

'Abraham agreed and emigrated with his family. We believe his twins stayed in London whilst he and Hannah set up home in Montana. Otto was then allowed to resign his position at the camp and concentrate on running the estate. Sadly, their only son Helmut lost his life during the war, and this was the catalyst that led to Hildegard taking her own life.

'Otto left the estate to be run by a man called Christian Schmidt whist he enrolled for the German Luftwaffe as an administrator in Berlin. We believe that he resigned in 1943 and then trained as a tank radio officer. Later he was sent to France.

'According to Father Benedict, Otto drew up his last Will and Testament and left everything to Christian and Ursula Schmidt who ran the estate and had become dear friends. Otto had received a visit from the Bavarian chief of police who was surprised that Otto was planning to leave the estate to the Schmidt's instead of to an organisation that they thought Otto would approve of, namely one that helped former Nazis who had avoided justice but had fallen upon hard times.

'Totally unexpected in 1949, the Schmidt's were deemed to have committed suicide whilst in their car with the engine running and a hose attached. Father Benedict thinks it is more likely that they were murdered in the hope that Otto would have no one else left to leave his estate to and would therefore name this organisation as his beneficiaries.

'It would appear that Otto would not have his mind changed. He made a new will this time leaving it to a Major McKee, but with the caveat that the will would not be discharged until the deaths of his housekeeper Tanya van der Leyen and the gardener, Frank Meyer. Frank passed away in 1997.'

'That is all very fascinating, but what has brought you to my office?'

'Otto was a fine artist. In his house are many paintings of his, all but three are of German landscapes. The exceptions being a beautiful painting of Leah and Eliana, holding their violins, the second is The Vienna Opera House and finally of an English High Street, which has your office in prominence. When we looked at the back there was a note that merely said, *This picture is of great significance.*'

'I still don't understand the connection. Why would Otto paint a picture with our office in it?'

'There is speculation sir, that before the outbreak of the war, many treasurers were brought to Abraham for him to hide and to keep safe until they could be returned. There is heavy excavation taking place in every single part of the estate. It is happening as we speak.'

'I see, and what do you think Herr Wagner's purpose in visiting my father would have been?'

'Well sir, I am clutching at straws here. It is good that we have confirmed that the Carmichael's in the painting is this very office. The reason why it took so long to discover me as the beneficiary is because Otto mistook the name McKay for McKee. By putting in the caveat that nothing was to be done until the death of either Tanya or Frank, would suggest that he was hoping to buy time and that the organisation with the passing of time would have folded. I am really speculating now when I surmise that perhaps Otto left you details of where the artefacts are actually hidden.'

George Carmichael let out a deep breath and then picked up his pipe that was on the desk, filled it with tobacco, lit it and then was lost in thought. Finally, he said, 'And what would you do if you stumbled across this hidden treasure?'

'Well sir, Louise and I have decided that the entire estate was in effect stolen from the rightful owner. Therefore, we have no desire to profit from another family's misery. We will not be taking over the estate. If we had knowledge of where the treasure was hidden and it was revealed, then we would ensure that it was all returned to the rightful owners.'

'May I say Doctor Packham that your decision deserves much credit. I would describe your situation as receiving The Unwanted Inheritance. Also, I congratulate you on your analysis which has brought you to this office. I might add that it was just in time, because I am retiring in two weeks' time, and as I have no children, the name of Carmichael's will be a thing of the past.' With that he lent forward and pressed a key on his phone. 'Alison, will you go to the safe and bring in the envelope marked Major McKee or his descendants?'

A moment or two later, a tap at the door. Alison entered clutching a brown envelope.

'Thank you, Alison. I have no idea as to the contents of this envelope. I do know that my father placed great importance that it should only be handed over to the person entitled to it. It has been a pleasure meeting you Michael, now I am off to lunch. I always go to the café opposite; I can recommend it.'

With that we both left the office together. George Carmichael crossing the road and me walking back to where I had left my car.

'Good afternoon, Carmichael's solicitors.'

'Good afternoon, I am wondering if I might be able to speak with George Carmichael? My name is Dieter Muller, I am the Senior partner of a law firm in Munich. I am telephoning about the disposal of an estate in Bavaria.'

'I am sorry Mr Muller, but Mr Carmichael has gone to lunch. However, I believe what you are ringing about has been resolved. Mr Carmichael handed over the envelope from Otto Wagner to Michael Packham just before leaving for lunch.'

Trying to maintain his equilibrium Herr Muller replied, 'Thank you so much, you have been most helpful. No need to mention my call to George. Good afternoon to you.'

Chapter 12

Before leaving the car park in Wetherby, I texted Louise with the message *'Hi Darling, just leaving now. Should be home by six. Have got sealed letter. Will open together, Love Michael xx'*

I pulled up outside our home at just after six. Although I had only been away for two nights, I had really missed Louise. I was wondering when we should set a date for our wedding. I unlocked the front door and there was my lovely over the stove cooking our meal.

We embraced fondly and then I removed the letter and said, 'Let us keep the suspense going. Have our meal and then with a glass of wine we will sit down in the lounge and open up to reveal the substance of Otto's wishes of nearly fifty years ago.'

'You tease you; I have been anticipating all day you revealing the contents. But you are right, thirty minutes more will not make a lot of difference. Will you lay the table please?'

'Certainly, what have you got on the go there?'

'This is some homemade mushroom soup. It is just coming to the boil now. This will be followed by roasted rack of lamb, your favourite.'

'Hmm, hmm, hmm,' I replied, 'it smells delicious.' My thoughts were interrupted by someone ringing our front doorbell.

No sooner had I opened the door than a large muscular figure barged in violently shoving me in the chest pushing me over backwards.

'You fucking bastard you, did you really believe that you could out fox me?'

Louise immediately saw the frightening sight of Johann in full rage as he reached into his pocket and started to remove a handgun, which she had no doubt that he would use. Without waiting Louise picked up the saucepan with the boiling mushroom soup and hurled it into Johann's face. Johann let out an almighty scream, I jumped to my feet but was unable to prevent Louise from bringing the saucepan down upon Johann's head with all her might.

Johann body immediately crumpled and fell to the floor motionless almost as though he had been shot dead. He was laying in the prone position with his right hand holding the gun. I quickly said to Louise, 'Get me a wet tea towel.'

Whilst she was doing this I felt for a pulse, thankfully there was one albeit not very strong. I told Louise to dial 999 and request an ambulance and the police. I then placed Johann on his back and wiped away with the damp tea towel the mushroom soup which I could see had severely burnt his face. I checked his pulse again; it was getting weaker. I then started the process of cardiopulmonary resuscitation. I continued with this until the ambulance arrived at the same time as the police.

I explained what had happened and the medics took over ensuring that Johann was connected to an oxygen supply before removing him to the ambulance. Four police cars had now arrived on the scene, two of them from a rapid response unit containing armed officers.

Louise by now was almost hysterical with grief. Folding her arms across her chest and swaying from side to side in floods of tears. She was inconsolable. The police sergeant who was the highest-ranking officer there and was part of the rapid response firearm unit, looked at the gun on the floor and remarked.

'That's a Glock 21, a very nifty and effective personal weapon.'

Louise was quite clearly in shock as indeed I was but to a much lesser degree. I briefly told the police officer what had taken place. I then requested that he returned tomorrow, or we could call in at the police station. He said that someone would call in on us at ten in the morning.

I then made Louise a hot chocolate and without her knowledge added quite a strong sedative. I took her to the bedroom. Helped her undress and placed her in the bed and then I quickly followed. It was only eight fifteen. I cuddled into Louise and within ten minutes she had stopped her shuddering weeping and drifted off to sleep. With all that had happened in just one day, it didn't take too long for me to follow.

I awoke at about five thirty. I was at first confused and slightly disorientated. Louise was still soundly asleep. I eased myself out of the bed and went and used the shower downstairs so as to minimise the noise level. After changing, I reflected on what had happened last night.

Although early, I decided to call the hospital and explain that I was unable to come in that morning. I felt guilty because Doctor Wilkinson, my boss had kindly given me yesterday off and I knew that by not going in today it would cause a problem. Whilst there I asked to be transferred to the emergency ward where I suspected Johann would have been taken.

When I explained who I was the duty nurse said, 'Hold on a moment, Mr. Mike Dean the surgeon is here.'

'Good morning Michael, this is Mike here, an early call is it not?'

'I agree, but a lot has happened in the past twelve hours, I was just ringing to find out about Johann Ballack who was injured last night?'

'Poor chap, had suffered a severe head trauma, I did my best, but it was not enough I'm afraid.'

'You mean that he's dead!?'

'He died just over an hour ago. I didn't realise that you had been involved in his care?'

'No, I wasn't, but I was involved in his death. I will catch up with you later Mike.' I put down the phone.

I looked at my hands and could see there was a slight trembling. My mind was in a whirl. I thought, 'come on get control of yourself.' It is strange how you can be totally reassuring and calm with other people and yet you lose that self-control when its personal.

It was as though I was paralysed with fear. I was just walking around in a daze. I just couldn't concentrate on anything. Just before nine, I heard the upstairs toilet flush. I made two coffees and carried them upstairs. Louise was in the shower, that, I thought was a good sign. When she exited the shower, I was there waiting with a nice rough bath towel. We hugged one another tightly.

Louise then said, 'I am sorry about last night Michael, I just saw him reaching for a gun, I had no time to think what I was doing, it was just pure instinct.'

'I know darling,' I said. 'You were incredible. He totally took me by surprise, he was the last person that I expected to find on our doorstep. I wonder how he knew that I had been to Wetherby and had been given the information that he was so desperate for?'

'I wonder Michael if you could ring the hospital and find out how Johann is?'

I looked at Louise and felt a sickening feeling in my stomach. 'I have some bad news. Unfortunately, Johann could not be saved and died about four hours ago.'

I could feel Louise's body go limp in my arms. She looked into my face tears rolling down her cheeks.

'Oh my God Michael, I killed him. I didn't mean to. Oh my God, what have I done?'

We hugged each other tightly, with me gently kissing her neck and wiping away the tears with the back of my hand.

'It was not your fault darling, the police will understand, you have nothing to worry about. It was self-defence. I doubt if you feel like eating anything, but a slice of toast and marmalade will do us both good. I suspect today is going to be difficult.'

The doorbell rang just before ten. There was a plain clothes police officer together with a WPC. I was pleased to see the WPC, I thought to have a woman present would be comforting to Louise.

'I'm Inspector Lockhard, no comments please, and this is WPC Annie Taylor. How are you both this morning?'

'It's difficult to say how we feel after last night.'

'Yes of course, quite understandable, a very traumatic experience for you both. Normally, I would interview you here and take your statements, but regrettably Mr Ballack did not regain consciousness and has since died from his injuries. We are now looking at a charge of possible murder. You have the right to remain silent. Anything you say can and will be used against you in a court of law. You have the right to an attorney. If you cannot afford an attorney, one will be appointed for you. Would you please follow me, Miss Johnson?'

'Can you give us ten minutes please Inspector to allow us to collect some clothing?'

'Yes of course sir. We don't need you at this time it is just Miss Johnson. She is the one whose actions have caused the death of Mr Ballack. We will interview you as a witness later on. Also. it will not be permitted for you to sit in when Miss Johnson is being interviewed. You might be advised in hiring the services of a good lawyer.'

I looked at Louise and was surprised to find how strong and determined she now looked. Back in control, with a grip on the reality of her situation.

'I did not murder him Inspector. It was an act of self-defence.'

As Louise left the house accompanied by the two officers, I was surprised to see a press photographer and a reporter from the local television station outside. I watched as Louise was encouraged into the police car with the Inspector putting his hand on the top of her head and pushing it down, as though she was not capable of getting into the car unaided.

I returned to the kitchen and sat down on a bar stool with a note pad in front of me. 'Things to do,' I thought. Everything had happened so quickly. Johann had been felled within sixty seconds of entering our house. The indisputable fact was that he was now dead and had died as a result of being struck by a saucepan wielded by Louise. I began to feel trepidation. What should I do? I knew exactly the circumstances that had taken place, but whichever way you looked at it, for the time being at least, Louise was in trouble.

I seemed to be making little progress with what I should do when the phone rang. It was my boss Doctor Wilkinson. 'Hi Michael, it is Stuart Wilkinson here. Look I have just seen the local television news, you must both be in a state of turmoil. I am sorry for what has happened.'

'What did the news channel report?' I asked anxiously.

'They said that a thirty-three-year-old German man, was taken to hospital last night, suffering from a severe head wound, a wound that he did not recover from and that he died earlier this morning. They have arrested a twenty-six-year-old female estate agent, a Miss Louise Johnson in connection with the incident and that the police are viewing it as a possible murder investigation.'

'My God Stuart, did they really say that? It was nothing like that. This man broke into our house and produced a gun. Louise just acted instinctively out of fear for our lives.'

'Look mate, you don't have to explain what happened to me. Under the circumstances you would not be in the right frame of mind to return to work at this time. Therefore, I am authorising that you take four weeks' compassionate leave. Good luck and give my love to Louise.'

'Thank you, Stuart, I appreciate your thoughtfulness. I will be in touch to let you know how things are progressing.'

No sooner had I put the phone down than it rang again, this time it was Kate, Louise's mum.

'What's happened Michael? I have had the local paper on the phone asking me for a comment. I asked them with regard to what, and they said that Louise was being charged with the murder of a German national who she attacked and killed in your house, surely this cannot be true?'

'Kate, it is not as it has been told to you. A German man broke into our house last evening with a gun. Louise acted promptly and struck the assailant over the head with a saucepan. I can only think that the initial contact must have been the edge of the saucepan which caused such a trauma. Stay inside, do not answer the landline. I will call you on your mobile this evening.'

I replaced the phone onto the cradle, and it rang immediately once more. 'Yes!' I answered now feeling a sense of anger growing within me.

'Michael, it is Louise. How are you faring?'

'It's not about me, the important thing is, how are you?'

'I'm good, everything has been explained to me by Inspector Lockhard. I've been given a cup of coffee and some toast and marmalade. I accept that the police are doing their job. This is the one phone call that I am able to make. I think it would be wise, given the seriousness of the charge that I am facing that we engage a lawyer to represent me. The only lawyer that I know and who impressed me was Daniel Watkins, of Hildreth and Watkins whose initial contact with us has resulted in my present sorry situation.'

Recovering a degree of composure, I said, 'Okay Louise, I will give him a call. Keep your chin up darling, it was a complete accident, you will be free in no time at all. Love you.'

'I love you too, and stay strong my darling, I am all right and I know that once fully explained I will be returning home. Bye love.'

I was struck by how calm and collected Louise had been. Even in her situation she was more concerned with my wellbeing than her own. I felt a wave of optimism run through my body and I felt reinvigorated with a renewed sense of determination and clarity.

I sat looking at the phone for several seconds before it rang again. This time it was the local press asking for a comment. I just put down the receiver before picking it up immediately and dialled a number in London.

'Good morning, Hildreth and Watkins.'

'Good morning, could you please put me through to Daniel Watkin's secretary?'

'One moment please, putting you through now.'

'Good margining Daniel Watkins's secretary.'

'Hello is that Carol?'

'It is, who is this please?'

'This is Michael Packham; I need to speak with Mr Watkins urgently.'

'Daniel Watkins is in court this morning, I expect him to be back at around three, I will get him to give you a ring then.'

'Thank you, Carol. Please stress to him that it is extremely important.'

Rather than sitting indoors I decided that I would drive to the police station in the hope that I could see Louise. As I left the house, I noticed that the knot of reporters had grown and now there were two television vans outside. Rather than ignore them I decided that I would make a statement.

'Good morning,' I tried to sound cheerful as a number of microphones and recording devises were thrust in front of me. 'Last night at around six thirty, a man broke into our house and threatened us with a handgun. My fiancée's quick thinking prevented the assailant from getting a shot off by striking him with a saucepan, her actions were borne out of fear and self-defence with our lives being in potential danger.'

'When did you realise that he had died?'

'Did you know the intruder?'

'Is Miss Johnson being charged with murder?'

I ignored the questions, got into my car, and drove away. 'Amazing' I thought, 'less than twenty-four hours ago, I was in Wetherby, and everything was fine.'

When I pulled up outside the police station there was again a group of newspaper reporters. I went inside and fortunately, just leaving was WPC Annie Taylor who was one of the arresting officers. She looked up and instantly recognised me.

'Doctor Packham, Louise has just appeared before a hastily arranged Magistrates court. Due to the seriousness of the charge, she has not been granted bail and is now in police custody.'

'What?' I was aware that I had raised my voice. 'Louise is not a criminal. It was an act of self-defence. She is not likely to abscond. It is a nonsense to keep her locked up. Am I able to see her?'

'That will not be possible until we have a full statement from you.'

'Am I able to be interviewed now? I am expecting a call from a lawyer a little later.'

'Yes, come this way, I will see if Inspector Lockhard is free.'

I was then taken to a small featureless interview room. Three plain walls, the fourth having an observation window, where you could look into the room but not be observed from those inside. There was a security camara in each corner.

I explained what had occurred, it took me less than one minute.

'Did you know the intruder?' asked Inspector Lockard.

I gave a full explanation as to the circumstances in which we had met. Starting at the beginning when Danial Watkins first contacted us and continuing on with our journey to Munich and to visit the estate. I also mentioned after advising us that he was making progress in tracing the family of Abraham Benowitz, how the genealogist Henry Winkler, had his offices firebombed and that he was now in intensive care.

'You say that you were working on a hunch about visiting Carmichael's in Wetherby, doesn't it strike you as odd, that Herr Ballack should turn up there on the very morning before you? How would they have come to the same conclusion?'

Up until then I hadn't given this apparent coincidence any thought. I shook my head in disbelief as the likely cause of their information struck me. 'I am shocked to say that I now believe that we must have been under audio surveillance.'

'You have told us that you travelled up to Wetherby on Saturday and stayed for two nights. Yesterday morning, you arrived early and took up a position where you could observe George Carmichael's office. Why did you suspect that Mr Ballack might appear?'

'During our last meeting with Dieter Muller he advised us that his consortium had increased their offer to eight million euros. Then before our meeting had finished, he got called away by a member of staff called Fritz. When he returned, he announced that the offer to buy had now been withdrawn. Later on, at the airport as we were making our way to the departure gate, we spotted Johann Ballack waiting to board a flight to Manchester.

'On the Monday, after we had arrived home, Louise telephoned to make an appointment with George Carmichael. She was told that Mr Carmichael was on holiday and would not be available until the following Monday. The first available slot was at noon. Louise was then asked, what it was in connection with? She told her that it concerned a will in respect to a German estate. The receptionist then suggested to come at twelve-fifteen. It seemed odd that she should change the time.'

'So, you set yourself up in the café opposite, what did you see?'

'Just before eleven, Johann Ballack appeared and entered Carmichael's. He left just before noon.'

'You went in shortly afterwards, and convinced George Carmichael that you were the rightful beneficiary to Otto Wagner's estate?'

'No, I explained to him that I was there purely on the back of a hunch. But it was clear from the painting, that Otto Wagner had been to this office. Mr Carmichael then asked me a series of questions. It would appear that the answers that I gave established in his mind that I was the heir of David McKay and he then handed me an envelope that Otto had given to Zachariah, George's father back in 1949.'

'And what were the contents of this envelope?'

'It had been my intention that we both opened the letter after dinner together.'

'So where is it now?'

'It should be sitting on the breakfast bar where I left it last night.' Just then my mobile rang. I glanced at the number and could see that it was an 020 prefix which I knew to be London. Quickly glancing at my watch, I could not believe that it was now after three, the interview had taken longer than I had expected.

'Do you mind if I answer this Inspector? This could be Louise's lawyer.'

'Go ahead, we can call it a day. We will be back in touch once your statement has been typed out for you to read and then to sign.'

As I thought, it was Daniel Watkins. I spent the next seventy minutes going through our entire experience since arriving in Germany and our returning home. He then confirmed that he would travel down from London to interview Louise the following day.

I had just reached my car when Louise's younger sister Samantha, rang.

In a voice full of concern, she said, 'Michael I heard what has happened. I went round to your house to see if there was anything that I could do. I suggest that you don't go home, there is a posse of news reporters camped outside. I suggest that you spend the night here at my place.'

'Thanks Sam, that does sound like a plan. I will see you shortly.'

The following morning, I received a phone call from Daniel Watkins, requesting that I meet him at the police station. His mood was grave as we shook hands before being shown to the waiting room. Louise came into the room without the escort. I thought this is prisoner/attorney confidentiality being observed. Louise and I embraced and kissed while Daniel pretended to be looking at some documents. Finally, we got down to business.

Louise and I answered all the questions that were asked. Daniel agreed that he would represent Louise and would try to arrange for her to be released on bail. While we were speaking, Daniel's mobile which was on the table started to vibrate.

He looked at the number and then said, 'Be absolutely quite I am going to put this call on speaker phone. It is none other than Dieter Muller.

'Good afternoon Dieter, I had not expected to hear from you again after we had traced Michael Packham.'

'Good afternoon Daniel. It is about Michael Packham that this call relates to, or not so much as to Michael, but more to do with his fiancée, Louise.'

'I'm intrigued, please do continue.'

'I was advised earlier this morning, that a trusted and highly valued member of my personal team has been murdered by Louise Johnson, who together with Michael were guests of ours here in Munich as recently as ten days ago.'

'What is the name of your employee who has met such an untimely and tragic end?'

'His name was Johann Ballack, he had been employed by me for five years since leaving the Special Forces Command of the German military.'

'May I enquire why it was that Mr Ballack was visiting England and more importantly why did he turn up unannounced at the home of Michael and Louise?'

'We recently came across information that cast doubt on the validity of Otto's will, by that I mean his true wishes.'

'I am slightly perplexed here, Dieter, and I must tell you that Louise and Michael have been in touch and have asked me to represent them in court. The reason for my being perplexed is that on the final day of their visit to Germany, you met with them at the estate and am I correct when I say that you represent a consortium of businessmen who were prepared to offer eight million euros?'

'That is so, an extremely generous offer.'

'Indeed, it was Dieter, a very generous offer. This provokes the question, why would a group of businessmen wish to pay maybe considerably more than the estate is worth?'

'It has been viewed very much as a business opportunity for the future with great potential. I don't need to tell you Daniel, a person who has an office in one of the most expensive parts of London, how quickly realty inflation is moving, it is the same over here. In just a few years' time, eight million euros will look like a steal.'

'It is interesting that you use the word steal. We have suspicions here and I don't wish to cast any aspersions on your firm's reputation as I realise like all of us in the legal profession, we are here to carry out the instructions of our clients. If as you indicate this was a steal, affording an opportunity to make a substantial profit in future years, why was the offer suddenly without any warning withdrawn.?'

'We received that very afternoon, information advising us that there was a small-town solicitor in the north of England who may well have been in possession of a letter left there in 1949 by Otto Wagner when he last visited Britain.'

'Forgive me for being naive Dieter, but you have been searching for Otto Wagner's descendants for over two years. Then when you had established that Michael Packham is the person you are looking for, he is with you and you have, I believe been quite insistent, forgive me if that is not the right word, in encouraging him that it would be in his best interests to accept an offer of seven million euros and return to England even without viewing the estate. He indicated that he would like to view the estate and then a further increase of five hundred thousand euros was made and then another increase bringing the total to eight million euros.

'Now, I am just puzzled how after all this time, that the information that has led you to send your emissary, the sadly departed Herr Ballack, to visit this firm of solicitors in Weatherby came to you on the very last day of my clients visit?'

'We have as you know Daniel kept the estate going since the death of the former gardener, Frank Meyer. It was the will of Otto that we do not seek the beneficiary to his estate until after the deaths of Tanya and Frank. Since then, we have employed staff to maintain the property and to continue running the estate as a viable business.

'One of the housekeepers, a lady called Ingrid, decided that very day to do a thorough clean in the library. By thorough I mean to take down the paintings and de cobweb and dust behind them. It was upon the removing of a painting by Otto of an English town scene that she noticed a note by Otto on the back indicating that the picture was of great significance.

'She brought this to my attention, and after a great deal of thought, I concluded that the significance must be the name of a solicitor, Carmichael which appeared at the forefront of the painting. I was acting purely on a hunch. As you are fond of saying in English, I was clutching at straws. But I requested one of my secretaries to research whether or not such a firm still existed and to my surprise we discovered a Carmichael's in a small town in the north of England.'

'May I ask Dieter, what you did next?'

'We then made an appointment for Johann to visit and speak with George Carmichael who like you and I was following in Zachariah's, George's father's footsteps by taking over the firm after his father retired.'

'Were you not concerned that this was a law firm run by a Jew? Or were you prepared to overlook this in order to achieve your client's wishes?'

'Without wishing to be rude, Daniel, that is most unworthy of you. My firm is merely carrying out the wishes of our clients.'

'Do you have any reason to believe that your clients current views reflect the views that were held by many during the thirties in Nazi Germany?'

'I am not sure what the purpose of that question is? But it is irrelevant in seeking to execute the wishes of our former client, Otto Wagner.'

'I realise that this is not of importance, but I am told that Otto was a member of the SS, were you aware of that?'

'Vaguely, I recollect hearing something about that.'

'You may therefore be surprised to know that Otto was an SS member at the very first concentration camp set up by Himmler at Dachau. After the war many of the guards at such establishments were prosecuted for war crimes and sent to prison or worse. But many escaped detection and took on new identities, I am wondering why it was that Otto neither felt the need of a new identity nor was never prosecuted?'

'I have the answer to neither, Daniel, but I feel we are moving away from why I called you.'

'My apologies, please continue.'

'Johann had hoped to make an appointment with George Carmichael last week. He had flown to England only to discover that unfortunately, George was holidaying in Heidelberg of all places. This meant that that Johann had to return to Germany the day after he had arrived in Manchester. He flew out again on Sunday and was able to visit Carmichael's on Monday morning.'

'Does that mean he saw George Carmichael?'

'He did. But George Carmichael would not let Johann have whatever document that Otto had left, because George apparently had looked at a copy of the will that Otto had made and noticed the addendum that the will was not to be executed until the deaths of Tanya and Frank.'

'So, you will agree then Dieter, that George Carmichael acted entirely appropriately as you and I would have done?'

'I would have agreed with you had Michael not turned up a little later. George Carmichael handed over the letter to him from Otto, something that he should never have done.'

'You and I both know Dieter, that Michael is the only surviving heir of David McKay, a position that you have endorsed and in fact were keen to buy the inheritance from him for eight million euros. I cannot but ask myself, how you knew that Michael had been given the envelope? and why it was that Johann was so keen on retrieving it for you Dieter?'

'I telephoned to speak to George after Johann had advised me of the situation. When I mentioned to his secretary what it was in connection with, she apologised because George was at lunch and told me that everything had been dealt with and that Michael had received the letter written by Otto.'

'Why was it so important that Johann visit Michael and retrieve what was rightfully Michael's which Johann had no business to interfere with?'

'That is because the letter was addressed to the survivors of David McKee and most definitely not David McKay.'

'An enormous amount of effort was made in tracing McKee, and it was concluded that there was no one remotely connected to a field hospital in Normandy during July and August 1944 by that name. The only person who could possibly have attended to Private Otto Wagner at that time was Major David McKay. On that we both agreed.'

'That certainly was our initial thought that the right person had been found but now we are contesting that we have all been duped.'

'My dear chap, I know that you don't believe that to be the case for a single moment as in fact neither do I. I am more disturbed by the reality that a member of your personal staff should turn up uninvited at my client's home, barge in and assault Michael by pushing him to the ground and then proceeds to produce a loaded Glock handgun. Could you explain this to me please Dieter?'

'Indeed, I can Daniel. It was clear that Michael knew exactly the extraordinary value in monetary terms that the estate was now worth. Therefore, Johann considered that his life would be in danger if Michael knew that he was on to him. Therefore, he had to make it an unannounced surprise visit and use the gun in order to deter any act of aggression against him from Michael. Regrettably, he hadn't considered that Louise was capable of killing.'

'I understand that Johann was around six foot four inches tall, a muscular thirteen stone and an extremely fit individual. That he had spent ten years in the German armed forces the equivalent of our own S.A.S., was an expert in unarmed combat as well as being a highly skilled marksman. In other words, he was a trained killer. Whereas on the other hand, Michael is a doctor working daily in the stressful environment of Accident and Emergency at his local hospital. He is trained to save lives. I am therefore of a mind to dismiss your theory that Johann imagined that he would be in any sort of danger.'

'I did not ring to argue with you Daniel. I am deeply distressed that a personal employee of mine has been murdered by a client of yours whilst disputing the authenticity of a will.'

'May I put it to you Dieter, that in normal circumstances you would be carrying out this transaction without any doubts as to who is the rightful beneficiary is? I believe that what is concentrating the minds of the consortium who you represent, I am told that they call themselves 'The Brotherhood', a strange name, if I may say so for a group of businessmen, but that is neither here nor there.

'No, the main reason is the speculation that has existed for many years now, that a treasure trove was hidden somewhere on the estate. Apparently a five-week search took place by the Bavarian police department after the war when Otto was a P.O.W. and wasn't there. Nothing was discovered. And now during the past two years whilst you have been looking after the estate, a serious and thorough systematic excavation of every field has been occurring. Could you confirm why is this happening?'

'We had already explained to Michael, that it is alleged that a Roman village or small town quite possibly existed here. It is a fact that in 788 Charlemagne incorporated Bavaria into the

Carolingian empire for a short time. Bavaria became a part of the Holy Roman Empire in the tenth century. We are excavating the estate in the belief that evidence of this will be found and so confirm what historians and archaeologists have always suspected.'

'According to Michael's observations, it looked like a crude search with mechanical diggers. Normally for an archaeological dig of this sort, there would be many people on their hands and knees sifting with trowels. My interpretation of why Johann was desperate to get hold of the letter given to Michael, is that Otto would have revealed the details of where this treasure trove was hidden. Is that not the case Dieter?'

'Now listen here Daniel, my patience is beginning to run thin. You are representing as indeed is your right, a person who has cold bloodedly and without provocation murdered an employee of mine in the execution of their duty. I need to know where the letter is that had been left by Otto Wagner and given to Michael and importantly, if that letter has been opened?'

Daniel looked across at Louise and winked at us.

'Your capacity for patience is clearly thin my friend but is of no importance to me. It is interesting that you should use the word describing Johann as executing his job, because I suspect that he would have had no second thoughts about executing both Louise and Michael in order to obtain the letter.

'There does seem to be a bit of a pattern developing. First of all, there was the apparent suicide of Christian and Ursula and then only last week the premises of Henry Winkler who ran a business in tracing people and their family tree, we call them here in England genealogists, his office was firebombed shortly after you heard that he was making progress in finding out what happened to members of the Benowitz family.'

'You have said enough Daniel. It is of crucial importance that the letter written by Otto is not opened. I will arrange with your Crown Prosecution Service if they permit me to prosecute on their behalf in this case as it involves a German national as well as a will written by a German national in connection with an estate in Germany. Goodbye Daniel.'

Chapter 13

Because of a backlog in cases the Crown Prosecution Service were unable to bring Louise to court for eleven months. She had spent the entire time in Holloway Prison in London. She became very adept at taking care of herself and indeed protecting some of the more vulnerable inmates, not by her physicality but by the power of words.

Being such an attractive young woman inevitably brought her to the attention of several highly sexually charged and deprived women. But Louise dealt with them kindly and assured them that they were wasting their time. It soon became apparent to the prison governor that Louise was a good influence. She began helping other women to read as well as assisting in the prison library.

I had been offered a new job in Addenbrookes Hospital which I would have taken had it not been for Louise being incarcerated. I felt an anger every day, but Louise just accepted the circumstances in which she now found herself. She was determined to make every minute count and subscribed, somewhat surprisingly, that no matter how long you nurse a grudge, it will never get better. She had no doubt at all that she would soon be free again.

The first day of the trial held at the Old Bailey attracted a good deal of press coverage. Our case was to be heard in the famous Court Number One, that had served as a court since it opened in 1907. Trials such as the case against Penguin Books on the charge of obscenity by publishing D.H. Lawrence's *Lady Chatterley's Lover* and the trial of Ruth Ellis for murder resulting in her being the last woman in Britain to face the hangman's noose had taken place inside this courtroom.

The public gallery was filled to capacity. It had been agreed that both cases would be linked together. The charge of murder and the inheritance which was deemed to have been an integral part leading to the trial.

Louise was escorted into the seat which is reserved for the accused. There was a male prison officer on either side of her. Having spent almost a year in prison had not diminished her poise, confidence or beauty. Because of her status as being a trusted prisoner, she had been able to spend 45 minutes in the gym each day. She had taken full advantage of this privilege.

Dieter Muller had been given leave to prosecute the case on behalf of the CPS, a most unusual occurrence for a foreign prosecutor to take the lead in an English Court of Law. Dieter and Daniel greeted one another with courtesy and handshakes.

The Jury were sworn in and Mr Justice Langholme took his place, this being his final case before entering retirement after fifty years' service involving criminal justice.

There was no doubt about it, Dieter cut a very impressive figure in outlining the case for the prosecution. Although he spoke good English, his German accent meant that those present had to be extra attentive to hear and understand what it was he was saying at all times.

Dieter for the benefit of the jury covered what he had already outlined to Daniel. A client of his law firm had written a will leaving his entire estate to an Englishman called McKee. After engaging a London Law Firm Hildreth and Watkins, the best that they could do was to come up with a Michael Packham who was the grandson of a Major David McKay. The prosecution case, therefore, is that this is an instance of mistaken identity. The will clearly indicated that should no descendant of McKee be located then the estate would be left to a consortium borne out of an organisation of which Otto himself was a member.

Dieter called no witnesses and strode back to his seat with the air of a man who had kept things very simple for the jury and easy for them to understand the facts. Namely that Michael Packham was not the beneficiary of the will of McKee.

Daniel Watkins remained seated for a moment or two before standing and making his way before the jury. He smiled at them as if he were greeting acquaintances that he had not seen for some time.

'Ladies and gentlemen of the jury. This case I would suggest has its roots right back to before the Second World War. The estate in question was owned by a Jew by the name of Abraham Benowitz. In 1938, a Nazis decree ordered that any commercial business owned by a Jew must be transferred to an Aryan. Abraham had twin daughters and in the year of 1907 Abraham and his wife Hannah employed a governess called Hildegard to educate and teach their daughters music. Hildegard quickly became a member of the family.

'In 1921 Hildegard married a man called Otto Wagner. They spent their honeymoon as guests of the Benowitz family. Otto had met Adolph Hitler in Vienna in 1912, they were both Austrian. After the First World War, Germany was in disarray which led to the creation of many political parties. One of these was called the German Workers Party and was founded by a man called Anton Drexler. Otto became an administrator for Anton and a little while later Adolf Hitler joined the Party and a year or so later took over as leader and at the same time renaming the party, the Nazi party.

'After Hitler failed to gain power in 1923 in what was to become known as the Munich Putsch, he was imprisoned. A little later Otto, who was a talented artist, managed to get himself a position teaching art at a private school. He and Hildegard were the proud parents of a son called Helmut who was born in 1922.

'Then in 1927 out of the blue, Adolf Hitler who had been released from prison after just a few months, knocks at Otto's door and offers Otto a job as one of Hitler's main administrators. Apparently, Hitler had been very impressed with Otto's efficiency. Otto took up the offer and worked in the Munich headquarters. Hitler then set up a headquarters in Berlin. Otto had little contact with the Führer after that.

'Then out of the blue, in 1933 Otto was summoned by Hitler to Berlin where he also met again Himmler, Goebbels and Goering. It was at this meeting that Hitler appointed Otto as administrator for a new project called Dachau, and in order to give Otto a rank of authority, Hitler appointed him as a member of the SS.

'Both Hildegard and Otto became increasingly concerned by what they were witnessing. At first Dachau had been a concentration camp for political opponents, many of them were communists, whose policies Otto did not support. But as time went on the background of those being detained at Dachau changed. They now included priests, academics, gypsies, and Jews. Otto although not approving, realised that it would be dangerous for him and his family if he were to voice his concerns. Therefore, like huge number of Germans at that time, he remained quiet.

'Then on 9th November 1938 a date that was to become known as "The Night of Broken Glass" when Jewish business and synagogues were attacked and set on fire. That very evening Leah and Eliana Benowitz the daughters of Abraham were picked up and taken to Dachau. Members of the jury call it what you want, "An act of God, divine intervention or fate" whatever it is, it was fortunate that Otto was the administrator and managed to persuade the commandant to release the girls.

'Quickly after this came the decree about transferring assets from Jews to Aryans. I suggest to you that it was probably because of Otto being a member of the SS and the fact that many high-ranking officials knew that he had been a friend of the Führer's that Otto was permitted to be the recipient of Abraham's estate. The family Benowitz then managed to move abroad. We believe the twins stayed in London whilst Abraham and Hannah settled in America.

'Three significant things happened over the next five years. First of all, Helmut Wagner who was a Luftwaffe pilot lost his life in Russia. This had a devasting effect on Hildegard who sadly took her own life. Otto then left the estate in good hands, worked in Berlin for a while before volunteering as a Panzer tank radio operator.

'It was in August 1944 that Otto was shot and injured during a battle near Falaise in Normandy. It was here that his life was saved by a British army surgeon by the name of Major David McKay. Please ladies and gentlemen remember the name McKay. Otto then spent almost four years as a prisoner of war in Yorkshire.

'Upon his release he returned to run the estate. In his absence the farm had been very well managed by his estate manager Christian Schmidt and his wife Ursula. They were Otto's best friends. Before Otto's return a thorough search lasting for more than five weeks was undertaken at the behest of the Bavarian chief of police. It had been rumoured that many valuable artefacts mainly from churches, synagogues and wealthy Jews had been hidden on the estate. Nothing was discovered.

'Otto then made his will which was drawn up by the father of my learned friend Dieter Muller. In the will, Otto had left the entire estate to the Schmidt's. Then in 1949 Christian and Ursula were found dead in their car. The cause of death was recorded as suicide. Now if you please Your Honour, I would like to call my first witness, Father Benedict.'

After Father Benedict had been sworn in Daniel went back to his desk and picked up some papers before resuming. 'Thank you, Father Benedict, for travelling here today to assist us in the pursuit of justice. Could you please tell the court how it is that you know the defendant, Miss Louise Johnson?'

'Certainly, sir. I am the priest at the Roman Catholic Church of the Virgin Mary which is in the village of Bischofswiesen in Bavaria. It was about a year ago, upon entering the church I discovered two visitors who introduced themselves as Michael Packham and Louise Johnson. They advised me that they had inherited the farm estate known as *Schlachthaus*.

'This for me was a big deal. The estate of *Schlachthaus* had played an important part in village life for many years. Two years prior to my meeting Michael and Louise, the estate had been handed over to be managed by a consortium. I therefore invited Michael and Louise to join my sister, Elizabeth, and I for tea.

'I ran through the circumstances of how the estate had been transferred from Abraham to Otto. I could tell that they were shocked when they heard this. Otto had given his word to Abraham that he would merely be looking after the estate until such time as Abraham could return. He carried on with Abraham's policy of helping villagers who needed help. He confided in me that the place was subject to an intense search authorised by the Bavarian Chief of Police.'

'Could I ask Father Benedict, what were they hoping to find?'

'In 1938 it became apparent where the government policies were leading. Jews and others were being victimised and it was thought that a large group of church leaders and wealthy Jews, looking to the future, when the nightmare would be at an end, decided to hide some of their most valuable possessions.'

'What sort of possessions?'

'It was rumoured that a good deal of artwork and other precious artefacts, especially from churches and synagogues were hidden.'

'Did Otto ever indicate that this was the case?'

'He gave no indication whatsoever that this rumour was true.'

'We have heard that the estate had been successfully manged during Otto's absence by Christian and Ursula Schmidt. Otto named them in his will as I believe that he had no surviving heirs to be his sole beneficiaries. They then retired and a few months later, their bodies were found together in what appeared to be an act of suicide. Did this come as a shock to you?'

'It came as a total shock. They were probably the happiest married couple that I knew. They had a comfortable lifestyle and had thrown themselves into village life and gave a lot of their now free time working for the community.'

'Does that mean that there were doubts over whether this was something other than suicide, murder perhaps?'

Dieter jumped to his feet. 'Objection Your Honour, we are here to listen to facts and not speculation or opinions.'

'Objection sustained, please move on Counsellor.'

'After Otto's death and the consortium taking over the running of the estate, did you notice any changes?'

'Yes sir. A man by the name of Heinrich Merkel was appointed to manage the estate. The first thing that he did was to cancel the support that had been given to the many villagers.'

'Was this Heinrich Merkel an aggressive individual?'

'Objection Your Honour, Counsel is leading the witness.'

'Objection sustained.'

'I have no more questions Your Honour.'

Dieter had decided on the tactic of remaining as passive as possible.

'The prosecution has no questions for this witness Your Honour.'

Justice Langholme banging his gavel. 'In that case we adjourn for lunch and resume at two this afternoon.'

I looked towards Louise as she was taken by her escorts, not before she had blown me a kiss, that I returned.

At the resumption, Dieter Muller rose and walked towards the jury box. 'Members of the Jury, you have heard my learned friend ask that you concentrate on the name McKay. He is absolutely right; this you must do. The wishes of Otto were to leave his entire estate to the descendants of a man called McKee and not as the defence would have you believe, a man called McKay.

'The defendant before you, is charged with the brutal murder of Johann Ballack. Why would she murder someone who she scarcely knew? Indeed, had only met him two weeks before and had been shown great respect by the now deceased, who had endeavoured to be of help at all times. Johann Ballack, who as you know was an employee of mine, had met Michael and Louise at the airport, had given them a tour of Munich, had driven them to the estate and then the following day taken them to Salzburg. He had done everything he could to make their visit an enjoyable experience.

'So, why murder him? It must be remembered that Louise worked as an estate agent. She was merely an employee. It was not her business. She earnt a reasonable salary but no more. Her fiancé, Michael Packham is a doctor working at a local hospital in the Accident and Emergency Department. His salary was greater, but nothing out of the ordinary. They lived in a property that had a mortgage. You could say they enjoyed a good stand-ard of living, but nothing exceptional.

'And then totally unexpectedly they receive a letter advising them that they may be the beneficiaries of a substantial proper-ty and farm estate in Bavaria. The value of which is put at sev-eral million euros. This is wealth beyond her wildest dreams. With such wealth, there would be no need ever to work again. The drabness of having to go to work every day and show cli-ents around properties that she would have no interest in. She and Michael could now afford a substantial house in the coun-try of their own. They could purchase top of the range cars, even a yacht, they could employ servants. They could travel the world.

'Members of the Jury, can you imagine this happening to you? And then there is doubt, that they are the beneficiaries of these unexpected circumstances and that everything that Louise was dreaming of, could be taken away in an instance.

'I suspect that they would have known that if the descendants of this McKee were not found then the wishes of Otto, that his estate be passed onto an organisation that he was once a mem-ber of would be fulfilled.

'This prospect would have horrified Louise. On the day that they left Germany to return to England, somehow, they discov-ered in the library behind a picture of an English town scene, that Otto, who incidentally, members of the Jury was an accom-plished artist, had a painted, there was a note stating that this pic-ture was of great significance.

'In the forefront of the picture was an office of a solicitors called Carmichael's. Louise feared that Otto might have left something during his visit to England in 1949 that would repu-diate Michael's claim. She therefore researched this and discov-ered there was such a firm that was still in practice in the small market town of Wetherby.

'Apart from fearing being denied what she considered now to be Michael's property, I put it to you that she had also realised that there may be substantially more. The rumours that there might be a treasure trove and if discovered would be worth many millions would be worth killing for.

'I am the partner in the law firm that was originally entrusted with carrying out the wishes of Otto Wagner. By sheer coincidence we also deduced the possible significance of Otto's painting. I then authorised Johann to visit the offices which had a sole solicitor by the name of George Carmichael.

'Mr Carmichael confirmed what we had suspected, and that was that Otto had left a letter with George Carmichael's father the late Zacharia Carmichael in 1949. He confirmed that he had no idea what the contents of the letter were as it was addressed to the descendants of McKee. Please note members of the Jury, the name McKee and not McKay. George Carmichael did not hand over this letter to Johann, stating that he needed to conduct further enquires.

'It was by pure chance, that when I telephoned George Carmichael to speak with him that I discovered through his secretary that the envelope had been given to Michael.

'Members of the Jury, you can imagine my absolute horror that a fraud of great magnitude was in the making. Michael could destroy the envelope and say afterwards that the contents were of no importance. One thing is for sure, this letter would not have been addressed to McKay. It could though, as have been alluded to reveal the whereabouts of this mysterious treasure trove.

'Once I had established that Michael had wrongly been given the envelope, I contacted Johann to advise him it would be good if he could see Michael and explain to him the situation as I have explained it to you. That unfortunately there had been a mistake and that Michael was not the beneficiary.

'I was aware in instructing Johann that I could be placing him in great danger.

Anyone who had been misled that they were to receive a huge windfall and then to be told that it was all a mistake and that they were not the beneficiaries, well, I put it to you, we would all be angry wouldn't we? I therefore advised Johann to be incredibly careful as I considered that Michael and Louise could be dangerous and would do all in their power to retain the illusion that they were the rightful owners of this estate.

'Johann who had spent many hours with Michael and Louise and therefore knew them quite well, must have also realised the possible danger and therefore took a small gun in with him for self-defence purposes only. The police will confirm that a knife and fork were found in the hallway. I put it to you that with this knife Michael was about to use it to stab Johann. Johann, according to Michael himself managed to shove him to the ground. It was then out of fear for his own life, that Johann withdrew the pistol from his pocket.

'There was no time for Johann to explain that he had merely brought the pistol for his own self-protection. He was immediately and savagely attacked by Louise with a scolding saucepan of soup. It is assumed from the coroner's report that the soup was thrown first and that she then hit Johann as hard as she could on the side of his head. This resulted in a traumatic head injury of which Johann was to succumb just a few hours later.

'My learned friend for the defence will, have you believe that this was an act of self-defence on the part of Miss Louise Johnson. It is more than likely that throwing the scolding soup into Johann's face would have been enough to disarm Johann. Can you imagine the pain that he was feeling with his skin being instantly burned?

'Therefore, members of the Jury, I leave it to you to decide. Why would Miss Johnson after disabling Johann with boiling soup when it would be apparent that Johann would not be a threat, did she deliberately hit him again with such force that he died very soon afterwards? The answer is simple. She did not wish Otto's estate to pass to anyone else but Michael Packham. This is her fiancé, and she was bound to benefit with life changing results. A life that would now be filled with fun and adventure instead of the daily trudge to earn a crust working as an estate agent.'

Dieter again did not ask to question any witnesses, but instead went to his position on the right-hand side of the court and sat down.

Justice Langholme, looking at his watch, banged his gavel and declared. 'It is now three thirty on a Friday afternoon. I think this is a good time to stop now. We will resume at ten a.m. Monday. Members of the Jury, I know that there is no need to remind you, but it has been a habit of mine to do so anyway, but you must not discuss this case with anyone whilst outside of this courtroom. I wish everyone a good weekend.'

'All stand,' called the court usher.

We all stood as Justice Langholme disappeared into his back office before no doubt leaving London, bound for his home in the county of Hampshire and a weekend of pheasant shooting.

Dieter Muller and his team left while I turned and once again exchanged blow kisses with Louise.

The following morning, I visited Louise in Holloway. I was amazed how calm and upbeat she was. It was clear to me that she had no doubt that she was innocent and would be released after the trial.

'Hello, my darling, how are you bearing up?' I said.

'I'm fine,' she smiled. 'Dieter did an impressive job of making me look greedy and bad and gave a compelling reason why I might have deliberately murdered Johann. I am confident that the truth will prevail, but it did make me consider how many innocent people have been put away because of the convincing arguments made by those prosecuting?'

'Well, you won't be one of them, my love.'

CHAPTER 14

'All rise,' instructed the court usher.

Justice Langholme took his seat and then peering over his half-moon spectacles hoped that everyone had enjoyed the sunshine of the weekend?

'Are both Counsels ready to resume?' he inquired with a benign smile. Both Counsellors nodded. 'In that case, Mr Watkins you may continue.'

'Thank you, my Lord, I would like to call George Carmichael to the stand.'

George Carmichael cut an imposing figure as he took the oath.

'Mr Carmichael, would you please tell the jury what your occupation is and where you ply your profession?'

'I was a solicitor in the Yorkshire town of Wetherby, I retired just over a year ago.' Anticipating what Daniel's next questions would be, he continued. 'My father Zachariah Carmichael, established the practice in 1920 and I took over from him in 1960.'

'I thank you for your explanation. Could you please tell the court the sequence that has brought you here today?'

'Two weeks before my retirement, just over a year ago now, I had returned from taking a week's holiday in the beautiful German town of Heidelberg. During my first morning back, my secretary had arranged several appointments. The first two were to do with neighbour disputes, but the third and fourth I could see and so could my secretary, that they were connected. After dealing with the first two appointments, I then waited to see who was to be my next visitor.'

'Could you tell the court who that was?'

'The gentleman was a German national by the name of Johann Ballack.'

'Do you have a large German clientele seeking your services in Wetherby?'

George gave a gruff chuckle. 'It may surprise this court to discover that in almost fifty years, this gentleman was only the second German to set foot inside of the offices of Carmichael's.'

'Could you tell the court, who the first German national was?'

'In 1949 my father Zachariah Carmichael took instructions from a German client called Otto Wagner. Otto explained to my father that he had been a prisoner of war from late 1944 to 1948. It transpired that Otto's life had been saved by a British army surgeon, whose name he was not entirely sure of, but it sounded when he had asked, like McKee.

'As Otto had no living relatives, he had decided to leave his estate to this McKee. He advised my father that the original copy of his will was lodged with a German law firm called Muller and Schneider. This was the second will that he had made. The first had left the estate to a loyal couple who had served him well called Christian and Ursula Schmidt. They unfortunately had died just a few months earlier. It was listed as suicide. Otto however, firmly believed that they were murdered.'

'Objection your honour,' Dieter said springing to his feet. 'The death certificate clearly shows death caused by carbon monoxide poisoning and concluded as a hose was attached to the car that the most likely cause of death was suicide.'

'Indeed,' replied Justice Langholme, 'but again this is just an opinion of the coroner, no one witnessed their deaths, so there could be room for doubt. Continue Mr Carmichael.'

'Thank you, Your Honour. Otto explained that there was no reason for them to have taken their own lives. They were well respected by their peers and did a lot of good things for the village in which they lived. Otto then went on to explain that an organisation representing ex-Nazis who had avoided criminal proceedings at the end of the war were putting pressure on him to leave the estate to them. This would provide them with a regular revenue stream from a profitable farm operation.

'This organisation must have discovered that the Schmidt's were childless and also had no relatives to leave their estate to. Therefore, Otto surmised that the organisation believed that if the Schmidt's were disposed of, then Otto would have no choice but to leave the estate to them.'

'Objection your honour.' Interrupted Dieter. 'This is pure conjecture.'

'Is this pure conjecture, Mr Carmichael?' asked judge Langholme.

'No sir, it is not. My father had a reputation for being extremely thorough in everything that he did. He wrote down almost in verbatim what had taken place. Also, when he retired and handed over the business to me, he explained everything concerning Otto Wagner in great detail and emphasised the importance that Otto's wishes be carried out.'

'So, what were Otto's wishes?' Daniel asked.

'My father was shown and given a copy of Otto's final will. It was his wish that his entire estate pass to the descendants of Major McKee. But he inserted a clause or addendum stating that the two employees who had replaced the Schmidt's a certain Tanya van der Leyen and a Frank Meyer, be permitted to continue living on and running the estate in the same manner as Christian and Ursula Schmidt had done. Only after their deaths could the search begin for the relatives of Major McKee.'

'Now the court has been told by my right honourable friend that Otto left an envelope with your father, is that correct?' Daniel asked.

'It is Sir. A sealed envelope was left with my father. The details on the outside of the envelope merely said To Major McKee or his descendants.'

'Could you tell the court what the contents of that envelope were?'

'No sir, Otto had expressly given instructions that the envelope was only for Major McKee or his decedents.'

'Now Mr Carmichael, may we return to the visit to your office of Johann Ballack? What was the purpose of that visit?'

'He mentioned that he was representing a well-respected Munich law firm called Muller and Schneider. They were the executors of a will that was drawn up on behalf of a man called Otto Wagner. It would seem that Otto had left his estate to a man called McKee who had saved Otto's life during the war.'

'Forgive me for interrupting you Mr Carmichael, but did you say that Johann acknowledged that the reason for Otto's request was because his life had been saved by an Englishman or perhaps Scotsman, called McKee during the war?'

'That was what he said. He then continued to advise me that Muller and Ernst had obtained legal authority to run the estate whilst they pursued exhaustive enquiries to locate this McKee. Forty-eight years had passed and regrettably as no descendant of McKee has been found that the Statute of Limitations owing to the time that has passed has been applied for in the German courts.

'He then went on to suggest that they had reason to believe that Otto Wagner visited Wetherby in 1949 and may have seen my father, and perhaps left a document which would help establish their credentials.'

'That seems perfectly reasonable to me Mr Carmichael. Did you hand over the forementioned letter?'

'No sir, I didn't.'

'And why was this?'

'Before Johann had arrived, I took the trouble to read Otto's will once more. It clearly stated he wished for his will not to be executed until after the deaths of Tanya and Frank. Frank died in 1997. Therefore, the Statute of Limitations did not apply.'

'What happened then?'

'Mr Ballack left in an angry mood advising me that my actions could be viewed as conspiring against the wishes of Otto Wagner in denying that his estate be passed to the rightful custodians. As he was leaving, he told me that I was likely to receive a call from Dieter Muller.'

'And then what happened?'

'A little while after that Michael Packham arrived on time for his appointment.'

'What was the purpose of his visit? It must have seemed odd after all the years with no one contacting you, that you should receive two visits from different people on the same morning?'

'My secretary Alison, who is a smart cookie, drew my attention to this unusual event, so I was very much on my guard. It was too much of a coincidence.'

'What persuaded you to give the envelope to Michael?'

'Michael gave a full account of what had happened and how he and Louise were acting on a hunch owing to discovering a note on the back of a painting by Otto Wagner that showed the office of Carmichael's. He then explained in great detail the events that had led to his being named as the beneficiary.'

'I imagined that he was ecstatic about his newly found status as a wealthy landowner and one would presume an extraordinarily rich man?'

'I would have agreed with you and would have expected this to be the case. However, Michael and Louise were appalled that the land had in their view been stolen from Abraham. He also mentioned, something that Johann had not, and that was that there was much speculation that a treasure trove had been concealed at the estate before the outbreak of war.'

'If this treasure trove were to be discovered,' Daniel asked, 'I imagine that any item that cannot be returned to its original place, would then become the property of Michael's?'

'That is exactly what would happen.'

'So, Michael and Louise would be exceedingly wealthy, would they not?'

'What you say is true if that were the wishes of Michael and Louise.'

'I don't understand, what do you mean by that?'

'It was because of the circumstances in which Otto had acquired the estate and that he had made clear to Abraham, that he was only looking after it until such time as Abraham returned that Michael and Louise decided that they did not want to benefit from this unexpected circumstance.'

'That's extraordinary. What were they planning to do?'

'After visiting the estate for the first time, they then engaged a firm of genealogists to track down the provenance of the estate and then to locate any surviving relatives of the Benowitz family.'

'Were they successful in doing this?'

'They employed a company in Vienna that was established by a Henry Winkler. He told them about the provenance with regard to the original owners being Abraham and his forefathers. Abraham was the third generation. Michael then instructed Henry Winkler to trace any descendants of the Benowitz family.

'On the day that they were due to depart Germany. They were at a meeting with Dieter Muller at *Schlachthaus* when Henry Winkler telephoned. Michael put his phone on speaker so that those present could hear what Henry Winkler had to say. Henry Winkler then explained that he was making progress and would be in touch. Within the week, the premises of Henry Winkler had been firebombed and Henry Winkler died from his burns two months later.'

'What you are saying Mr Carmichael is shocking. The possibility of tracing members of the Benowitz family that was heard by Dieter Muller, resulted in Henry Winkler losing his life and all of his records destroyed?'

'Objection Your Honour!' snapped Dieter Muller. 'The inference here is that I had something to do with the unfortunate incident in Vienna which cost the life of Henry Winkler.'

'I apologise Your Honour, I will withdraw the question,' said Daniel, knowing full well that he had just sewn a seed in the minds of the jurors. 'What had Michael and Louise planned to do?'

'Michael made it perfectly clear that they had no wish to benefit from this and would try to establish the rightful owners and then return it to them.'

'What you are saying, completely contradicts my learned friend for the prosecution, when he states that Louise's motive for killing Johann was borne out of greed. That she and Michael could live a life of luxury. A big house, servants, a yacht and continuous travel.'

'That was the case, yes.'

'So therefore, the death of Johann was not caused through a desire to hold onto something for their own personal gain, but perhaps more to do with self-defence?'

'Objection your honour, this witness cannot possibly know what motives Louise had for murdering Johann, he wasn't there to see what happened.'

'None of us were there Herr Muller. The law of probability as you know is often taken into account when reaching a verdict.'

'I have no more questions Your Honour. Your witness.'

'The prosecution has no questions for this witness Your Honour.'

'In that case we will break for lunch and resume at two this afternoon.'

Everyone filed out of court and headed in most cases for the local eateries. I looked at Daniel and asked, 'How do you think things are going? I notice that Dieter has not chosen to cross examine anyone.'

'It is going very well my boy, there is no need for you and Louise to be concerned. My team have carried out a good deal of research. I hope that the court will be surprised by our findings.'

Chapter 15

Just before two, everyone was back in court and safely if their seats. Louise then entered the court flanked by her security officers. After which Justice Langholme opened the proceedings.

'Good afternoon everyone.' He spoke as he was leaning forward, whilst looking over his half-moon glasses. 'I trust that everyone has now been fed and watered and we are ready to resume?'

'I now call upon the Prosecuting Council, Herr Muller, to call the next witness.'

Dieter stood to his full height and then looking towards the jury said, 'Alas the main witness for the prosecution in respect of the will, would have been Johann Ballack. But as we are acutely aware, Johann is unable to be with us because of the murderous actions, caused through greed, of the defendant, Miss Louise Johnson. This has resulted in the second part of this trial being necessary. Without my main witness Your Honour, I have no witnesses to call.'

'Thank you, Counsellor.'

'Therefore, I invite Mr. Watkins to call his next witness for the defence.'

'Thank you, Your Honour. This is a most unusual case and an extraordinary sequence of circumstances. In all my years and I would also think yours too, Your Honour, I have never been in court with an overseas lawyer prosecuting a case on behalf of the Crown Prosecution Service.'

'I agree with you,' Justice Langholme confirmed.

'But what makes this even more extraordinary, is why the Crown Prosecution Service would have allowed such a thing, and secondly why Dieter Muller was insistent that this case should be prosecuted by him. I realise that the case concerns a German Estate, left in the will by a German national and that it was a German citizen who has lost his life. But Dieter Muller is very much part of the jigsaw in this case. He is in a unique position to throw light on several matters.

'I would therefore in these highly unusual circumstances call as my next witness, Herr Dieter Muller.'

'Objection your honour, it is Louise Johnson who is on trial, not me.'

'That is perfectly so, Herr Muller. But as the Counsel for the defence has suggested, you are in a unique position to shed light on several of the events, especially as the sadly deceased Johann Ballack was an employee of yours.'

Dieter then rose and walked from behind his desk and entered the witness box. After taking the oath to tell the truth and nothing but the truth, Daniel Watkins, then approached with a genial smile.

'I am grateful to you Herr Muller for agreeing to be a witness in what after all is totally unprecedented. But as His Honour has pointed out you are a key component in this trial.'

'I will do whatever I can, rest assured,' Dieter confirmed, 'in assisting that justice is done especially for Johann's wife and family who are seeking closure.'

'Yes of course, we all want that. The firm that you are a partner in, Muller and Schneider, is remarkably similar to my own Hildreth and Watkins. You and I have taken over from our fathers. Can you confirm please that you first met Otto Wagner, when you were a junior at Muller and Schneider back in 1949?'

'That is correct, I met Otto Wagner when he came in and my father wrote out his Last Will and Testament.'

'Did your father conduct any other work during the war? For example, was he a member of the Nazi party?'

'Your Honour, we are here to discuss this case, are we not? Not to discuss my family.'

'I am interested to see where Mr Watkins questions are taking him, so I will permit it. Please answer the questions,' instructed Justice Langholme.

'My father was just a solicitor and nothing more. Like many Germans, he kept his head down during the war.'

'I only ask the question because my team have done a good deal of research. Members of the jury, none of you would have fought during the Second World War. Indeed, looking at you, it appears that we have a very youthful jury. So please allow me to give a quick report on what it was like to live in Germany during the war.

'We are all fortunate to live in Britain where our police are regarded as friends, people that we might call on in a time of need. A road accident, a burglary or an assault or even helping to locate a missing person. The only ones to fear the police in our country are the criminals and law breakers.

'Sadly, this was not the case during the Second World War in Nazi Germany. There were several police forces in operation, but the most feared was a force called the Gestapo. Not everyone was in uniform. The Gestapo relied heavily on paid informers. The Gestapo were able to operate carte blanche without judicial review. Any person that they considered was against the regime of the Reich, they would put into a thing called protective custody.

'This protective custody was a euphemism for the power to imprison people without judicial process. An oddity of the system was that the prisoner had to sign an order declaring that he or she had requested to be imprisoned for their own safety.

'The research done by my staff has revealed that in Munich from 1943 until just before the war ended, that there were two solicitors, one called Gunther Muller and the second was named as Pieter Schneider both of whom held the rank of SS-Hauptsturmführer in the Gestapo. Just to be sure that we had the right names, it would appear that they had both fathered one son each. Their names were Dieter and Ernst.

'Another fact that we discovered, a man who was to become the Bavarian chief of police immediately after the war, was a gentleman by the name of Hans Adenauer. He was also a member of the Gestapo with the rank of SS-Oberführer.

'Now, I ask you again Herr Muller was your father a member of the Gestapo?'

'I cannot believe what I am hearing Your Honour. My father was a loving, caring husband and father.'

'That may be so, Herr Muller,' agreed Justice Langholme, 'but we do need you to answer the question.'

'No! he most certainly was not!'

'I imagine,' continued Mr Watkins, 'that you would have known the Bavarian chief of police, Hans Adenauer?'

'Yes of course, he was a very important man in the State of Bavaria, particularly following the end of the war when there was much crime.'

'Were you aware Herr Muller that Hans Adenauer was also a member of the Gestapo during the war?'

'I was not aware of that, no.'

'The entire legal profession works under a code of confidentiality. There has to be an unbreakable trust between a client and their legal representative. Would you agree with that Herr Muller?'

'Absolutely, no question about it. This is why firms such as the one that you work in and my own have prospered for so many years. Our clints come to us in the knowledge that they will be represented well. In the case of disputes, we give a fair and accurate appraisal for our clients. If we think that they are making a claim that is not justified and therefore will not result in a positive outcome for them, then we say so at the start. We don't wish for our clients to waste their time and more importantly, their money.'

'That's a very noble principle Herr Muller. It is not one regrettably that is observed by all law firms.'

'I agree, but it is by adhering to this that Muller and Schneider have built such an impeccable reputation over many years.'

'I am wondering, Herr Muller, if what you are telling this court is actually true. The reason that I say this, is why would a will of Otto Wagner's which only you would have known about, attract a visit from Hans Adenauer, the Bavarian chief of police? Hans Adenauer aggressively interviewed both Christian and Ursula Schmidt.'

'Objection your honour,' Dieter Muller interrupted. 'How would anyone know if Hans Adenauer was being aggressive?'

'Sustained, move on please Mr Watkins.'

'Thank you, Your Honour. The main point is that the Schmidt's were visited by the chief of the Bavarian police, who knew that the estate had been left to them in Otto Wagner's will and not to an organisation that Hans Adenauer belonged to.

'Now it begs the question, how would Hans Adenauer have known?

'Herr Muller, would you please identify who this organisation is please? I believe that they may be called The Brotherhood, is that correct?'

'You know Mr Watkins as well as His Honour here, that I am not able to disclose the details of any clients.'

'I would agree with you if that had always been the case. But in the instance of Otto Wagner's will I would suggest to the court that details of the beneficiaries were leaked to Hans Adenauer. We know, and I have documents to prove it, that Gunther Muller, Pieter Schneider and Hans Adenauer were all in the Gestapo together. If you like they were a Brotherhood.'

'Your honour?' interrupted Dieter Muller. 'May both counsels approach the bench?'

'Of course,' responded Justice Langholme.

'Your Honour, I have found myself in a totally unexpected situation, one that I was not prepared for. It is causing me a huge amount of stress. The suggestions of the counsel for the defence are outrageous. I have been suffering for a little while now from a duodenal ulcer. I am feeling very unwell at this moment, and would request that I be excused from the witness box?'

Justice Langholme then looked at Daniel Watkins. 'Mr Watkins, it is not unusual for a witness to feel ill whilst giving their testimony. We both know that very often this is related to anxiety. What are your views please?'

'Your Honour, Herr Muller here is an experienced lawyer. He has I suspect just like me, stood up thousands of times to address a court. For him, he would be the principal actor in a theatre in which he would use his extensive knowledge of words. Those words would be used to persuade members of a jury to agree with whatever he was articulating.

'His becoming ill has resulted in his being made very uncomfortable by facts that he knows I am going to reveal to this court. I would recommend Your Honour that Dieter's request for an adjournment is denied.'

'Gentlemen,' began Justice Langholme, 'this is my very last case in which I sit in this famous Number One Court. I wish as always to be seen to be even handed and respectful to all that are part of these proceedings. I agree with the counsel for the defence that it does seem to be a bit of a coincidence you falling ill whilst being cross examined. Having said that, I would not wish to be the reason why your condition deteriorated. Will you be okay for the morning in which to continue with your testimony?'

'That is very considerate of you Your Honour and I thank you.'

'I am prepared then to adjourn today's sitting. However, being a foreign national and being a key witness to these proceedings, I am sure that you will understand Herr Muller, that I must request that you surrender your passport until the end of the trial.'

'Is it a request or are you insisting?' Dieter Muller responded.

'I am insisting. It is possible that you may decide to travel back to Germany which would give us a problem. The defendant, Miss Louise Johnson has already spent a year in prison, so it is vital for her that the charges against her are heard and resolved without further delay.'

With that the two lawyers resumed their normal positions and Justice Langholme explained that the court would be adjourning until the following day.

Chapter 16

I arrived at the court at ten minutes before ten and met once more with Daniel Watkins. We took our seats and a moment or two later, Louise was escorted in. The clock on the wall opposite the jury box showed that it was now a quarter past ten. Justice Langholme had yet to take his seat. Another noticeable absentee was that the chair of the crown prosecutor also remained empty. A murmur of low conversation took place. A few minutes later, the court usher addressed the packed court room.

'All rise.'

Justice Langholme slowly and calmly walked in and took his seat. Arranging some of his papers and taking a sip from the glass of water, he addressed the court.

'Ladies and Gentlemen, I apologise for the delayed start in this morning's proceedings. I can confirm that Herr Muller will be joining us in a few minutes time.'

Everyone in the court room just sat there and started to speak in whispered voices. A few minutes later, there was a noise at the back of the court and in came Dieter Muller with a police officer on either side of him. He was escorted to the table of the prosecutors and took his seat. The police offices then departed.

Justice Langholme, looking directly at Dieter Muller then delivered his opening remarks. 'Ladies and Gentlemen of the jury. I suspect that you are puzzled as to why Herr Muller for the crown prosecution has arrived late in court this morning and accompanied by two police offices. When the court adjourned yesterday, I directed that Herr Muller surrender his passport. This he did.

'After listening to the counsel for the defence yesterday, I felt unsure that Herr Muller would abide by my decision that he is to appear in this court today. As a precaution, I alerted our border force agency that Herr Muller might try to travel back to Germany using another passport.

'My instinct proved to be right when I received a call from Dover last night shortly before I was due to retire to bed advising me that indeed Herr Muller had presented a high-quality forged passport. They were able to apprehend Herr Muller, because we had taken the photo from his genuine passport and sent that to the agency. If they had not been on the lookout for the man in the photo, then the details in his forged passport would have got him through.

'I don't need to tell you Herr Muller that what took place last night was a serious offence. But it is one that I will deal with at the end of this trial. It is important that this trial continues in respect of being fair to the defendant, Miss Louise Johnson. So, we will carry on as if everything is the same. Mr Watkins, would you like to continue where you left off yesterday?'

'Thank you, Your Honour. I would like my learned friend Herr Muller to retake the stand please.'

Dieter Muller moved slowly across the court room floor. Not showing the same confidence or arrogance as he had on the first day of the trial. He took his seat and was sworn in once more.

'Herr Muller,' Watkins began, 'I hadn't realised that your gastro enteritis was so bad that you felt the need to flea England back to Germany in order to get emergency treatment. We do have good doctors here. But I am pleased as indeed we all are that you have made it to court this morning.'

Dieter Muller averted his eyes towards the floor.

'Members of the jury, just to recap from where we left off yesterday. If you remember, I had established that the two founding members of Muller and Schneider were during the war, middle ranking officers of the Gestapo. Another member at the same time was a man called Hans Adenauer who at the conclusion of the war became the chief of police for Bavaria.

'It must be acknowledged that not all members of the Gestapo wore the dreaded black uniform with the chilling insignia. Many members were civilians who were paid informers. I suggest that both Gunther Muller and Pieter Schneider used as cover their law practice to conceal a more sinister side of their activities.

'We have established that Otto Wagner directed Gunther Muller to draw up his will. Also present was our witness here this morning, Dieter Muller who was just starting out on his journey as an attorney at law. Otto had left his entire estate to his two devoted friends Christian and Ursula Schmidt.

'Whilst Otto was away in England as a prisoner of war, the Schmidt's received a visit from Hans Adenauer the chief of police questioning why it was that they had been left everything instead of to the organisation that Otto, according to Dieter Muller was an active member of.

'A little while later the chief of police returned once more with a search warrant personally signed by himself and a small army of officials and tore the place to pieces. This we now know was because of speculation that a treasure trove had been hidden on the estate shortly before the outbreak of war.

'Otto was then repatriated in 1948 and returned to take up the reins once more. The Schmidt's then retired and threw themselves into community projects. They were in their own way, civic leaders and were much respected.

'Otto was then visited by our friend Hans Adenauer, who once more questioned Otto as to why he had not left his estate to the organisation. Let me remind members of the jury, that Otto was a member of the SS. It was not a position that he had sought, it had been conferred upon him by no other than Adolf Hitler who he had met some twenty-one years earlier whilst they were artists in Vienna.

'Otto did not support the actions of what amounts to as ethnic cleansing. Otto questioned Hans Adenauer why it was that he thought this treasure trove had been hidden on the estate? Apparently, a priest had supplied the information which Adenauer confirmed must have been false intelligence. According to Adenauer the priest had met with an unfortunate accident, falling whilst out walking in the hills and hitting his head on a rock. Members of the jury, please note that Otto was led to believe by Adenauer himself that this was no accident, but that the priest had been murdered. This is death number one.

'The following year in 1949, the Schmidt's who were apparently enjoying their retirement, to the great shock of everyone who knew them, appeared to commit suicide. It begs the question why would a loving couple, who were happy and enjoyed life, were comfortably well off do such a thing? We have already heard from Father Benedict that many believed that this couple were murdered. And before my honourable friend objects, I agree that this is just speculation and that there is no proof that they were murdered. But suspicion, nevertheless, remains. These are now deaths two and three.

'After the Schmidt's were buried, Otto made out a new will in which he left everything to a man who had saved his life, called Major McKee. But as we have heard he included an addendum that his two live in staff were to stay there and that his will was not to be acted upon until they had both died. Now, we have to ask ourselves, why would Otto make the request that Hans Adenauer receives a copy of his will? We can only speculate that it was to make Adenauer aware of this clause and that others might also have knowledge of this. Therefore, it would appear too much of a coincidence if both Tanya and Frank were also to unexpectedly die.

'We can also surmise that Otto was hoping that he could buy some time. By that I mean that should either Tanya or Frank pass away in the late 1990s, which they both did, that this mysterious organisation would now be defunct.

'What could this organisation possibly be? Members of the Jury, you may or may not be familiar with a very distinguished English author called Frederick Forsyth. He first came to prominence with a brilliant book called *The Day of the Jackal*. It was about an anonymous Englishman who was hired to assassinate the then French president, General Charles de Gaulle.

'A subsequent book was titled *The Odessa File*. This involved a secret organisation consisting of ex Nazis whose purpose was to provide new identities for Nazi war time criminals many of whom managed to escape to Argentina. Adolf Eichmann was a good example of this. In the end Eichmann was kidnapped by Israeli agents and returned to Israel to face trial in 1960 where he was found guilty of war crimes and sentenced to death.

'I suggest that this organisation known as The Brotherhood, was a similar organisation, except that it was for lower ranking Nazi members. SS and Gestapo who will tell you that they were merely following orders. But many of these middle ranking officials were responsible for acts of unimaginable cruelty very often leading to death. Otto's estate would offer a regular source of income, but the main prize would have been to discover this treasure trove as it was believed to be concealed somewhere on the estate.

'We are now up to date. Frank Meyer dies in 1997. Muller and Schneider then seek to find the surviving beneficiary to Major McKee. They instruct a London firm, Hildreth and Watkins.' At this, Daniel Watkins makes a low bow towards the jury. 'We spent two years and engaged a genealogy company to trace one Michael Packham as being the only surviving relative of his grandad, David McKay.

'Members of the jury, we have heard from Dieter Muller himself that they accepted that this was the rightful person who they were seeking. They accepted that it was not Major McKee but Major McKay and that he was the only one possible who was in the right place at the right time. It was he who removed the bullet from Otto's shoulder. This was the person who Otto Wagner wished to thank for saving his life and therefore left his estate to this man or his surviving relatives.

'This was not disputed by the firm of Muller and Schneider. In fact, they agreed to purchase the estate from Michael Packham by offering eight million euros, which was considerably above the true market value. Now why would anyone do this?

'We can only speculate that they were certain that they would locate this mysterious treasure trove, which is believed to be worth at today's prices many millions, perhaps hundreds of millions of euros. This would keep members of The Brotherhood enjoying a good standard of living until their dying days.

'So, what changed their minds? We have heard Michael say in his testimony that he and Louise did not wish to inherit this estate because of the circumstances in which the estate was given over to Otto. Instead, they were determined to find if Abraham had any living relatives. During their meeting with Herr Muller on the final day that they were in *Schlachthaus* they received a telephone call from Henry Winkler the genealogist who advises that they are making progress and that he should have some news soon.

'Shortly after this call, Herr Muller leaves the room and returns to say that all offers of a purchase have now been withdrawn. Now what caused this? And then Johann visits George Carmichael on the same day as Michael. We must draw the conclusion that this was not a coincidence of one in twenty million, it was gathered by eavesdropping on Michael and Louise. You will agree with me, a shocking thing to happen to anyone.'

Daniel continued, 'A few days later, the offices of Herr Winkler are firebombed. Now, I return Your Honour to asking our witness Herr Muller, the question, did you have anything to do with the firebomb attack on Herr Winkler's offices which ultimately led to him dying from horrific burns?'

After sitting in the witness box and listening to Daniel Watkins for such a long time Dieter Muller was clearly finding it difficult to contain his anger.

'Your Honour, these suggestions by Mr Watkins are utterly outrageous. They are a slur on the reputation of Muller and Schneider. I can tell you now, that I will be suing Hildreth and Watkins for slander and causing loss of reputation. A reputation that has been built up over a course of seventy years plus.'

'That is for another day Herr Muller, in the meantime we would like you to answer the question,' interjected Justice Langholme.

'I'm sorry Your Honour, what was the question?'

'Were you responsible in any way for the death of Herr Winkler? The fourth person to have died in connection with this case.' Daniel Watkins enquired.

'Absolutely not. No. No. No!' shouted Dieter Muller.

'I must remind you Herr Muller, that you are still under oath.' Daniel Watkins continued. 'May I remind the court that Johann Ballack had spent ten years in the German equivalent of the Special Air Services or better known as the S.A.S. These units consist of highly trained men. We know that Johann amongst other skills was an explosive expert.

'I am pleased to announce to the court Your Honour, that I have been able to obtain the records of Johann Ballack's mobile telephone. On the day before Winkler's office was firebombed Herr Ballack received a text message from none other than Herr Dieter Muller. It said and I quote, "Do what is necessary to stop information from Winkler's." The following day, the same day in which the offices of Herr Winkler's were firebombed, Johann sent a message of his own which read, "No further worries. Job done."

'Would you care to comment Herr Muller on these two texts?' Daniel asked.

'I am not aware of these texts.'

'Does that mean Herr Muller, that you were also unaware that Johann was in Vienna?' Daniel continued.

'What my staff do in their spare time away from work is, quite frankly, none of my business.'

'Your Honour, I would like to show the jury and Herr Muller some photographs if I may? These are the images captured by CCTV on the night that Henry Winkler's offices were attacked and destroyed. The images were taken from a CCTV camera two hundred metres from the offices in question. Please Herr Muller, could you look at the photograph and confirm that the man there is one Johann Ballack?'

Holding the photos at arm's length and endeavouring to give the impression that he was scrutinizing the photos with great care and concern. Dieter Muller finally looked up and said, 'These photos could be one of many men. The man in the photo, it could be argued is similar to Johann Ballack, but certainly no one would be able to say conclusively that it is him.'

'I agree with my learned friend.' Daniel Watkins continued, 'we cannot be one hundred per cent certain. Fortunately, we do have three other photos, which if it please Your Honour I would like to share with you, Herr Muller and the Jury.'

Daniel handed the photos to the clerk of the court who then handed them out.

'This photo shows very clearly a brand-new top of the range BMW series 3 saloon car. We checked with the German Vehicle Licencing Authority, and they confirmed that it is a company vehicle registered to a Law Firm in Munich, by the name of Muller and Schneider.

'The car is seen leaving the Altstadt Hotel in Vienna shortly before the attack on the offices of Henry Winkler. We have contacted the hotel and they have confirmed that a Johann Ballack stayed there that evening and that his credit card was assigned to a company called Muller and Schneider.

'Herr Muller,' continued Daniel, 'I suggest that your father and his partner together with Hans Adenauer, belonged to an organisation which we cannot be totally sure of, but we suspect is called The Brotherhood. This organisation was set up to aid middle ranking Nazis officials from evading justice for crimes they might have been charged with, due to their activities during the war.

'Unfortunately,' continued Daniel, 'all three of those gentlemen are now deceased. However, a new generation has taken over, which you Dieter Muller are used as the front and giving the appearance of respectability. Would I be right to assume that it was information given to this organisation that resulted in *Schlachthaus* being visited during the time that the Schmidt's were running the estate, which resulted in a five-week search being undertaken?

'And then, when nothing was found, the priest giving this information met with an untimely accident. A euphemism Your Honour, for murder me thinks. Then after the return of Otto Wagner, a person that you claimed must have been killed during the war, because you had no knowledge to the contrary, despite a full list of German prisoners held by the Allies and sent to the relevant German authorities. An unannounced visit by the chief of police then took place.

'We believe that Otto was pressured by Hans Adenauer to leave the estate to The Brotherhood. After it became apparent that Otto was not prepared to do this, his two beneficiaries, Christian and Ursula Schmidt are deemed to have committed suicide. We suspect that they were murdered.

'Our research has also revealed that Johann Ballack, the four people looking after the house, Max Schlesinger, Fritz Spiel, Ingrid Scharaditch and Annaliesa Schwartzman as well as your two female personal assistants, are children of middle ranking German officials, that is true Herr Muller is it not?'

Looking quite pale now, Herr Muller responded. 'None of us can be held responsible Your Honour for the actions or beliefs of our parents. We are all victims of circumstances.'

'Members of the Jury.' Daniel continued, 'There were many German children who after the war condemned the actions of their fathers. But that was not the case with either Herr Muller or Herr Schneider. They actively encouraged and participated in the organisation to facilitate the evasion from justice of many who had committed terrible crimes.

'Herr Muller has reasoned that this trial in order to convict an innocent woman of murder, was revealing more about his own involvement than he had anticipated. The charges against Louise Johnson are merely a distraction. With the spotlight now turning on him, Dieter Muller last evening took the decision to run for it using a forged passport, that I am told was of extremely high quality.

'How is it that a man who proclaims that he is on the side of right, should then commit a brazen criminal act of possessing a forged passport? Where could he possibly obtain such a passport? And why should he wish to flee this country in the middle of a trial that he has insisted on and persuaded our own Crown Prosecution Service that he must be the trial prosecutor?'

'These are all lies!' shouted Dieter Muller. 'None of what you have been told is true. We have a woman in the dock who is guilty of trying to obtain an estate falsely which has led to her murdering one of my staff.'

'That will be enough, Herr Muller,' interrupted Justice Langholme at the same time banging his gavel as pandemonium broke out in the court. 'Order! Order!' shouted Justice Langholme. 'The court must come to order. I suggest that we now take a break for lunch and resume at two this afternoon. In the meantime, Herr Muller, you will be placed into custody until the end of this trial.'

'Your Honour, you cannot do that!' shouted Dieter Muller.

'Officers, take Herr Muller to the cells and return him here at two.'

'Court arise,' instructed the court bailiff, as Justice Langholme made his way down from his perch behind his bench.

Chapter 17

Everyone took their seats early for the afternoon session. The press and the public gallery were chocker block. Louise came in once more, looking remarkably relaxed considering the strain that she undoubtedly was under. Dieter Muller was once more escorted in by two police officers. He took his place behind the prosecutors table.

Justice Langholme after taking his seat, looked around the court before directing Dieter Muller to take the witness stand, where once again he was sworn in. He then invited Daniel Watkins to continue.

'Thank you, Your Honour,' Daniel Watkins began. 'Members of the jury, we have heard several times now, the background to this case. I believe that you will conclude that there is no doubt at all, that Michael Packham is the rightful beneficiary of Otto Wagner's estate.

'Whether or not there is a concealment of riches, we don't know. We do know that a thorough search took place in 1948 which lasted five weeks. As we speak the estate which is being managed by Dieter Muller on behalf of an organisation is continuing a systematic search in the hope of finding these treasures.

'I now move onto why we are here. For a year now Miss Louise Johnson, who is a young woman, engaged to be married, might already have been married by now had it not been for the dreadful events of that evening when Johann Ballack entered her home uninvited whilst she was preparing an evening meal.

'We have already heard from George Carmichael that Michael Packham and Louise Johnson had made it clear that they had no intention of benefitting from what they regarded to be, ill-gotten gains. So, the suggestion advanced by my learned friend for the prosecution that Louise murdered Johann out of greed is untrue.

'The prosecution has also stated that Michael threatened Johann with a knife. When Johann rang the doorbell, Michael was laying the table in readiness for their evening meal. He then went to open the door still holding the two knives, two forks and two spoons, which he was about to place as part of the table setting. I think we can all agree that he opened the door without any thought of attacking anyone with a knife, fork and spoon.

'He was though taken aback when Johann Ballack pushed him in the chest resulting in him falling over backwards. Now I ask you to consider, do you really believe that Louise, who is preparing the evening meal with her fiancé had murder on her mind? What would have triggered her reaction into throwing a saucepan of soup at Johann? I will tell you members of the jury; it was the sight of Johann producing a handgun.

'We know that Louise is a quick-thinking intelligent woman. Her action that night was provoked entirely out of fear from seeing the gun. Her actions were instinctive. No time at all to consider. She sensed that they were in real danger. We would all be shocked if someone were to enter our homes and pull out a gun. Why would anyone do that? Why did Johann do it? We don't know for sure; we can only speculate.'

Walking over to the jury, Daniel stopped and paused for a moment or two before continuing, ensuring that he looked at every member of the jury. 'This young woman before you has been charged with murder. The definition of murder is the unlawful premeditated killing of one human being by another. The important word here is premeditated. That means that she would have planned to murder Johann Ballack.

'Everyone can see that this is not the case. This is a good example of cause and effect. Johann Ballack has burst into her home unannounced carrying a loaded gun. That's the cause. The effect has been an instinctive reaction of self-defence. There is only one victim in this case and that is Louise Johnson. You would have noticed that the counsel for the crown prosecution has not asked a single question to anyone. They have instead presented a picture of what they wish you to believe. It has been baseless.

'Your Honour, I request that the charge of murder is dropped entirely and that the nightmare that this young woman together with Michael Packham and their families be brought to an end with her immediate release, with no charges pending. Also, that the Last Will and Testament of Otto Wagner is honoured by acknowledging that Michael Packham is the only living descendant of David McKay. I rest my case Your Honour.'

Looking over his glasses once more, Justice Langholme then spoke to Dieter Muller. 'Herr Muller you have brought this case and convinced the CPS that you could secure a guilty verdict. Unfortunately, the Crown Prosecution Service like many public organisations are always chasing figures. Successful prosecutions are always welcomed by the CPS as it strengthens and justifies their existence. During this trial it is true that you have relied solely on your own interpretation. Do you have anything more to add?'

The court was entirely silent. Dieter Muller sat in the witness box looking like a broken man. He looked ahead but ensured that he did not make eye contact with Louise. 'No, Your Honour, I have no more questions. I will seek a meeting with the Crown Prosecution Service and recommend that we withdraw the charge.'

'Ladies and gentlemen of the jury.' Began Justice Langholme. 'This has been an unusual case. Normally murder trials can last several weeks. We have been here for just a few days. A unprecedented occurrence. You have heard all of the evidence. Normally at the conclusion of such a trial the judge would give his summing up and then guidance to the jury.

'An occasion such as this is unlikely ever to occur again. To have as prosecutor a foreign lawyer who is intrinsically involved in the case. He and his father before him are and were principal players in this whole charade. I have to advise you Herr Muller, that I have contacted the German authorities. At the very least you will be charged with gross professional misconduct and potentially your involvement in the deaths of Christian and Ursula Schmidt and I would think certainly authorising the killing of Henry Winkler.

'Before that happens, you will remain in custody and will be charged with a serious passport offence. I would like to direct the jury to finding Miss Louise Johnson not guilty on the charge of murder and therefore to release her as of today. The second issue, the one that led ultimately to this charge of murder, is the disposal of Otto Wagner's will. There can be no doubt that Michael Packham is the correct person that has been found. I, therefore, direct the jury to find in his favour.

'Now ladies and gentlemen of the jury, I now invite you to retire and consider my recommendations. If you need any guidance or further advice, then please notify the court usher and he will relay your wishes. You may take as much time as you need to deliberate. Thank you.'

It would seem that we had only been out of the Number One court room for a short while before we were given notice that the jury were about to return to give their verdict. Everyone returned. I looked up at Louise and gave her my broadest smile, fervently hoping that we would not be let down, and that Louise would be free imminently. This was the first time that I could see that she was nervous. Our eyes met and I detected that hers were almost pleading, that the nightmare would soon be over.

I glanced over at Father Benedict and at George Carmichael who had both agreed to stay on until the end of the trial should they be required to take the stand again. They were sitting next to each other in quiet conversation. Dieter Muller looked decidedly unwell. Once Justice Langholme had taken his seat, the jury returned.

'Thank you, ladies and gentlemen,' Justice Langholme began. 'Foreman of the jury have you reached your verdicts?'

'We have Your Honour.' Both verdicts were reached unanimously. 'The jury have found that the Last Will and Testament of Otto Wagner be executed in favour of Major David McKay's only living relative, Michael Packham.'

There was a stirring in the court as people fidgeted and an air of optimistic expectation gripped us all.

'On the second charge,' continued the foreman, 'we find the defendant, not guilty of murder.'

It was most unusual for the verdict of a murder trial to be greeted with such elation. Many applauded, people hugged one another, and everyone was laughing. I glanced across at Louise and finally observed that she had cracked. Tears were streaming down her cheeks. She was now crying uncontrollably. This made me also well up, but I had to restrain myself. Justice Langholme, also smiling let the emotional outburst proceed for a couple of minutes before he called for order.

'This as you know,' he began, 'is the last time that I will sit as a High Court Judge. This trial will be remembered for a long time, as being perhaps one of the shortest murder trials ever to have taken place. I commend the jury for carrying out their duty. Having sat in judgement for so many years, there are times when I have experienced the feeling that justice has not been served well and that an innocent person has been found guilty. That was a possibility in this case. It would have been a travesty of justice. After the not guilty verdict for murder, it is usual to then look at the charge of manslaughter. A killing of one person of another which was not premeditated as has occurred in this case. However, Herr Muller acting for the Crown Prosecution Service has withdrawn all charges.

'Herr Muller, you will be taken and held in custody on the charge of passport offences. Once this has been dealt with, then you will be escorted by officials from the Home Office, back to Germany, where you will be handed over to the German police authorities. Miss Louise Johnson, I have to say how sorry I am that you have been falsely accused and have experienced such an awful last year. The good news is, that you are now free to resume your normal life. Thank you everyone.'

'Court rise,' instructed the usher.

Two police officers then came in and this time handcuffed Dieter Muller. As he was led away, he looked across at Daniel Watkins and gave a slight bow, before being ushered out. Louise had stopped crying. Her mascara had run down her cheeks and being aware of what she must now look like, pulled out a tissue and started wiping away furiously. I immediately went towards her and hugged and kissed her. We then both started laughing almost uncontrollably. By this time Louise's sister, and parents were there together with George Carmichael and Father Benedict. Last to join us was Daniel Watkins.

All of us surrounding Louise, sensed the presence of Daniel and parted. Louise and Daniel stood for a moment looking at one another before Louise held out her arms and they both embraced. Everyone cheered and started to pat Daniel and Louise on their backs.

Daniel then stood back and said, 'Listen everyone, this was a verdict that I fully expected. The evidence was compelling. I am not sure if Herr Muller had considered us to be lazy or negligent, but I am surprised that he did not consider that we would be checking on the whereabouts of Johann Ballack to see if there was a connection with the death of Henry Winkler. There are eight of us here, I have arranged for a celebration buffet at my office which is just a few minutes away. So, let us go and celebrate.'

CHAPTER 18

The eight of us arrived at the offices of Hildreth and Watkins. We were met by Carol, Daniel's personal assistant who took us upstairs and into the boardroom, a room that Louise and I had not seen before. Like Daniel's office very warm and comforting with the oak panelled walls. A wonderful spread had been laid on. There were four ice buckets containing a bottle of Dom Perignon in each one.

There was a good deal of excited chatter. Everyone was in conversation with someone. Our champagne flutes kept being refilled without us really taking much notice. One moment they were empty and the next they were full again. The buffet was superb. Not the sort of quality that I was used to. For me it was usually egg mayonnaise sandwiches and Asda pork pies. Everything here seemed to have been supplied by Fortnum and Mason. It included crab and oysters.

It was about an hour later. Everyone had had the opportunity to chat with everyone else. There was such a spirit of joy in the room. Then Daniel tapped the side of his champagne flute with a spoon and a hush immediately descended.

'Louise, Michael, Father Benedict, George, Kate, Stephen and Samantha, what a day? And what a result?'

We all broke into applause, and I hugged Louise once more. Daniel continued. 'This was a result that I had felt would be delivered all along. I find it difficult to believe that the CPS allowed Herr Muller to try the case. It was never a case of murder. At best they may have achieved a verdict of manslaughter. But it matters not a jot now. It is all behind us. Louise and Michael, you can look forward to starting a new life together, one which I am sure will be full of adventure.

'In anticipation of this outcome, we have been busy working behind the scenes. I am most grateful to Father Benedict and to my colleague George Carmichael for their efforts in achieving a post-trial positive scenario. The immediate problem will be the transition of Otto Wagner's estate which is currently being run by staff of, we will content ourselves with calling them The Brotherhood, over to Michael.

'George Carmichael here, flew to Munich and to the legal department concerning German wills. In the strictest of confidence, he outlined what the situation was at our trial and how he considered that Dieter Muller would be, at the conclusion of our case open to charges of serious professional misconduct. As George Carmichael was in possession of the final will of Otto's, it was deemed that this one would be enacted upon, and that George was given the authority to proceed.'

Again, spontaneous applause broke out and Louise gave George an affectionate hug.

Daniel continued. 'I am also indebted here to Father Benedict. He has been on a covert recruiting mission and now he has a group of people who have been waiting and are ready to go and manage the house and the estate. Father Benedict is flying home this evening. I think it would be good if the rest of us flew out on Monday. Please before leaving here today, give Carol your details; passport numbers and personal details that she will need for purchasing the flight tickets.'

I put up my hand and Daniel nodded his consent that I may speak.

'We have waited so long for today. Now that it is here, I can hardly believe that it has happened. All so quick. I think that Dieter Muller will reflect, I hope whilst he is serving a prison sentence, that his biggest mistake was in engaging Daniel Watkins.' Again, applause broke out. 'Louise and I will be eternally grateful for your support and professionalism in conducting your own investigation into especially what happened in Vienna and the death of Henry Winkler. Without that, the outcome could have been quite different.

'Louise has shown such fortitude during her incarceration. You have no idea how incredibly proud of you I am darling.' I could feel my voice cracking, so I paused for a moment before continuing. 'I feel lucky that Kate and Stephen, Louise's parent's and of course my future sister-in-law, Samantha never lost faith and were convinced of this outcome today.

'I am also grateful to Father Benedict and to George Carmichael for their support and input into achieving today's result and for their time and commitment into establishing the way ahead. I am concerned about the cost of our flights to Munich. You are indicating Daniel that you are footing the bill for all of us? In fact, I am concerned about the entire cost of this case, because so far Daniel we haven't paid you a single penny.'

'My dear boy, there is no need to worry. Dieter Muller gave me authority to charge whatever is necessary until I receive notification that this arrangement has ended. Clearly, Herr Muller doesn't keep track of all of the various bank accounts under his control. Quite unwittingly, Muller and Schneider or The Brotherhood have been paying for Louise's defence costs for the entire time. Poetic justice me thinks.'

Once more laughter and applause greeted this news.

'Now I suggest,' Daniel continued, 'as Father Benedict is travelling back this evening that the rest of us go over next Monday, and arrange to stay there for an entire week. We can instantly dismiss the staff, of course making sure that they are given what is due to them for redundancy. I suggest that we give them five thousand euros each on the day and then make arrangements for whatever else is owing to them.

'It has been a wonderful day. I think that we are all sufficiently fed and certainly more than well-watered, I suggest that no none gets behind the wheel of a car for a good few hours. And George it would be lovely to have you as my guest until we leave on Monday.'

As Louise and her family including her sister lived near us, we decided to hire a minicab taxi for the one-hour journey home. We dropped off Kate and Stephen first before stopping at the convenience store near Samantha's home to pick up some much-needed groceries. Louise and Samantha hugged one another outside Sam's house once more. Again, the tears weren't far away.

By the time that I opened our front door it was dark. It was difficult to imagine that the last time Louise had left through her front door was twelve months ago on the occasion of her arrest.

As soon as the front door was closed, we were in one another's arms, hugging, kissing and giggling. We were both feeling exhausted, the emotional energy that had been expended had finally caught up with us. We decided to order an Indian takeaway. We were advised that it would be thirty minutes before delivery. Enough time in which to take a shower together.

'Our first time of love making before I left for Wetherby.'

The water flowed over us. We were exploring each other's bodies, satisfying ourselves that they were the same. Louise had kept incredibly fit during her prison stay and was still firm everywhere. Without noticing it, I was now carrying an extra seven pounds. Louise didn't comment. We made love in the shower that was so intense and so passionate, that it left us breathless.

The takeaway arrived. It was I must say delicious. Louise told me that after a year of eating off the prison menu, all meals would by comparison be delicious. We then retired to the bedroom. We must have made love six or seven times during the night and into the early hours of the morning. We both knew that we would be sore in the morning, but to hell with that.

It had gone past ten before I woke. Louise was still fast asleep. I got up and had a shower, came back in and dressed. By this time Louise was stirring.

'What time is it darling?' she enquired.

'It's just before ten thirty,' I replied.

'I haven't enjoyed a night like that ever before. Our lovemaking first of all and then such a sound sleep on a comfortable mattress. I am determined never to take anything for granted again. Starting with freedom.'

The next couple of days went in a whirl. We had so many friends and neighbours knocking at our door. All wishing Louise well and expressing their sorrow at what had happened. I had been granted indefinite leave by the hospital, so there were no work considerations for either of us to take into account this time for our second flight to Munich.

Daniel's secretary Carol had arranged for a minibus to pick the five of us up as we lived close to each other to take us to Gatwick Airport. There we met Daniel and George before making our way through the necessary procedures before boarding our British Airways flight to Munich.

We arrived at the Franz Joseph International Airport just before eleven. Kate and Stephen were impressed by how modern the airport was. I mentioned that it had only been opened in 1992 and so was still very new. A minibus had been ordered. After climbing aboard with Daniel insisting that Louise and I go up front we set off once more for Bischofswiesen.

When we arrived instead of turning into the drive of *Schlachthaus* we continued into the village and to the home of Father Benedict. We were met by Elizabeth who welcomed us into their home. We were then ushered into the dining room where a large table had been set for nine placings.

Father Benedict then spoke. 'Welcome to our home. I believe Michael that you are very partial to Shepherd's pie, so guess what Elizabeth has prepared for our lunch today?'

The lunch was lovely. Everyone was in good humour and chatty. Then Father Benedict held up his hand so as to attract our attention. We all ceased talking.

'My friends I have staff who will replace the existing staff on the estate tomorrow. They will arrive at nine. I spoke with Ingrid at the house yesterday and made an appointment to see the estate manager, you may remember him Heinrich Merkel?' Louise pulled a face. 'As far as I could tell they are not aware of what has happened with Dieter Muller.

'Our appointment is for twenty minutes time. I also took the precaution, knowing what a brute this Henrich can be to request from the local police chief that he also attend accompanied by two offices. This he has agreed to do. He will be waiting for us in a layby near the gated entrance. I suggest that we prepare to leave now.'

We all gave Elizabeth a hug and thanked her on the way out. As Father Benedict had advised, the police car was waiting in the layby. We slowed down and passed, and they pulled out and followed behind. We turned into the driveway and stopped at the gate. Father Benedict pressed the buzzer.

'Good afternoon Father,' came the unmistakable voice of Ingrid. 'We assumed that you would be alone. Is anything the matter? I notice a police car behind you.'

'I will explain everything when we arrive.'

With that the wrought iron gates parted and slowly opened to permit access. Samantha was blown away at her first sight of the house as we pulled up outside. There to greet us was Ingrid but also an angry Heinrich Merkel, who was clearly puzzled, especially upon seeing Louise and I stepping out of the minibus.

'What the hell is going on?' were Henrich's first words of welcome.

The chief of police then stepped in front and spoke. 'Herr Merkel, we will all go inside. Please arrange for all of the estate's staff to be assembled as quickly as possible.'

Heinrich grunted some sort of instruction and waved Ingrid back inside I suppose to make the calls. Without waiting to be invited in, Louise followed her, closely followed by everyone else. There in the kitchen was Annaliesa baking some biscuits. Sitting at the table opposite was Fritz reading a newspaper.

'Good afternoon, Fritz, Annaliesa, nice to see you again.' Louise then continued. 'We will be going into the dining room, could you bring some of those biscuits and two pots of tea for us please Annaliesa? When all of the staff have been assembled, would you please come in and join us?'

Heinrich could not contain his anger any longer. 'Who the hell do you think you are? Walking in here and giving us orders. I suggest that you leave right now.'

I could see how wise Father Benedict had been in inviting along the chief of police who then answered Heinrich's question. 'Herr Merkel, just carry out as has been asked. Everything will be made clear to you and your colleagues in a few moments. In the meantime, we look forward to having some tea and biscuits in the dining room.'

It was a long table, the same one that Abraham and Hannah must have sat at and enjoyed their meals with their daughters sixty years previously. We all sat around, and a few minutes later there was a knock at the door and in entered Annaliesa pushing a fully laden tea trolley. We drank our tea and ate the scrummy biscuits while admiring the interior of the dining room at the same time. No sooner had we finished, then in barged Heinrich Merkel, closely followed by Fritz, Max, Ingrid, Annaliesa and two farm hands who we did not know.

It was Father Benedict who spoke first. 'Thank you for coming everyone. I'm not sure when you were last in communication with Dieter Muller?'

'Dieter has been abroad for a little while now, so we have had no contact,' Ingrid responded.

'You remember,' continued Father Benedict, 'that you met Michael and Louise a year ago now. You will recall that that this estate was originally owned by a man called Abraham Benowitz. Shortly before the war, it passed to Otto Wagner, and he left the estate in a will to the descendants of a Major McKay which turned out to be Michael here.'

'No that is not the case,' interrupted Heinrich. 'It was being challenged in court that Michael was an impostor and that the rightful benefactors of the estate was a society called The Brotherhood.'

'Yes, that is what you may have been told Herr Merkel,' continued Father Benedict. 'The fact is that it has now been verified that Michael is the only relative of David McKay and therefore the estate has legally passed to him. All other claims such as The Brotherhoods, are bogus and without foundation.'

I could see that Heinrich was in a rage, he clenched his fists. This was a man that was not used to being contradicted. The chief of police also recognised these signs and before Heinrich could say anything he said, 'Heinrich, I can assure you that what has been said is correct. Now stay still and be quiet.'

This last command didn't help to improve Heinrich's demeanour, but he stopped himself from saying anything further.

'Thank you, chief of police,' continued Father Benedict. 'The new owner of the estate is Michael Packham. He would like to return the running of the estate in a similar manner as occurred before you took over. Namely, to be run with a social conscience, looking after the villagers who need assistance.

'This is a policy we know that you do not agree with, especially you Herr Heinrich, who made it quite clear to me that you were a business and not a charity. A decision has been made that apart from Martin and Jurgen who I don't believe you have met Michael, the rest of the staff your terms of employment have been terminated as of this moment.'

And then raising his hand to discourage an outburst he went on. 'The five of you will receive five thousand euros before you leave now and then the full entitlement of any redundancy package will be worked out and sent to you. Please gather your personnel effects and be gone within one hour.'

Heinrich, Max, Fritz, Ingrid and Annaliesa all looked stunned. By having the chief of police present with two officers endorsed the reality of what Father Benedict was saying. After the five had left to gather their belongings, Father Benedict then introduced Martin and Jurgen.

'Michael, Louise, this is Jurgen, and this is Martin, they have been employed on the estate for a year now. They are good lads and from the village. They are fully experienced in everything that is connected to the farming side. They are both members of my church and are poorly paid. I hope that you will be able to review their salaries and give them a suitable increase?'

'Pleased to meet you both,' I said. 'I have always subscribed to the principle of a fair day's wage for a fair day's work. I am sure that you are both deserving an increase.'

Both men looked relieved that they were not to be sacked and happy that they might receive an increase in their pay. 'Carry on lads,' I said giving my first instruction as lord of the manor.

In less than an hour the cars belonging to Heinrich, Max and Fritz were just finishing being loaded. All the estate keys were handed over to Father Benedict. Max and Ingrid travelled together and Fritz and Annaliesa also. Not surprisingly, Heinrich's personality had never appealed to a woman, so he was single living as a bachelor. There was no waving goodbye as the three-car convoy left for the very last time. Once they were gone a sense of relief settled on everyone.

It was Louise who let out a whoop of delight as the final car disappeared out of sight. 'Thank you so much, chief of police, I was so pleased when Father Benedict had advised us that you would be with us this afternoon. Would you and your officers care for a drink?'

'No thank you mam, we are still on duty. I am pleased that we have played a small part in getting rid of that bunch and look forward to seeing your social changes being implemented.' And with that they turned and went.

For the next hour Louise and I gave a tour of the house. Everyone looked at the beautiful picture of the twins holding their violins. When we entered the library, I went over to the painting showing Carmichael's. I took it from the wall and handed it over to George.

'A gift from Otto at this time I would think is appropriate.' Daniel patted George on the back, 'A reminder of your many years of practice?' commended Daniel.

CHAPTER 19

The following morning there was a buzz of excited anticipation in the air. We assembled in the kitchen just after seven where Louise and her mum were busy preparing a traditional English fried breakfast. Even Daniel and George were impressed by the house and the gardens.

Before everyone had gone to bed the previous evening, Louise, Kate and Samantha had stripped the three beds of the previous occupants and replaced with clean bedding. Everyone had slept soundly. Before Louise and I got into our bed, I thoroughly checked the room, looking behind mirrors, checking the phone and examining vases. The last thing that I checked was the picture that hung over our headboard.

'Look at this darling,' I said, as I took down the picture. Sure, enough there it was. A wireless microphone still in situ.

'That was the night that you proposed to me Michael do you remember?'

'How could I forget?'

'Well, whoever was listening in, I don't think that they would have been in any doubt as to how happy you made and make me still. But clearly that is how they discovered the connection with George Carmichael.'

As we were finishing breakfast, there was a knock at the door, and without waiting, in walked a beaming Father Benedict.

'Good morning Father,' Kate said. 'You are just in time for coffee.'

'Thank you my dear,' replied Father Benedict. 'During the past two months I have been discreetly recruiting personnel for the estate. Yesterday you met with Martin and Jurgen. They are both hard working young men and had nothing to do with the regime that employed them.

'This morning first up you will meet Lucas Fischer. He is thirty-four years old and has been manager of a large farm just north of Salzburg. His wife Frieda was housekeeper at the same estate. She is an excellent cook, they have two young children, a son aged nine and a daughter aged seven. I think it would be nice if a family atmosphere could be revived as it always was up until 1938. When I approached this couple, they were so enthused. Lucas will be the perfect fit for managing this estate. He enjoys a great reputation with his present employer, but they have failed to recognise the contribution that Lucas and Frieda have made to the success of the estate. Therefore, I feel no guilt in pinching them for your benefit. They will be able to start immediately.

'I have chosen as assistant housekeeper to Frieda a young woman called Zelda Koch. She is nineteen, a local girl with loads of personality. Her family are extremely poor and had always been helped out by the estate up until two years ago. She is very much a roll your sleeves up type of young woman, who will turn her hand to anything without question.

'Finally, I have chosen Zelda's fiancé Tobias Weber. You may not think this is a good idea, but trust me, he is a fine young man. He is twenty-three years old. Attended Munich University where he achieved a First-Class degree in Business Management. Having been brought up in a rural environment, he would love the challenge of making an estate such as this as profitable as possible. Lucas would be in overall charge for the day to day running, with Tobias taking care of the office side of things and bringing in new ideas.'

All eight of us sat around the breakfast table and chatted away with the various people that Father Benedict had selected. They were all perfect. We felt an instant connection with them all. The children were delightful. With eight bedrooms, it was decided that Tobias and Zelda would occupy the bedroom in the west wing, whilst the Fischer family could have three bedrooms in the east wing. It still left four bedrooms available.

The next five days flew bye. By the end of the week all the staff had taken up their positions. It was important to Louise and me, that we created a family atmosphere, with all staff, where they felt equal and an integral part of what we were aiming to achieve. It was lovely having the joy of the two children, hearing their laughter and we all delighted in their enthusiastic energy and running around.

Two days before we were due to leave, I spoke with Father Benedict. I explained that neither Louise nor I were religious. But would he consider officiating at our wedding? And could the ceremony be conducted at *Schlachthaus* the following evening? He confirmed that he considered both Louise and me to be good, kind people and he would be honoured to officiate and would set off immediately to obtain the necessary documents permitting the ceremony to take place.

I received a call later in the afternoon from Father Benedict confirming that all arrangements were in place. I then invited him and his sister Elizabeth to join us for dinner that evening. I immediately went into the kitchen and found Frieda and Zelda both busy baking. I felt very conspiratorial when I told them that I was intending to ask Louise to marry me tomorrow and that I wished to announce it over dinner that night and that I had invited Father Benedict and Elizabeth. I would leave it up to them to decide what we should eat that evening. Both women gave me a hug and kissed me. I could tell that they were genuinely pleased for me and then shooed me out of the kitchen so that they could make plans.

Samantha was the first to notice that there had been two additional place settings. 'Are we expecting company?' she asked.

'I thought as we are going home the day after tomorrow, that it would be nice to have Father Benedict and Elizabeth join us.'

'What an excellent idea,' Kate remarked.

The best silver had been brought out, along with the best china. Two candelabras with lighted candles were placed midway towards each end of the table. A beautiful hand-made Madeira lace tablecloth was also a feature. Wine glasses were there next to the champagne flutes.

'This is absolutely lovely,' remarked Elizabeth. 'I hope that it is not going to be the last supper?'

The wine a product from the estate was poured and then the first course was served. It was homemade pate with toast. And then we were treated to Vienna schnitzel which brought back memories. Again, beautifully cooked, and well presented. Louise didn't say anything, but I think she suspected something because we were being waited upon by Lucas and Tobias. And then after me discretely nodding at Frieda, Zelda and Tobias appeared with two bottles each of the estates sparkling wine. It was the same wine that Louise and I had celebrated with when I had proposed to her.

'I sense something is happening,' observed Louise's dad, Stephen.

I then stood up and looked around at all the expectant faces. 'First of all, I would like to thank Frieda and Zelda for cooking us such a fine meal and also to thank Lucas and Tobias who volunteered to be our waiters.' A ripple of applause as people raised their wine glasses and toasted the four.

I then continued. 'Just two weeks ago, we were in the high court awaiting nervously the outcome of the case against Louise. We were lucky in having the services of a brilliant lawyer and also the help of George Carmichael and Father Benedict. I knew the circumstances in which Louise had found herself. It was not her fault. Louise has told me that whilst in prison, she had met several women who in her opinion had been wrongly convicted. So, our outcome was not as assured as I had hoped.

'We have sadly lost an entire year of our lives. I found it exceedingly difficult to concentrate in my duties as a doctor but working in A&E was a welcome distraction. Louise tells me that she does not consider that she has lost a year of her life. It was not as she would have chosen to have lived it, but it gave her a new perspective on members of our society with whom she had had little dealings before.

'It was almost a year ago that I proposed to Louise in the garden at the back here. With all the principal people in our lives, here in the one room this evening, I took it upon myself to see if it were possible that Louise and I could be married tomorrow, here in *Schlachthaus* and the service conducted by Father Benedict.

Fortunately, Father Benedict has secured the relevant documents to make this permissible and has agreed to conduct the service.

'I promise you Louise that this is the last time I will ever do anything behind your back without your knowledge. Please forgive me on this occasion, but would you please do me the honour of becoming Mrs Packham tomorrow?'

A hubbub of sound emerged, and all eyes turned to look at Louise as silence then took hold. Louise looked a picture of serenity. She then stood up and I sat down.

'To our family and friends,' she said taking in everyone, including the standing Lucas, Frieda, Zelda and Tobias.

'A good deal has happened during the last twelve months. I have constantly questioned myself, could I have avoided killing Johann Ballack? I certainly had no intention of killing him or even causing him harm. Everything happened in the blink of an eye. Michael being pushed to the ground and then the sight of Johann reaching for a handgun. I just reacted, there was no thought whatsoever. Whichever way I look at it, my actions have been responsible for the death of a husband and a father. For that I am truly sorry. It is something that I will live with for the rest of my life.

'During my incarceration, I never felt alone or abandoned. I received weekly visits from mum, dad, sister Samantha and the love of my life, Michael. I now consider Daniel as almost a surrogate uncle, and George and Father Benedict have also recently been a big part of my life. This is the perfect gathering and setting for us to marry. Tomorrow would be ideal, although I do not have a Bride's gown, so it will be an informal affair. Of course, I would like all of the staff of *Schlachthaus* to be present.'

This was met with applause, and everyone went over to kiss and hug Louise and then came and hugged me, with the men shaking my hand and the ladies giving me a kiss. It felt wonderful. We then charged our champagne flutes and Daniel proposed a toast to our happiness and also to the change of fortune for the estate. We agreed that the wedding would take place at five p.m. This would have allowed enough time for Martin and

Jurgen to have milked the cows, quickly shoot home to change and then to return.

Most weddings I have observed, can be very fraught affairs, especially for the bride and groom. It is natural to worry about so many little things that could go wrong. When no one else is worried. All guests are there because they are pleased to have been invited and are happy for the couple being married.

Because I had announced the wedding only one day before, there was little time to plan. Ours was indeed such a simple wedding, it was relaxed right from the start. It was a normal day until around two in the afternoon. Louise decided to take a bath whilst I took a shower. Daniel had very kindly agreed to be my best man. Another of George's interest happen to be photography and so he volunteered his services as the wedding photographer.

It is at such an occasion, that unknown talents are revealed. Tobias was a competent pianist whilst Zelda was a fine violinist. I immediately thought how appropriate with the love of music that the Benowitz family had encouraged. The wedding was outside on the patio. The piano had been pushed outside with Tobias sitting on his stool. Next to him was Zelda, clutching her violin and looking very pretty. Father Benedict stood waiting behind a lectern.

I sat in the front row on the right next to Daniel and then Martin and Jurgen. On the bride's side, Kate, Elizabeth, Lucas and Frieda. Then Father Benedict, with a nod, a signal for Tobias and Zelda to commence playing Bach's Air on a G string. A rehearsal must have taken place without my knowledge because Louise on the arm of her dad, had timed their arrival to be at my side to coincide exactly with the final bar of the music. Samantha was closely behind holding a posey of flowers and acting as bridesmaid.

The entire service was beautiful. Louise looked stunning. She had clearly decided to take a good deal of time with her hair and makeup. She was wearing her favourite summer dress with high heels. I could not have been prouder. I noticed the look of joy in her family. I felt remarkably close to them after all that we had been through.

After the ceremony we then retired to the dining room. Frieda and Zelda had prepared the most wonderful buffet, I suspect with the help from Lucas and Tobias. The speeches were brief and then someone put on some dance music. Louise and I were invited to take to the floor first.

'What are you thinking?' asked Louise.

'I was just thinking about my plans to remove your lipstick later on,' I replied.

'Yes, that would be good. I hope that there will be other things that you would like to remove as well,' Louise said giving me a squeeze.

I returned her squeeze and looked around. By now Zelda and Tobias were dancing and looking affectionately into one another's eyes.

'I don't think it will be too long before those two become one,' I said.

'I agree. Isn't it lovely to see my mum and dad looking so happy? I have rarely seen them dance. By now Lucas and Frieda had joined us and surprisingly Samantha had got Gunther to dance. The entire evening was marvellous. It was a shame that we were to return home the following day.

After the wedding breakfast, Daniel suggested that he and I go for a walk in the garden.

'It has been quite an unexpected adventure, hasn't it?' Daniel said. 'What are your plans going forward?'

'I feel that we are leaving the estate in excellent hands. One thing that we will do before we leave is to ensure that the gates at the entrance are left permanently open, as they had always been. I have spoken with Father Benedict, and he is going to liaise with Lucas to ensure that the villagers are taken care of which would have been the wish of Abraham and Otto. I don't feel that it is necessary for Louise and me to constantly be visiting. It is still our desire to discover who should rightfully be the owners here.'

'What will you do?' enquired Daniel.

'I'm not totally sure. Louise does not wish to resume her job as an estate agent. She now feels that she has a calling in helping women in prison. When we get back, she intends to contact the Governor of Holloway. If she manages to find a position, then I guess we will move nearer to London and perhaps I will apply for a job at Guys Hospital.'

'I have to say that I am impressed and always have been from my first meeting with you and Louise. You uphold all the standards that I aspire to. It is not complicated, is it? Just to be honest, decent and reliable. I respect you and your family. This whole case has resulted in several unexpected friendships. George and I have become firm friends. He has invited me to his home for a week's fishing and also to watch Yorkshire play cricket against Middlesex. This I look forward to.

'There is one final piece of advice that I would like to give Michael. Not once have you enquired about the envelope that was left by Otto with George who has passed it over to me. I am happy to hold onto this envelope. I would suggest that you do not seek the contents of this letter until one year has passed. There is still much speculation that a treasure trove was hidden somewhere on this estate. People will be watching and asking. Therefore, if nothing happens for a year, it will be concluded that no such thing existed.'

'Thank you, Daniel, I will heed your advice. Also, we cannot thank you enough for what you have done. You deserve to enjoy a happy retirement.'

After saying goodbye to the staff and Father Benedict and Elizabeth, we made our way back to Munich Airport for our return flight home to Gatwick.

CHAPTER 20

We kept in weekly touch by phone with the staff at *Schlachthaus*. Everything was running smoothly. Louise had become very good friends with both Frieda and Zelda. Their calls to each other lasted for over an hour each time. It amazed me the endless subjects that women find to talk about. Not once did I hear them mention Chelsea Football Club or Bayern Munich FC.

As I had suggested to Daniel, Louise qualified to work as a prison educator in Holloway where I soon found at that she was well liked and respected by all. Instead of working in Guys, I found a position at St. Thomas's just opposite The Houses of Parliament. We bought a property in Epsom. At weekends, we would play golf or tennis and sometimes went for a walk along the Downs. Everything was ideal.

We ventured across to visit the estate twice and stayed for two weeks on each occasion. Louise's mum and dad came along as did Samantha who brought the new man in her life, Robert who was a graphic designer. It was always such fun. Our last visit there was even more delightful with the news that Tobias and Zelda had become engaged. We held a big party for them with many of their friends from the village in attendance. We opened up the barn. It was all decked out and there was a superb swing band playing.

Because we had now got into a routine at home in Epsom and with our jobs, I had quite forgotten about Daniel Watkins. This was rectified one weekend when the phone rang. It was no other than Daniel.

'How are you and Louise, Michael?' he began. 'No little Packham's on the horizon?'

'Not just yet,' I replied. 'Louise is on a mission at the moment, in trying to make a difference to the lives of many women in prison.'

'I'm not surprised,' Daniel continued. 'She has a very caring nature. I retired almost ten months ago now but am still a sleeping partner in the firm. During this time, I have tasked myself with investigating the possible whereabouts of any Benowitz family members. You will remember that we were advised that Leah and Eliana had stayed behind in London and had found employment with the Bank of England? They had a love of music and joined a local orchestra. It was here that Leah met a Cellist called Thomas Smith. They fell in love almost immediately. They were married in February 1940. Thomas was at that time serving as a Royal Naval officer on board the Battle Cruiser *HMS Hood*. He was on leave in October 1940 when Leah became pregnant.

'He returned to his ship shortly afterwards. On 24th May 1941, early in the Battle of the Denmark Strait, *HMS Hood* was struck by a shell fired by the German Battleship *Bismarck*. The shell detonated a rear magazine, holding the 15-inch shells and cordite propellants for the guns. It was incredibly unlucky for the *Hood*, resulting in her sinking within three minutes. There were only three survivors of the 1,418 men. Sadly, Thomas was not one of the three. On 23rd July, Leah gave birth to a daughter who she named Susan.

'In February 1941 Eliana left the Bank of England and signed up for a secret military mission whereby she was parachuted into France to gather intelligence. She spoke fluent French and proved to be an effective agent. It ended very badly when she was betrayed to the Gestapo. She was taken to Lyon where she was tortured personally by Klaus Barbie, who had the notorious distinction of being known locally as 'The Butcher of Lyon. Eliana revealed nothing at all, which sadly led to her death.

'In 1961, Susan married a motor mechanic called Howard Watson, and they have a son called Abraham born in 1963 and a daughter called Hannah, who was born a year later. They both work for Médecins Sans Frontieres. At the present time they are together in Ethiopia assisting with the humanitarian relief as a result of the famine in that country.'

'Well, I'm staggered,' I replied. 'The fact that Susan named her children after her own grandparents tells us that she knew a good deal about her family heritage. What do you think we should do?'

'I would suggest my dear boy, that now is the time to open the envelope and reveal once and for all why the contents have assumed such importance. Then we can decide how we wish to play things. May I suggest that you and Louise visit the office next week? Carol is always asking after you.'

'Certainly, we can do that,' I replied.

The following week, we were warmly greeted by Carol who showed us into the Boardroom, as Daniel no longer had an office. He greeted us warmly. Carol then brought in tea and chocolate biscuits again served on a silver tray with bone china. It immediately took me back to our first meeting with Daniel.

We exchanged pleasantries for around fifteen minutes concluding how fortunate we had been to have had Father Benedict as such a useful contact. Then without warning, Daniel reached inside his jacket pocket, removed a buff envelope, and handed it over.

I held it in my hands and was conscious of the silent anticipation and the watching eyes of Louise and Daniel.

'It's funny,' I said, 'but after all this time, I feel so nervous. It is as though I am holding a live hand grenade.' I looked at the envelope, upon which were the words, *To Major David McKee or his surviving descendants.* Daniel handed me a paper knife to open the envelope.

I then retrieved the one page inside and proceeded to read aloud what was written.

'To whom it may concern. I Otto Wagner owe my life to an English Army Surgeon, whose name I believe was Major David McKee (but I could not be certain). This Major saved my life in Normandy in 1944. I am the legal owner of a farm estate in Bavaria, Southern Germany called Schlachthaus in the village of Bischofswiesen. I sincerely hope that this letter finds the true beneficiaries of my Last Will and Testament. There is an organisation consisting of ex Nazi members that will stop at nothing in order to gain control of this estate.

The reason why they are so keen to get their hands on this estate, is because a Roman Catholic priest by the name of Father Braun who was trusted by Abraham Benowitz, was the bookkeeper in recording in great detail many items of great value that were brought to Abraham for him to hide.

Abraham received these items always after darkness in the great barn, where Father Braun recorded them. They were then hidden by Abraham and a man called Christian Schmidt who Abraham had complete trust in. These were the only two who knew where the items were hidden.

On his last day at Schlachthaus just before leaving for exile, Abraham confided in me where the treasures had been hidden. There is a disused quarry on the estate. There was a disused tunnel of around one hundred metres. This is where all the items have been hidden. Once they had taken delivery of the final item, Christian and Abraham spent many evenings mixing concrete to the exact blend of the rocks. They then cemented the entrance to a depth of around two metres. The last thing left in place was the ledger by Father Braun. It is my wish that all the items are returned to their rightful owners.

Thank you.

Otto Wagner – 3rd August 1949

Daniel was the first to speak. 'If I were you, I would gather together your trusted employees on the estate. Explain the circumstances and insist that none of them discuss with absolutely anyone, what you are about to do. And then proceed to chisel away at the entrance.'

'That's great advice,' Louise commented. 'It would be nice if both you and George were present as you have been very much involved in reaching this situation, also Father Benedict.'

'I can speak on behalf of George who like myself would welcome being witnesses to the unveiling of this mystery which has been the cause of at least five deaths.'

One week later we descended once more on the estate. The staff were happy but surprised to see us. I then called all of them to a meeting in the library. It was there that I explained the purpose of our return. All of them seemed genuinely excited by the prospect of discovering what had long been rumoured. They all swore that they would tell no one.

We gathered the following morning in the quarry. It was apparent that a previous attempt had been made to blast away the entrance. Rocks lay strewn around on the ground in front and to the side. It looked as though they had gone in for a distance of one metre and then concluded that it was a waste of time.

Lucas suggested that we didn't use explosives as we were unsure of how thick the rock might be. If it were not very thick, we could potentially damage whatever was inside. It was agreed that pickaxe and shovels together with a pneumatic drill would be used. All four lads took fifteen-minute turns on the drill. After four hours further inroads of about two foot had been made. Then the welcome sight of Frieda and Zelda appeared carrying a picknick hamper and several bottles of locally brewed beer. We all gathered round eating, drinking and talking. It was strange. All of us came from various backgrounds and yet we felt like family. It was extremely comforting.

After an enjoyable hour, Frieda and Zelda gathered up the remnants of the picknick and made their way back to the house. The men started once more attacking the rock face. George was there with his camera recording the events. It was when Tobias was on the drill that it suddenly broke through.

I then requested Martin and Jurgen to fetch the arc lamp that was in the barn together with some more petrol for the generator that had been used for the drill. And added that on the way back to alert Frieda and Zelda. I wanted us all to be there to witness this together.

The two lads quickly followed by Freida, and Zelda arrived back. It took a further hour before the entire entrance had been cleared. We had made the entrance almost back to the original size of around seven foot high by nine foot wide. The natural daylight did not penetrate far inside. We then connected the arc light. I was the first to enter followed by Louise and then the others.

The air was so musty that it was initially unpleasant and difficult to breathe. We advanced about ten metres in, and I stood the arc lamp facing inwards. Just a few yards in front of us was a table upon which were three thick books. I picked up the first and blew away a thick layer of dust. It was a very old copy of the Christian Bible. The second book was written in a language with which I was not familiar. Zelda, looking over my shoulder immediately advised us that it was a copy of the Tanakh, which is the Jewish Bible. The third was a thick ledger. One page had been dedicated to each individual item. It had been signed as a true record by Father Braun.

We then proceeded for a further ten metres or so. It took several moments to appreciate the enormity of what Abraham and Christian had achieved. The cave continued for almost eighty metres. Along the sides of the walls were stacked or leaning, boxes or containers of all shapes and sizes. It was evident by the shape that many contain works of art. We slowly took in the scene and then retraced our steps to the outside again after thirty minutes or so.

'Phew,' remarked George. 'A real Aladdin's cave by any imagination.'

Father Benedict was the next to speak. 'I would suggest that we leave everything for now and return in the morning. We can then transfer all the items to the large barn on the back of the farm wagon. In view of what we have just seen, it is important that the local chief of police be in attendance with perhaps an officer or two. I will impress upon him the importance of keeping this information to ourselves.'

Everyone agreed that this was the correct thing to do. After the evening meal, I suggested that Zelda and Tobias entertain us with their live music. My word they were good. Their repertoire seemed to know no bounds. They played classical music from the compositions of Igor Stravinsky, Sergei Prokofiev and Bela Bartok and then the second half consisted of George Gershwin, Elvis Presley, Bob Dylan.

The last piece that they played was John Lennon's *Imagine,* a song that Louise had originally confided in me, should be the Anthem of the World. Surprisingly, everyone knew the words and sang with feeling. It was a wonderful evening. The time was approaching ten o'clock. Father Benedict announced that he would go home. He mentioned before he left that he had requested that the chief of police and his men arrive not before nine fifteen, after Frieda's two children had gone off to school. The rest of us bade him goodnight and Zelda made us all coffee before we eventually turned in for bed.

The following morning, once again, we all experienced this feeling of anticipated excitement. We were very fond of Frieda's children, but on this occasion, we could hardly wait for them to leave for school. At nine fifteen the chief of police arrived with two of his officers.

It was like a real posse of workers as we made our way to the quarry and to the entrance of the cave. Martin drove the tractor towing the trailer wagon. The Chief of Police, Albert Swartzman and his two officers went in first. I put the arc lamp on. We then formed a human chain gang. The first items to be removed were the two holy books and the ledger. I noticed that all items had a large number painted on the outside of the container. Inside the ledger were the details.

It took nine trips of the tractor and trailer to transfer every item from the cave to the barn. It was now approaching four in the afternoon, and we knew that the children would soon be returning from school.

The chief of police spoke. 'Look everyone, I realise that there is a desire to keep everything low key until we have established what it is, we have here. But I suspect that you are too, amazed by the amount that has been concealed. The last container number read as 1,148. It will take an enormous amount of manpower to catalogue and reconcile all these items.

'It is going to be almost impossible to keep this a secret for too long. When word gets out, it could encourage criminal activity of the worst kind. Putting it bluntly, I believe that you would be exposing yourself to danger. My suggestion is that we allow two news outlets, one for television and the other a newspaper and for them to share with the rest of the news agencies. That we arrange tomorrow for security vehicles to pick up what is here and take it to the German National Museum in Nuremberg.'

Father Benedict responded first. 'I believe what Albert here has suggested makes a good deal of sense. Once it is known that everything is now in the safekeeping of the museum, there would be no reason for anyone to come looking here. The only request that I would like to make is that most of us here would like to be present at the initial inspection when the protective cases are removed?'

'I think that is a perfectly reasonable request,' responded the chief of police. 'I will make the arrangements now. In the meantime, I will be placing two offices outside the barn all night as security.'

The following morning two big, long lorries turned up. The television newsman and the newspaper reporter were told that they could not file their reports until the lorries had left and had arrived at the National Museum. It was a busy day. Everything was loaded by two in the afternoon and the lorries slowly moved down the driveway and disappeared from view.

Frieda then announced that Zelda had been busy baking cakes and that she could organise afternoon tea in twenty minutes. Albert Swartzman and his officers were also invited. It was just a babble of conversation with everyone talking to someone. The Curator of the museum had agreed in Nuremberg that the unpacking and recording would start promptly at nine the following morning.

The distance to Nuremberg from where we were was around 360 kilometres, realistically a three-hour drive. We decided it would be best if I drove with Louise in the front passenger seat with Father Benedict, Daniel and George in the back. I was grateful to Lucas for the loan of his Opel car. We left at six in the morning after coffee and bacon rolls. The traffic was reasonably light, and we arrived at the museum at ten minutes to nine.

Chapter 21

Because of the breaking news the evening before, after the two lorries had arrived at the National Museum, there was huge media attention. When we stepped out of the car, we were immediately surrounded by reporters and newsmen, all wishing to know how and when the discovery had been made. We eventually pushed our way through to the back entrance where the Curator, Mathius Spielberg was waiting to greet us.

He was as excited as anyone could be. We were invited into the staff dining room and offered refreshments whilst the unloading took place. After the refreshments we then followed Mathius and three of his assistants into a large hall. This we were advised was a depository.

The porters were all wearing blue dust coats as they brought in the pieces and carefully placed them in numerical order. Mathius Spielberg had placed the ledger of Father Braun's on a table before him. He then took out and put on a pair of white gloves. A young female assistant stood next to him, pen in hand holding a clipboard.

'Right ladies and gentlemen,' he said. 'Let's get started. According to Father Braun's ledger, item number one is a painting by Friedrich Overbeck. This is a German artist, if I remember correctly who was born in 1789 and died in 1869. *Adoration of the Kings* is a well-known work of his. According to the ledger the piece we are about to see is called *The First Miracle*, painted in 1847. The last owner, presumably the person who had entrusted this work to Abraham lived in Durnstein, Austria, a village I know quite well, which lies on the banks of the River Danube.'

We all stood back about ten yards so that everyone would get a sighting of the picture when the porters had removed the protective casing. Great care had been taken in the protection. Every item was encased in wood. When the porters had unscrewed the screws and removed the front panel, beneath was scrunched up newspapers and straw. This was removed eliciting an audible gasp from those of us watching.

We were viewing a picture that had been hidden from all human eyes for sixty years. The picture was oil on panel and in size was about 20 inches by 30 inches.

Depicted was The Lord Jesus turning water into wine at a wedding in Cana, Galilee. It was stunning. Everyone broke out in applause. It seemed an odd thing to do, but it was so spontaneous. Everyone had a broad smile or grin on their face. After a lengthy examination by Mathius, the porters moved it to one side as another two porters brought in lot number two.

Mathius looked at the next page of the ledger, number two. 'This is another painting we have here. Oh, my word!' he exclaimed. 'I can hardly contain my excitement. If this is genuine, we have a painting here by Rembrandt van Rijn, called *Two Old Women Disputing.*

'I know that he painted in 1628 a picture that he called *Two Old Men Disputing*, which I believe is in the National Gallery of Victoria, Australia. But I am not aware of this work. As you know Rembrandt was a Dutch Master who died in 1669 at the age of sixty-three. Like many artists, he struggled when he was alive and just before his death, he considered himself to be a failure. If only he were to return now and see how utterly revered his pictures are today.'

Once more we waited in anticipation as the porter unscrewed the final screw and removed the front panel. Again, inside, the picture was protected with straw and newspaper. Once cleared, as with the Overbeck, it induced a gasp from all of us. You did not need to be an art expert to recognise this as being a Rembrandt.

'This is unbelievable,' exclaimed Mathius, in a rapturous voice. 'Quite amazing. Item number three,' Mathius continued. 'Ah I can see why our porters are struggling with the weight of this. This has been deposited by a Duke with attachments to the Hohenzollern Castle which is an impressive castle to the south of Stuttgart. Inside we should find thirty gold ingots.'

The fourth box to be opened up came from a Frankfurt Synagogue. There were six solid silver candle holders and a gold cross measuring three foot high and eighteen inches across. Each container's contents were taking roughly an hour to examine and then to record and remove to somewhere safe.

We decided that we had time to stay for one more item to be opened and revealed. This was another work of art. Instantly you could see that this was more modern. The picture was entitled *Springtime* and was painted by an artist by the name of Wilhelm List. Mathius with a number of reference books on the table grabbed one that said *Impressionists/Art Nouveau*.

'Here it is!' he exclaimed. 'This is not an artist that I am familiar with. Wilhelm was born in 1864 and died at the end of the First World War in 1918. Apparently, he studied at the Academy of Fine Arts in Vienna and then in Munich and Paris. It goes on to say that he was one of twelve illustrators of a catalogue produced in 1902 which was dedicated to Beethoven. What a delightful picture?'

I looked at my watch and advised Mathius that we must be on our way as we had a bit of a journey in front of us back to Bischofswiesen. We all shook hands with the ecstatic Mathius whose enthusiasm was almost orgasmic.

The journey back to the estate flew by. There was so much conversation between the five of us. Louise said that she particularly liked the last picture to be revealed, the one painted by Wilhelm List.

We had telephoned Lucas before we left Nuremberg and advised of our arrival time. Frieda and Zelda had cooked us a lovely lamb stew accompanied by a bottle of the estate's own red wine. There were so many questions being asked.

Tobias then said, 'I think there is an opportunity here. This discovery has brought our village to national attention. I feel that there are many who would like to visit the quarry and see where these treasures were hidden. We could open it to the public. Have a tea house, have tours of the farm, children from urban areas would love that. We could have an educational centre.

We have a very pretty village, think how becoming a tourist attraction would give our local economy a boost?'

We all agreed that the idea was good and that the four of them should work on that. I made it clear that it was them who would run the operation. They had the knowledge and the skills and so it was entirely up to them to be as innovative as they would like. I stressed that we would always like Father Benedict to be kept in the loop as he had proved to be such a wise head.

The following day we returned back to England and resumed our normal lives. Almost a month had gone by when I received a call from Daniel.

'Michael,' he opened. 'I am in your neck of the woods tomorrow, may I call in and see you and Louise at around seven in the evening?'

'That's wonderful,' I said. 'It will be good to see you.'

Louise had prepared a nice meal of rack of lamb, followed by apple pie and custard. Daniel was enquiring how the estate was doing. Every week either Louise or I would telephone and were given a brief update. Father Benedict's choice of personnel had been inspirational.

'That's good to hear,' Daniel observed. 'I have two pieces of news for you. I received a call from Mathius Spielberg yesterday. They were slowly making progress. Everything had been so well documented. The problem was that as so much art had been looted by the Nazis, it has not always been easy to return them to their rightful owners. He was wondering if you and Louis would consider donating or giving a long-term loan to the Museum of works that could not be repatriated?

'I of course, knowing you both as I do, said that I didn't consider that to be a problem. Apparently, this discovery has created massive interest and already the advanced ticket sales to the Museum are a record high. You are a fine couple. You have both continued working and have never sought any financial benefit from these unexpected circumstances. During Louise's year as a guest of Her Majesty's Prison Service, it would have been difficult financially for you to have survived. But to your credit you did.

'You have never sought any income from the estate. Therefore, I suggested to the curator that in view of this unexpected exhibition that would be of huge financial benefit to the museum that he make a payment of five hundred thousand euros. Money to be transferred into the account of Mr M.G. and Mrs L. Packham. He almost bit my hand off!' Daniel concluded with laughter.

'Ho, ho, ho,' Louise broke in. 'I knew my boy would turn up trumps with his unexpected inheritance. Thank you, Daniel, that really was kind and very thoughtful of you. I think that calls for another glass of wine.'

'There is another piece of news I wish to share with you both,' Daniel continued. 'You will remember that I had located the whereabouts of Leah's grandchildren, Abraham and Hannah and that they were working for a humanitarian agency in Ethiopia? Well, they have now returned to England and are residing temporarily in a small Cotswold town called Stow-on-the-Wold.

'As I know that you are both very busy, I took the liberty of contacting them and have explained the entire set of circumstances in respect of the estate that was owned by their great grandparents after who they have been christened. As you can imagine, they were both thrilled to have discovered something of their family history. Did I mention that Abraham was born in 1963 and his sister a year later? At this time, they are both still single. They sound delightful. As you can imagine with their work with Médecins Sans Frontieres, they are very caring. I have arranged for them to fly out accompanied by myself and I hope the two of you to view the estate in a week's time. Will this give you enough time to make work arrangements?'

'I will have no problem,' said Louise. 'It might be more difficult for Michael, I realise that the NHS is struggling to find enough doctors to work in the A&Es across the country.'

'I will see what I can do. Alistair, one of my colleagues I covered for recently, he might well reciprocate, especially if I bring back a couple of bottles of the estate's sparkling wine.'

'That's great,' concluded Daniel. 'I will make the arrangements.'

A week later Louise and I travelled up to Gatwick. We were excited about the prospect of meeting Abraham and Hannah. Daniel had suggested that after we checked in our baggage that we meet for breakfast at Wetherspoons. We made our way to the first-floor restaurant which was busy and searched around looking to see if we could spot Daniel. Suddenly I felt a hand on my shoulder and there he was.

'Hi Michael, glad you could make it.' Then shaking my hand and kissing Louise on the cheeks, he said, 'Grab your breakfasts, we are situated in the far-left hand corner, we have been fighting off people desperate to take your seats.'

We chose our breakfasts, paid for them and then made our way to join Daniel, Abraham and Hannah.

It is amazing how there are some people who you meet for the first time and you instantly bond with them. Both Abraham and Hannah were absolutely delightful. They immediately came across as being genuine, sincere, and caring. We chatted continually on the flight and during the journey to *Schlachthaus*.

We arrived in the early afternoon. We were met by Zelda who advised us that Frieda and Lucas had gone shopping for the day in Salzburg and that Tobias was working in the farm office. We followed Zelda into the house.

'You must be peckish?' Zelda enquired. 'I have made some sandwiches and cake. Afterwards I can take you to your rooms. And then looking at Abraham and Hannah. 'I understand that you have been working abroad?'

'Yes, that's right,' said Hannah. 'We have been working in Ethiopia. Another beautiful country which has been so poorly governed and created so many poor people as a result. Totally unnecessary. What is wrong with the world? Why is it that there are so many greedy dictators who are concerned only about their own personal wealth? This is particularly true in Africa. We are hoping that since Nelson Mandela became South Africa's President in 1994 that he will be an example to others of how to govern a country with honesty, integrity and fairness. Thank you for the sandwiches Zelda, you were right, we were peckish.'

'Not any more now,' Abraham chirped in. 'If you can show us to our rooms, then that would be good.'

'Certainly, come this way,' Zelda encouraged.

Following behind Zelda, halfway up the stairs, Hannah let out a gasp and grabbed at Abraham's arm.

'Look, look Abraham!' she exclaimed. 'There's our grandmother and her sister, Eliana!'

Louise then came and joined Hannah and Abraham. We all stood gazing admiringly at the beautiful picture of Leah and Eliana as two beautiful eighteen-year-olds clutching their violins.

'Do you know which is your grandmother and which is her sister?' Louise asked.

Abraham looked closely. 'Mum told us that Eliana had died during the war whilst in France, we would have been too young to have known her. They really were identical, weren't they? How could anyone tell them apart?'

'I wouldn't know,' Louise continued, 'but there is no mistaking looking at you two, that one of these beautiful girls is your grandmother. You have both inherited the good looks of the Benowitz family. I have never asked Daniel, but your mum Susan was born in 1941, there has been no mention of her.'

'Sadly, mum died of breast cancer just three years ago,' concluded Hannah.

After being shown to their rooms, Abraham and Hannah went for a walk around the gardens. When they came back, they discovered that Frieda and Lucas had returned from Salzburg and that Tobias had just finished in the office. Everyone greeted each other. The remarkable thing was that Abraham and Hannah both shared a presence. They exuded a calmness. A reassurance that everything was quietly under control.

Father Benedict joined us after the evening meal and we retired to the lounge. I then decided this was the moment to speak.

'Hannah, Abraham, we are aware that Daniel has explained everything to you in great detail. I am not surprised that you both speak fluent German and play the violin. Your mother must have been keen to keep the family traditions alive. But you know that we inherited this property from Otto Wagner who had promised to look after the estate until your great grandad or a descendant of his could return and reclaim what is rightfully theirs.

'As Louise and I explained on the journey over, it would be one of the most satisfying things in our lives and would have made everything worthwhile if you were to agree that we transfer the entire estate over to you. What you have told us, we are in no doubt at all, that you would continue the tradition laid out by Abraham. The first, in using the estate for the benefit of others. What do you say?'

We all looked eagerly at the pair. Hannah reminded me so much of Louise, in that she was a total equal and very self-assured. It was Hannah who summed up how they felt.

'Phew! Where do I begin to say how we both feel? The call from Daniel did not come as a surprise, but as a huge shock. The call lasted for over two hours in which Daniel explained everything to us, historically right up to the present. He also sent over a good deal of information for us to read and to gain a feel of the situation.

'My brother and I feel absolutely overwhelmed and touched by such kind generosity and honesty. There would have been nothing to have prevented Louise and Michael from owning this estate and living well as a result. Indeed, even now there is no requirement for you to hand back to us if you choose not to.

'Abraham and I have discussed this wonderful opportunity which we regard as having been heaven sent. If Michael and Louise transfer over to us, then we pledge that the wishes of our great grandparents will be upheld. This would include taking care of anyone in the village who needed help. Neither my brother nor I are materialistic. As long as we have a roof over our heads, clothes on our backs and food then we are thankful. Daniel has advised us that through the combined efforts of Lucas, Tobias, Frieda, Zelda and others that the estate is now making an impressive profit.

'The poverty of many of the children in Addis Ababa, is appalling. The lack of education and opportunity, things that we take for granted, is not there for those kids. It would be wonderful if we could move in and use two bedrooms. We would not interfere with the running of the estate. However, we would like a substantial part of the profits, say 75 percent nett profit, if you are in agreeance to help us establish a school in Addis Ababa and give the kids there some hope of a happy future.'

It was now the turn of Louise to speak. 'Whilst you were speaking Hannah, all that I could see were nodding heads. Nodding in agreement. We just knew from the first time this morning, that you would do everything right. That you will look after the staff here. I call them staff, but that is not the correct term. Everyone here is family. Everyone has a voice, and everyone wishes to do what is right. What you and your brother have proposed, I would think that if your great grandparents were looking down, they would be mightily proud.'

After spending two days with our friends on the estate we then returned home. Abraham and Hannah moved in a week later and seamlessly became part of the fixtures. Daniel sorted out the paperwork which was signed, ratified, and sent over six weeks later.

Louise and I returned to our work. Then in the following April Louise announced that we were to be parents. Wonderful news.

We had supper that evening and quite unexpectedly, Louise said, 'Michael, now that we are to become parents, would you consider making a fresh start?'

'What do you mean?' I asked.

'I would like to move into the country. I have enjoyed my work at Holloway prison, but it is that daily commute into town every day, is something that I could do without.'

'Where would you like to go?' I enquired.

'You grew up in Frome. You have memories of your grandparents and parents in that area, why don't we look there? I am desperate to be a full-time mum and a loving housewife to my man. I have never lived in the country. To wake up each morning to the sounds of the farmyard and to smell fresh air.'

'I am all for that,' I said. 'First of all, I will see if I am able to get a transfer to the Royal United Hospital in Bath, I have a couple of ex colleagues who work there.'

We had no trouble selling our house in Epsom. We decided that we would take a week's holiday and booked into The Royal Crescent hotel in the beautiful Georgian city of Bath. This was a special treat for us, we would never have considered such a hotel had it have not been for the windfall from the Nuremberg Museum.

Each morning we would travel around looking at houses. On the third day I received a call from Daniel, advising us that Dieter Muller had committed suicide whilst awaiting his trial in prison. All three of us, concluded that perhaps this was poetic justice. At the time we were looking at a house in Saltford, between Bath and Bristol.

We looked at houses in Shepton Mallet, Frome, Warminster and Westbury before falling in love with a mid-terraced cottage in the village of Dilton Marsh, in Wiltshire. It had open fields in the front and rear as well as a good size garden for our children to play. Louise had been told the week before that she would be giving birth to twins.

We moved in at the beginning of September. A week later I began my new job in the A&E department of the Bath Royal United Hospital. It was on the evening of 8th November that Louise began to experience her labour pains. I drove her to the RUH. She was in labour for several hours. At precisely one in the afternoon on 9th November she gave birth to twin girls. The first to arrive weighed in at six pounds seven ounces and her sister, a few minutes later, was not far behind at six pounds three ounces.

Louise was exhausted but deliriously happy as she cradled her two daughters together. The nurse took a photo of the four of us. The first of many to come I thought. We had deliberately requested that we were not told the sex of the babies during the pregnancy. We had not even considered possible names. 'Well done darling, you did great, now we need to agree what to call these precious darlings.'

Louise looked at me. 'Today is 9th November, on this same day back in 1938 it was known as Kristallnacht and two Jewish girls were taken by force and ended up in the Dachau Concentration

Camp. They were both beautiful girls, as indeed I am sure our own daughters will be.'

'I know what your suggestion of names will be, and I totally agree, it is almost as though the names have been ordained. How though will we tell which is Leah and which is Eliana?' I asked.

I leant forward and kissed Louise, who was now very sleepy. The nurse took the babies off to the nursery. I left the hospital for home and on the way, I called Louise's parents and sister with the good news.

Born to an unmarried mother in 1949 Graham
Sutherland spent three years in a children's home.
His mother married and he was returned to her
in 1952. He lived in London before moving to
Ashford in 1953. His stepfather worked at Ashford
Railway Works. Graham left school at sixteen to
take a six year printing apprenticeship as a compos-
itor then linotype keyboard operator.
He married in 1973 and moved to Frome in Som-
erset working as a printer for Butler and Tanner.
In 1975 he established his own cleaning business.
Graham has two sons and a daughter. In 1995 he
returned to Ashford and is now retired.

The publisher

*He who stops
getting better
stops being good.*

This is the motto of novum publishing, and our focus
is on finding new manuscripts, publishing them and
offering long-term support to the authors.
Our publishing house was founded in 1997, and since
then it has become THE expert for new authors and
has won numerous awards.

**Our editorial team will peruse each manuscript
within a few weeks free of charge and without
obligation.**

You will find more information about
novum publishing and our books on the internet:

w w w . n o v u m - p u b l i s h i n g . c o . u k